30p

ZITA

Also by RICHARD DEACON:

THE PRIVATE LIFE OF MR GLADSTONE
MADOC AND THE DISCOVERY OF AMERICA
JOHN DEE
A HISTORY OF THE BRITISH SECRET SERVICE
A HISTORY OF THE RUSSIAN SECRET SERVICE
A HISTORY OF THE CHINESE SECRET SERVICE
THE ISRAELI SECRET SERVICE
THE SILENT WAR: A HISTORY OF WESTERN NAVAL
   INTELLIGENCE
SPY! SIX STORIES OF MODERN ESPIONAGE
ESCAPE
THE BRITISH CONNECTION
A HISTORY OF THE JAPANESE SECRET SERVICE
WITH MY LITTLE EYE

ZITA

A Do-It-Yourself Romance

Richard Deacon

Frederick Muller Limited
London

First published in Great Britain in 1983 by
Frederick Muller Limited, Dataday House,
Alexandra Road, Wimbledon, London SW19 7JZ.

Copyright © Richard Deacon 1983

All rights reserved. No part of this publication
may be reproduced, stored in a retrieval system or
transmitted, in any form or by any means, electronic,
mechanical, photocopying, recording or otherwise,
without the prior permission of Frederick Muller Limited.

British Library Cataloguing in Publication Data

Deacon, Richard, 1911–
  Zita.
    Rn: Donald McCormick
    I. Title
    823'.914[F]   PR6063.A/
    ISBN 0–584–31162–1

Phototypeset by Input Typesetting Ltd, London SW19 8DR
Printed in Great Britain by Billing & Sons Ltd, Worcester.

ONE

I had just signed the register at my favourite hotel in the Île St-Louis on the River Seine when, while the receptionist was looking at my passport, I happened to glance at the signature immediately preceding mine.

The name was "C. A. Walters", but the handwriting was that of a man I knew as Charles Wetherby. It gave me a nasty shock because at one time I had been in the habit of receiving memoranda from Wetherby when he had been my immediate boss. Thus his calligraphical characteristics were truly engraved in my mind.

It may seem curious to be so sure about a mere signature, but part of my work at that time included analysing both typing and handwriting in a quest for establishing whether or not certain letters and documents were forgeries. Apart from that, the capital "C" and capital "W" in this signature were unmistakably the pen-prints of Wetherby – the elaborate, rather grandiloquent, flowing "C" and the "W" which was practically a triangle. If I had not been a handwriting expert, then I should have dismissed this signature as merely being remarkably similar to that of Wetherby. But not only was I trained to spot forgeries, I had also studied Wetherby's handwriting from the viewpoint of trying to read his character. This was a mere recreational sideline and not one particularly valued by my controllers who dealt in hard facts rather than theories. But it enabled me to decide beyond all doubt that this was the real Wetherby writing and not that of any other person.

This might seem to be a rash assessment to make on the spur of the moment. Normally, when analysing suspected handwritten forgeries, it is the practice to select, if possible, at least ten diagnostic characteristics of the questioned handwriting. On this basis, with ten as the top mark, one could make a fairly reliable judgement. I felt I did not need to make any such references. At least ten, if not more of Wetherby's calligraphic eccentricities were firmly fixed in my mind, and among these ten were the eight letters of the alphabet employed in the "C. A. Walters" signature. What the devil was he doing here when he was essentially assigned only to the London office and had never been given any foreign assignments in recent years?

I saw that the receptionist at the desk was regarding me with quizzical eyes as I kept studying the page in the register, so I hastily took my key and passport and went up to my room. I should have liked to ask for a description of "C. A. Walters", but decided this might arouse too much attention. What I most regretted was having signed the register in this particular hotel, as I was sure that Wetherby would spot it sooner or later. It would be quite natural, with his type of mind, to find some excuse for glancing at the register each day.

It was an unreal, almost twilight world in which I operated at that time. Though I have long since "gone private", as we say in the jargon of the Intelligence fraternity, it seems just as unreal today. With most of my colleagues I had complete rapport, but for Wetherby I had nothing but contempt. I never got along with him very well. I think that the Wetherbys of this world should be shown up for what they are, even though most of my ex-colleagues take the view that a cover-up is better than a "tell-all".

What I am about to relate is factional rather than fictional. Or, let me put it this way, it is only fictional in certain parts of the narrative where some expression of fantasy is needed, or where risks of breaking the Official Secrets Act could create a problem of conscience. It was the foregoing incident, however, which finally pushed me from a career in Intelligence to the vocation of a novelist. From time to time I had made attempts to write a novel, but every time I had done so I was interrupted by a signal sending me on another mission. I had written a few non-fiction books, but a novel had always eluded me. It was the start of each book which bothered me. I never seemed to get it right. So it was with a mild degree of exhilaration that in the silence of my hotel room I suddenly realised that the episode of the signature in the register made as a good a beginning as I was ever likely to get. So I wrote it down while the idea hit me.

Nevertheless I was very worried about that mysterious signature and I still felt sure I couldn't have made a mistake about it. I had been given six weeks' leave and had decided to spend it somewhere tranquil and beautiful, stylish but not particularly fashionable, remote, yet close to the heart-beat of a great capital city so that I could combine the best of two life styles. In such surroundings, I decided, I might make one more, possibly final, attempt at writing a novel. In six weeks, with a modicum of luck and some self-discipline, I might actually finish one at last. It may have been a pipe-dream, but where better to indulge it than in the Île St-Louis, an island in the heart of Paris, a fairy-tale world of its own, linked to the city by a bridge across the River Seine.

Still puzzling over the Wetherby mystery, I put on a pair of corduroy slacks and a T-shirt covered with a pattern of palm trees with a setting sun behind each, and set out on a ramble around the island. I had stayed at the hotel here only once before and almost instantly regarded it as one of my six favourite hostelries in the whole world. But it was more in my mind's eye that I looked upon the Île St-Louis as probably the perfect setting for the opening of my novel. I had read about it in that splendid artist's notebook by Robert Gibbings, *Trumpets from Montparnasse*. Gibbings had explored most of the islands of the Pacific, yet he wrote, "Without casting one grain of coral dust at the 'desert' islands on which I have spent idyllic days and nights, I must admit that it was the Defoe form of solitude that I found and enjoyed on the Île St-Louis. There in the heart of Paris, with the river flowing past either side, I was as isolated as a lake dweller, yet within easy reach of any sophistication that might momentarily become needful to the soul."

Wandering around the ancient architectural gems of the island, their nobly proportioned facades, the anecdotal tablets here and there and the wrought-iron balconies seemingly specially designed as a stage-setting for Juliet's sighs for Romeo, was to me a great serendiptitious adventure. I was enthralled by the pageant of delight which opened up for me at every turn; and I had briefly paused at the admirably designed Square Barye at the neatly pointed tip of the island, when I suddenly saw Wetherby turning into the Rue de Bretonvilliers. There was no mistaking him, though he was out of sight again in a matter of seconds. But I had an uneasy feeling that perhaps he might have seen me before I spotted him.

What could he be up to? Why was he using another name for signing the register, the implication being that he must have a false passport too? Wetherby's work was essentially indoors at an office desk, not that of an agent in the field. A secret assignment with a female? Or perhaps even a male? Either idea was laughable, for Wetherby was regarded as being wholly indifferent, or totally impotent, as far as sex was concerned. I recall once meeting Kim Philby in a bar in Beirut not long before he defected, and he asked me: "How's old Wetherby these days?"

I must have made some non-commital comment to the effect that he was "much the rather disagreeable dog he always has been," as Philby guffawed and replied: "Oh, a dog is frisky, but Wetherby must have been born without balls, cock or heart."

I didn't pay much attention at the time, for even then Philby was considered the bright boy of the Middle East by some in the office. But, looking back, I think that he might have been trying to pump me, a mere apprentice in the trade at that time. Not that he learned anything of importance, though I was perhaps unwise not to hide my personal opinion of him.

Bugger Wetherby, I said to myself. Here was I hoping to settle down to a holiday and book-writing and somehow he appeared out of nowhere to distract me at every turn. I wanted to avoid him at all costs, as I had an allergy to his presence. He, too, hated contact with his immediate staff, preferred to communicate by memoranda and insisted on "my subordinates", as he called us, making contact with him in the same manner. To try to put him out of my mind, I popped into a bar and ordered a Pernod, being reasonably sure I shouldn't run into Wetherby in such surroundings.

As I sipped the Pernod, I tried to seek a logical explanation for the Wetherby presence on the Île St-Louis. Until now I

4

had tried to argue against myself regarding that recognition of the signature in the register. But now there could be no doubt about it. Was Wetherby actually being given some most unusual foreign mission? It seemed highly unlikely, yet what other explanation was there? I was also irritated because this was not the kind of subject I wanted to have to cope with on a holiday. This was even more the case as I was contemplating writing a romantic novel.

A rash holiday adventure, perhaps, but it was in that kind of mood I had come to the Île St-Louis. Wetherby was an unwelcome intrusion into my thoughts. Then, sipping my second Pernod, I was sharply confronted with a chance to research heroine Number One (or that was how I put it to myself in a kind of escapist bravado). She was the sort of girl one couldn't miss. I had to start sometime to find a model for a heroine, so why not right away as this promised to be the best possible antidote to Wetherby. Here she came, clippetty-clopping up to the bar, looking neither to the right, nor the left, indulging in the kind of callipygian contortions that the Greek poet Hesiod warned men against as long ago as the ninth century. This was not a whore-like wriggle, but the unselfconscious undulations of a girl who knows she looks rather good in tight-fitting jeans with flamboyant gold and red stripes. She quickly ordered a Cinzano and took it away to a solitary table quite close to mine.

I wondered how I could make a speedy but meaningful contact. After all, it was romance I was researching, not looking for a pick-up. Or was I kidding myself? I was at that time forty-two years old, still feeling as nimble as I was at thirty-two, but fully realising that as a man gets older he needs to step up his skill and improve his technique if he is going to have any luck in amorous adventures. I was divorced and fancy-free, somewhat of a loner, but reasonably well-informed about the women of my own generation.

But my age target for a heroine was someone well below thirty and preferably nearer to twenty. And the girl sipping the Cinzano seemed to be around twenty-three to twenty-five. On this occasion my obvious opening gambit was fairly simple. The Île St-Louis had traditionally been a haunt of artists and was for that reason a magnet for models and would-be models. Therefore it was not inappropriate that I should convey the impression that I was an artist and might want a model. I knew it was not unknown on the island to find a girl prepared to pose for one by waiting in a bar until a likely character called in. The red-and-gold-painted one, with her tumbling honey-blonde locks, did not look as though she was hard up for a few hundred francs. So the course I adopted was not to make the first move in chatting her up, but to take out a sketch-book and make sure she could see I was drawing her. Very soon she finished her Cinzano and, in coming up to the bar to buy another drink, had to pass by my table. As she waited for her glass to be refilled, she turned towards me and glanced at my sketch-book.

"It's certainly one of the quickest sketches I've seen," she commented in a friendly tone. "But it is not as good as those splendid palm trees on your T-shirt."

She had the richly dark-brown accents of the American South, though her language was a rather contrived mixture of English and Franglais. Replying to my question as to whether she lived on the island, she said: "No, but I come here *pour le weekend*. You see, I have *une affaire de coeur* with the Île St-Louis. I like to *forgettez* the Tower and give myself an eyeful here."

I winced at this strained, jokey Franglais. When she came in I had mentally given her marks as an assessment of her potential as a possible model for a heroine. I rashly rated her at seven out of ten for first impressions, but then knocked off two marks for the rather ridiculous, grossly overdone punning Franglais. Then I gave her back a mark for sharing my enthusiasm for the Île St-Louis.

"Will you have another Cinzano?" I asked when she had finished her second drink.

"*Oui, si* I *changeais* my medicine. I am a Bluegrasser, so I like to switch. Sometimes *le* Cinzano, *quelquefois le* paraffin pink."

"Bluegrasser? Paraffin pink?"

"I come from Kentucky. Bluegrasser is our state nickname. *Le* paraffin pink is what I call the *rosé*. But I don't want that now. I warn you when I am asked to have a drink. I make a habit of setting *une devinette*."

"A riddle?"

"Yeah, a riddle. Not a jimmy-riddle, but *une devinette*. This time I feel in the mood for a Tania's Blush."

I raised an eyebrow, said nothing, but walked over to the bar and asked the patron for this concoction of which I had never heard. Did he know what it was?

"Ah, *bien sûr, m'sieur*. It is *ma'mselle's* little joke. She likes to tease, to mystify, that one. It will take a short while to mix, but I promise not to keep you waiting long."

"Better make it two Tania's Blushes," said I, taking a risk as rash as dipping into a bran-tub at a Hallowe'en party.

While waiting for the drinks we resumed conversation. The girl told me her name was April, "because I was born in that month" and that, though she was a native of Kentucky, her real home was in South Carolina. I ventured the information that I was an artist (not strictly correct but I could sketch a little) and that my name was Richard.

Returning to the bar counter to watch the *patron* mix this mysterious drink, I saw him pour into a cocktail-shaker two large equal measures of Bacardi rum and vodka, adding two half-measures of Cointreau and then dashes of Grenadine and lemon bitters. Finally, having put in ice cubes, he vigorously shook the mixture into what he called *le mariage* and then swiftly filled two glasses with the frothy, pink libation.

As he handed me the drinks, the *patron* bent forward confidentially, "She's a strange one, that. She has some money, but she is a scrounger in a peculiar sort of way. She collects men's shirts and has a craze for asking for one, if it takes her fancy."

"A fancy to the man, or the shirt?"

He handed me the change, replying, "Maybe just the shirt, which she wears afterwards. Or maybe sometimes the shirt and the man."

"She's already hinted that she likes mine."

"Take care, *m'sieur*. She's already had one of mine. It was one night several weeks ago when she insisted on my taking off my shirt right here in the bar just as I was closing. She was *un peu zig-zag* at the time, but as she is quite a good and regular client, I relented."

"Thanks for the information. I'll play it by ear. But I'd better get back to her now, or she will think we are plotting something."

I must confess that Tania's Blush was so surprisingly good that I decided it was worth adding back again one of the marks I had deducted. It was fun to drink with a girl who was willing to explore the by-paths and alley-ways of alcohol. I had almost forgotten what a really good cocktail was like.

Beginning to look forward to the evening ahead, I had already decided to suggest a repeat order when in burst two *gendarmes*. There was a quick exchange of words with the *patron* and then we were all ordered to go quietly outside the bar as it was believed that someone had planted a plastic bomb at an adjacent table. April seemed somewhat agitated and strode ahead of me to the pavement outside, not stopping until she was some thirty metres away from the bar. I had experienced too many bomb scares in various capitals to be unduly worried by this warning. April turned round, put out her hand and said: "Thanks for the drink. It's a pity we couldn't stay on."

"Maybe we can go back in a few minutes. I dare say it's a false alarm. Why should anyone want to plant a bomb in the Île St-Louis?"

"I won't take the risk. If the bar is still standing tomorrow, I'll see you there at noon. But for now, I must be on my way."

"All right, tomorrow at noon then," I replied, somewhat disappointed at her abrupt departure. It was such a firm, positive goodbye for now that I didn't feel it was the moment to suggest walking on to another bar. Tomorrow, I hoped, would be the bonus.

I never saw her again. Heroine Number One vanished round the corner. Then everything began to happen at once. I was in no mood for further drinking on my own. So I wandered slowly back to the hotel with one ear cocked just in case there was an explosion back at the bar. But all remained quiet. I had just entered my room and was pushing back the shutters and opening the window when I saw a figure approaching the hotel.

It was Wetherby.

TWO

The moment I saw Wetherby walking towards the hotel intuition told me that trouble lay ahead. But I also sensed danger. That was illogical, for whereas I had disliked Wetherby and was even contemptuous of him, I had never regarded him as being in any way dangerous. Now I felt impelled to revise this view.

I still don't know quite why I did it, but instinctively I turned the key in my bedroom door. Pocketing it, I moved to a corner of the room that was out of range for anyone who might peep through the keyhole. I suppose that after one has had some unnerving experiences in the field from time to time one's mind becomes calmly geared to taking such minute precautions.

Somehow I was sure that Wetherby would come up to my room. I hadn't long to wait. Presently I heard the lift moving upwards. Then a clanking of the lift door and footsteps along the corridor. There was a brief pause and a brisk knock at the door.

I can well understand anyone thinking that I was reacting in a melodramatic, even paranoid, manner towards my former sectional chief. So, too, would my colleagues back in London. After all, it was just possible that Wetherby might be on some secret mission and adopting another name and was anxious to keep me informed. But my instincts told me otherwise and in this game one comes to rely on one's instincts in a crisis. I was not only anxious for personal reasons not to see Wetherby, but I was also frightened. I had suddenly remembered something I had heard once from a close acquaintance in the CIA. It was a hint that there were two oddities about Wetherby that had always puzzled him: "If you take the trouble to check up on his various postings, you will find that wherever he was something went wrong on each occasion. When the Russkies found out that Peter Lunn was your MI6 man in Vienna in 1947, Wetherby was on his first mission to the Austrian capital. What is more, Wetherby employed Sean Bourke for odd inquiries when George Blake was in the nick. And, as you dam' well know, Sean rescued Blake from Wormwood Scrubs."

This scrap of conversation rushed back into my mind as there was one more knock on the door, this time a loud one. But Wetherby did not try to open the door, though he may have peeped through the keyhole. He walked away down the corridor. I moved back to the table near my bed and listened. There was no sound of the lift moving and I became suspicious. Four – it may have been five – minutes later I heard and watched the door handle being turned. Finding it locked, he must have walked away. This time I heard the lift clanking its way below.

By now I was convinced that Wetherby did pose some kind of a threat to me personally, though I could not imagine what form this took, or why. But the immediate problem was what my next step should be. It was by now about eight o'clock on an early May night, hotter than usual for the time of year. If Wetherby had simply knocked at my door, and gone away when he got no reply, my hunch of impending trouble might have been ruled out as unjustified. But the fact that he had tiptoed back and tried the handle clearly showed me that he was up to no good, unless of course he merely wished to frighten me, which again made no sense. Either he was convinced that I was in the room, or he wanted to search it while I was out.

Most people in my position would probably have gone to look for Wetherby right away and asked him what the hell his game was. But an Intelligence officer's mind does not always tend to work this way. As he was a very senior executive, I knew that to tackle him face-to-face would put me at a disadvantage. True, he was no longer my immediate boss, but he was far senior to me and his influence at the Office was considerable.

There was just a chance, though I doubted it, that the person who had tried my door was not Wetherby. I rang down for room-service and asked for a sandwich and a bottle of Sancerre. When the *sommelier* arrived I inquired whether anyone had been asking for me.

"*Non, m'sieur*, not that I have heard."

"You have a Monsieur Walters staying here? Is he in the restaurant?"

"*Non, m'sieur*, he left the bar a few minutes ago."

"He went for a walk?"

"*Non, m'sieur*, he checked out. He suddenly decided to go and he paid his bill."

"Did he say where he was going?"

"Not that I know of."

I ate my sandwich and drank my wine, wondering what to do. I knew that a close colleague of mine would be on night duty at Century House, so I decided to ring London."

"This is Richard."

"Good God! Feeling so lonesome you want to make sure we are still in business?"

"It's not like that at all. I wish I didn't feel the urge to ring you, but several odd things have happened."

"Can you talk reasonably freely?"

"Well, I'm alone in my room, if that's what you mean. But to be on the safe side there ought to be some double talk. You'll probably have to fill in some deliberate gaps in the conversation. Did you know that Wetherby was in Paris?"

"No. That seems extremely odd, because only two days ago he had a talk with Uncle Bobs [that was our secret name for 'C'] and nothing was said about his going to Paris. Are you quite sure?"

I told Hanson the whole story, omitting nothing, not even the incident of the suspected bomb in the bar.

"Have you been drinking?"

"Of course I've bloody well been drinking. But I've not only seen the hotel register, I've seen Wetherby."

"I really do find this quite astonishing. The first thing anyone is going to say, and I include myself in this, is why the hell didn't you answer the door when you heard that knock-knock?"

"I don't exactly know myself. It was just a hunch I had."

"Well, I'll give you the benefit of the doubt and make some inquiries. You've spoilt my evening. Nobody, but nobody, is going to believe this. I'll probably ring you back in the morning. 'Bye for now!"

I began to regret that I had rung London. Wetherby must have covered his movements with a fairly sound alibi. If so, I should have stirred up a hornet's nest without any advantage to myself. I half expected Hanson to ring back and say, "It's OK, old chap, we do know all about this after all, so just pretend nothing has happened."

Just in case Hanson did telephone, I decided to stay in my room. I felt uneasy about the whole business of Wetherby and it was hard to concentrate on anything. To take my mind off this I finished off the bottle of Sancerre and tried to make a few notes for my novel. I wanted to create a book which would have as its underlying motive some hints on how to achieve a viable and contemporary spirit of rhapsodic living. Behind all these thoughts there was deep inside me a rebel reacting against what I prefer to call the "dull-dirty" novel of today. More against the dull than the dirty.

My objective was to escape from the literary landscape where everyone lived dirtily, drearily and unhappily to an Arcadia of the joyful-erotic, instilling into the novel some kind of *allégresse*. Thus by the end of the day, despite the unwanted intrusion of Wetherby, I knew exactly what I wanted to write. I went to bed and to sleep, feeling rather smug and content that Wetherby had gone away.

I was woken up at seven o'clock by a call from London. Hanson was just about to go off-duty. "Sorry to wake you so early," he apologized, "but it's orders from on high. You are to return to London today as speedily as possible."

For several seconds, words just would not form themselves on my lips. To have been given six weeks' leave only a few days previously and then to be recalled within twenty-four hours of arriving in Paris seemed incredible. But I managed to control my feelings sufficiently to murmur, "Has World War III broken out?"

"I know how you must feel. I'm dreadfully sorry to disturb you at this hour. But you really put the cat among the pigeons when you telephoned about our mutual colleague. There is a monumental flap on."

"Can you say more?"

"Not now. Not a thing. Just get back as quick as you can.

Uncle Bobs wants to see you personally. Can you make it to the Office by eleven o'clock tomorrow morning?"

"With luck, just about."

"Well, goodbye then, and, once again, I really am sorry."

There could be no question of my not returning to London, or trying to argue about it. Hanson knew exactly how I felt and he had underlined the importance of my returning by saying that "Uncle Bobs" (or "Wet Bob" as one or two of us irreverently called him) wanted to see me.

Baffled as I was by the peremptory request for me to return, I more or less prepared myself for further bad news. The situation was obviously serious, but I still had no inkling as to what it might be all about.

I had only seen "C" twice previously and then for not longer than ten minutes. The head of MI6 had held this post for barely a year and was still somewhat aloof and unrelaxed, or at least that is how it seemed to those of us who could remember the reign of the late Sir Maurice Oldfield. Full of amusing stories, a natural bon viveur despite his shyness, Oldfield could be great fun, especially outside the Office. One favourite yarn he told was of an ex-MI6 man who had become a prison visitor. He was talking to a prisoner convicted of burglary and it turned out that this man had once had a job which involved repair work inside MI6 offices. He remarked to the prison visitor that he had taken the opportunity to "case the joint. It was a queer place. People didn't talk to one another in the lifts and they left nothing on their desks. Nothing worth nicking there, guv'nor." Oldfield swore that if ever he wrote his autobiography, "Nothing Worth Nicking" would be its title.

The present "C" was ex-Foreign Office and had had no experience "out in the field". There was a school of thought inside the Secret Service, certainly shared by myself, that members of the Diplomatic Service made inadequate Directors of Intelligence, and actually hampered our work. They preferred to keep on the right side of the Foreign Office and the politicians and wind up with a knighthood than to improve the efficiency of the Service.

"C" was coldly conciliatory. "I regret we have had to break

into your leave like this, but it seems more sensible to sort out some problems informally now rather than formally later on." This was his way of saying that there was to be an inquiry unless I could satisfy him I had the right answers – or rather the answers he wished to hear.

"First of all," he pressed on, "I want to know if you stand by all your verbal allegations about Charles Wetherby made on the telephone last night."

"Absolutely."

"What would you say if I told you that you have made a grave mistake because Wetherby is not in Paris and has not been outside the country for the past seven months?"

"I should still stand by my report. Not only did I positively identify his handwriting under a false name in the hotel register, but I actually saw him on two occasions."

"Wetherby has a complete alibi, I assure you. Will that make you change your mind?"

"No, I am certain I saw him in Paris."

"I should have preferred to keep this matter entirely within the province of Six, but I fear that Five is now involved. That means the Home Office as well as the F.O."

"I fail to see why this should be," I replied, somewhat irritated and actually showing it. "What exactly does all this mean?"

"C" tightened his lips and put on his severe look. "If you stand by what you say, then there is absolutely no alternative but for you to be questioned by a committee of inquiry consisting of members of Five as well as Six, and an independent chairman."

"You mean the Fluency Committee is to be reactivated?" I enquired with what must have been stark incredulity.

"You could put it like that."

"But so soon? Is this to investigate Wetherby?"

"It is to investigate *you* and various other matters. Very wide powers of reference, I assure you. Swift action to silence loose tongues before the politicians start asking questions. I am very sorry about this and it is not my personal opinion that this is the right step to take. That is why I wanted to avoid a full-scale inquiry, even a secret one, by giving you a chance to retract anything you may have said. As you had not made any formal written report, you had this one last chance of being saved from the ignominy of an outside interrogation."

"There is no logical way I can avoid it. To do so would be to destroy my own credibility."

"You could still say you were mistaken and give an adequate reason for it."

I shook my head. I knew that a retraction might save me a lot of trouble, but it would certainly remain a black mark against me. In any event I strongly resented my word not being accepted. It came as something of a delayed shock to realise that by telephoning London from Paris while on leave I had precipitated what looked very much like the sack. All these years of hard graft and traipsing around the world – for what? Bitterly, I realised that my career might well be in total ruins.

"I am afraid life is going to be rather difficult for you for a while," "C" went on. "You are suspended from all duties as from now, of course, but on full salary. For the period of interrogation it will be a strict condition that you must stay at Cucking Manor. A car is waiting to take you down there."

I chuckled at this last remark. This talk about possibly being able to avoid an inquiry, if I admitted making a false report, was either eyewash or a trap. The fact that a car was waiting meant that a decision had been taken regardless of what I might say.

Cucking Manor was what we call a "safe house" in the heart of the Kentish Weald and used by the SIS when there were interrogations concerning both sections of British Intelligence. I still felt my hunch about Wetherby was right and that he had been up to no good. But somebody had obviously put the boot in for me. Maybe it was Wetherby himself who had boldly decided that to attack me was the best policy. The trip down to Cucking Manor from Century House was uneventful. I cursed my luck at not having been able to see April again. In the space of some minutes she had provided me with some promising material for the novel even though her Franglais was hardly the best kind of dialogue for a potential heroine. But she had looks and style and a nice taste in alcoholic exploration.

Seated in the back of the car I read in *Publisher's Weekly* that a "tip sheet" had been sent to authors by an American publisher to help them satisfy the demands of readers of romantic fiction. The formula they gave for the heroine was that she would be "aged twenty to twenty-nine, not to be naive and virginal, but rather a mature woman. Although the failure or loss of her first love may have made her suffer, she must never be portrayed as depressed or depressive."

That, I was sure, fitted April all right, though "mature", a horribly depressing word at the best of times, was hardly how I should have described her. I chuckled aloud at a silent joke which flitted through my mind. Vaughan, the driver, called back to me: "Sorry, sir? I didn't quite catch what you said."

"I didn't say anything, Vaughan. Just rather a silly thought struck me. Two nights ago in Paris I met a girl named April for the first time. I was to have met her again at noon yesterday, but I had to come back to London. Well, this is the flowery month of May and I was just thinking 'Oh, to be in April now that May is here'. A lewd thought, no doubt."

"Yes, sir," replied the taciturn Vaughan, making no further comment. I knew and doubtless he did, too, that anything we said was almost certainly being tape-recorded by some hidden microphone in the car. I might as well give the Fluency Committee the chance of a giggle, if indeed they were capable of such sentiments.

I won't go into details of my prolonged interrogation. Suffice to say that the Committee required to know every scrap of information about my movements in the Île St-Louis from the moment I crossed the bridge over the Seine to the time I left by the same route. They did not believe anything I said about Wetherby and I was soon convinced that they thought I was creating mischief by wasting their time on an invented story. I kept urging them to get the hotel register signature examined by an independent handwriting expert, but all they said was that my suggestion would be noted.

The main blunder I had committed in their eyes was that, by not confronting the man I claimed was Wetherby but actually avoiding him, I had laid myself open to the suspicion that I was concocting the whole story. Everybody seemed convinced that Wetherby's alibi was unassailable. I was not told what that alibi was, or how substantiated. But, as I tried to tell the Committee, "By lying low and pretending not to have seen Wetherby, I might have been able to find out more. I was not to know he would leave the hotel so speedily."

Of course, the question that really floored me at the inquiry was "Why should you suspect Wetherby?" They knew, and I knew that whatever reservations people might have about Wetherby he was regarded as ultra-conscientious and dependable. My only reason for *beginning* to suspect him was that faked signature and a vaguely recollected conversation with a CIA man that Wetherby had made an unsatisfactory impression on him. It would have been fatuous to cite anything the CIA man might have said because, put in as evidence, it amounted to nothing at all. In any case, I had no intention of betraying a confidence. I was reminded that I had not got along well with Wetherby when I worked under him and that there were two or three occasions when we had had serious disagreements. Wasn't this a question of my trying to get my own back on Wetherby? There was even a suggestion that I might be trying to hide something from the Committee of Inquiry concerning the alleged bomb-planting episode in the bar on the Île St-Louis.

There was no doubt that Wetherby had pressed for a swift inquiry into the whole affair before I had any chance of substantiating my case. My version of what happened in Paris was not accepted by the Committee and, after keeping me waiting alone in my room for nearly an hour, I was called in and told that "in the interests of the Service" I should resign. This really meant that I had got the sack, but with three months' paid salary and a farewell handshake of £3,000.

THREE

It was not until I left Cucking Manor that the reality of my career being terminated dawned on me. Clearly it was not just a matter of my being under a cloud, but of having my reputation totally destroyed – all because I had taken the trouble to ring up London. It was this realisation which made me desperately anxious to solve the mystery of why the powers-that-be should suddenly decide I was an undesirable person to be in the Service. I felt angry, hurt and resentful. If I had been in some non-Service post, I could at least have sued for wrongful dismissal and even fought for higher compensation. Three months' pay plus a mere £3,000 would not last for very long. Some redundant artisans got more than that. Comparing my removal from a post with that of Kim Philby many years previously, I was nobody's favourite son. I wanted to fight the injustice of the whole outrageous business, but I knew that this required an almost superhuman effort to find allies. I was realistic enough to know that I needed to concentrate on creating a new career for myself.

The life of a full-time writer appealed to me in that it combined the maximum of freedom with all manner of opportunities for making my "researches" both recreative and cash-worthy. Experience told me I might find more adventure this way than in MI6 where quite often it was a question of checking up on suspected forgeries, analysing handwriting and collecting rather boring and sometimes what seemed totally irrelevant information. As I had been travelling around the continent of Europe and the Middle East, in and out of suitcases, for years, having neither home nor family, the main problem which confronted me was finding somewhere to live.

My last home had been sold some twelve years earlier when my marriage broke up.

I toyed with the idea of buying a very small cabin-craft and mooring it somewhere on the upper reaches of the Thames. But I decided that finding the right kind of craft at the right price and again the ideal site for moorings would be too time-consuming. If I were to get down to work quickly, I must not be side-tracked in this way.

During the past six years I had only spent about ten months altogether living in London: the rest of the time I had been in Algiers, Athens, Beirut, Cairo, Cyprus, Istanbul and Prague. I was horrified to note how prices for properties and rents had rocketed in the British capital. I wanted something fairly cheap, not too far from the West End or the City, definitely not anything suburban, but preferably a run-down area still possessing some character. I found just what I was looking for – a two-room unfurnished flat with kitchenette and bathroom – in what is a most peculiar village in the metropolis, a picturesque but decaying area known as De Beauvoir Town, within sight of the City and with a square full of buildings in a fanciful Dutch design. The rooms were very small, there was no central heating and no lift to the second floor on which the flat was situated. Nevertheless, it was quite a bargain for £35,000 for the leasehold. With substantial help from my bank I clinched the deal.

I retained a distant link with "Six" through my friendship with Hanson, so I took him along to see the little pad I had acquired. It seemed sound tactics to let my ex-colleagues know where I lived and what I was doing. Smiling, Hanson commented, "My dear Richard, you could define this pad of yours either as a poor man's Islington, or a failed spook's last safe house. But I'm sure you will be able to breathe some semblance of civilization into it. By the way, on an informal basis, it might be a good plan to keep in touch with me fairly regularly."

"Any special reason?"

He grinned. "Well, just in case we want to reactivate you. Stranger things have happened. Just look how they got rid of Philby one moment and then engineered a job for him in the Middle East the next."

"Reactivated over my dead body," I replied grimly.

"Well, you never know. Yours is a complex case. In the firm there is a subtle difference between being sacked and being asked to resign. You could define being asked to resign as being sacked with honour. It's a dead cert that someone has put in a lot of poison for you and somehow you have fallen bang into the trap. One day that someone might just slip up."

"Any theories as to who that someone might be?"

"Absolutely none. The real puzzle is how MI5 came to be brought into the inquiry."

"Wetherby. Who else?"

Hanson shrugged. "Let's talk of other things."

This was what could be called a blatant evasion of an important topic. But Hanson and I understood one another, so he came along and helped me choose some second-hand furniture, as well as a brand new bed and settee to make the place habitable. The quest for decent second-hand furniture proved relatively easy as this whole area had at one time quite a reputation for furniture-making. *New Society* once described De Beauvoir Town as "the most interesting half-mile in London" and as we roamed around the gentrified terraces of Victorian artisans' cottages we found some quite astonishing bargains – a really huge, but unornamental desk with a splendid bookcase. The latter was just large enough to hold my personal collection of books which had long lain in store – a strange assortment ranging from atlases and street maps to first editions of Laurie Lee and Lafcadio Hearn, and from Boswell's *London Journal* to Hone's *Modern Textbook on Astrology*. Once the telephone was installed I would be all set to push ahead with the novel.

I don't believe in shutting myself away from the world in total solitude until I have finished a book. That, to my way of thinking, is a puritanical and ruinous attitude to one's work. I don't mind rising early and bashing away on a type-writer. But come midday, I begin to hanker for the great outside world.

So it was that one morning I sallied forth to Fleet Street and met my publisher at El Vino's. The choice was mine because there is something about El Vino's which makes for civilized conversation. The publisher had previously commissioned non-fiction books from me and I had had lunch with him several times. As a result I had noted two important rules for me to apply to any meeting with him. Rule Number One was never to try to sell him an idea for a book unless he was paying for the lunch, as, subconsciously, he would feel that unless he got a book out of this expenditure, he would be wasting his money. Number Two was that if I seriously wanted his views and reactions to an idea, then I must be sure I picked up the bill. It might sound cynical, but it meant that if his brain was being picked, he needed that extra encouragement to go through at least three courses and to drink in the relaxed style of one who doesn't have to worry about the expense.

This time he proved me wrong on Rule Number One, but right on Number Two. Though it was I who had asked him out, not only did he quite surprisingly agree to commission a novel that wasn't even written – just on the basis of a brief outline of what I was trying to do – but he enthusiastically gave me positive advice on how to proceed. He loved green Chartreuse with his coffee, and I plied him with it while he talked.

There was a preliminary discussion on the spate of what is both inelegantly and contradictorily called "factional" fiction in recent years, more especially in the genre of spy stories and thrillers. The publisher's first reaction was: "Why don't you do a spy thriller? You've got the background for it, you have lived in the sort of capitals where spies congregate and you could ensure that it was authentic enough to compete with other so-called 'factional' spy tales."

I protested that my idea in writing a novel was to escape from this kind of scene. "I want to imbibe other backgrounds, a different atmosphere. In any case, the Official Secrets Act and a score of other obstacles preclude me from attempting anything factual or factional of this nature. I should need to get clearance from the Office, and I'm fairly sure I shouldn't get it. Even John Le Carré had to get the OK from the Foreign Office when he wrote his first spy novels. What is more, he once had to change the name of one of his characters because he learned that, inadvertently, he had chosen the name of a real-life secret agent."

I had told my publisher that I had left the Service, but I hadn't told him why.

"Well, I think you are making a great mistake. But what have you in mind?"

"Well, why not a 'factional' romance? A Do-It-Yourself Romance. I go out and seek potential heroines in the real world, not in my imagination, but in the flesh, selecting one, or maybe two, who would evoke something of the spirit of romantic eroticism."

"A *factional* romance! Hm, that sounds almost a new genre. You may have something there."

When the wine was finished and the Chartreuse took over, my friend became more enthusiastic about the idea. "Every novel requires research, some more and others less, but no quality novelist approaches his work so far removed from his characters that he has to research them from top to bottom before he starts. They have to be more or less alive in his mind. The only way you can do a novel in this context you are exploring," went on my publisher, "is to describe what you are going to do as the plot – that is to say, going out to look for your heroines – and develop the romance from about that stage. It will be extremely difficult and sensitive to do and there are not many I would back to pull it off. If you did, it would make a marvellous novel."

This might not sound particularly explicit, but in the context of our talk over lunch we managed to achieve a mutual consensus of opinion as to how to proceed.

"While I am quite excited about this do-it-yourself romance with the author researching his own heroines, I would give you one word of warning," the publisher said. "You are not going to get this book finished quickly, or tackled properly, if you just go hopefully into bars as you did on the Île St-Louis and make the acquaintance of the Aprils of this world. That is too hit-and-miss. You must cast your net sufficiently wide at the very first stage of your research to ensure that you not merely have an adequate number of prospective heroines from which to make a selection, but that they realise the name of the game and are prepared to play it – either for fun, or to work off their fantasies. Anyway, I rather favour having more than one heroine in the book. Gives it more variety. So leave April in, despite her appalling Franglais punning. Remember what I said about you yourself needing to have some idea of what you want your heroine to be. You, too, must inject some romance into her."

Finally, he declared, "The only way to do all this is to advertise. I should start off with 'Author in quest of a Heroine . . .' and choose carefully in which journals you place your *cri de coeur*."

I was elated that the novel had got this far off the ground, but was fully aware of the pitfalls which lay ahead. One worry was that if I advertised for a heroine, this in effect gave the game away. Therefore I was wide open to all manner of exploitation by anyone who might think it would be a splendid spoof to "send me up." Probably I would spot any spoofer fairly quickly, but the point to be borne in mind was that, initially, at any rate, sex would not be the motivation here, but in its place the thrill or, if you like, the fun of becoming a character in a novel and of being able to pour out all manner of ideas and whims in a style which would not easily be possible in a straightforward male-female relationship. Yet this could be more of an advantage than a weakness in the arguments concerning advertising for a heroine. Simply by exchanging letters a unique relationship might be built up. The poser was at which point in the ensuing correspondence should the author and heroine meet. My instincts told me there was a risk that the magic of such a relationship could be destroyed unless one kept it on a strictly postal level for some weeks.

Another snag was that the age of letter writers seemed either dead or dying fast. No longer were there lengthy court-ships developed through the exchange of love letters such as the many written by Dorothy Osborne to William Temple, or Enid Bagnold to Frank Harris. "Do you remember Herm and the little house there?" wrote Dorothy Osborne. "Shall we go thither? That is next to being out of the world: there we might grow old together, and for our charity to some shipwrackt stranger, obtain the blessing of both dying at the same time." In somewhat different strains the young Enid Bagnold wrote to the ageing Frank Harris in May, 1917, ". . . to meet you again, it takes my breath away. It would be such a crown to everything. You say sometimes: 'I shall be old . . .' My dear, my darling, do you think any such trifle matters? As to what you can *do* I am indifferent, it is yourself, your voice, your standard, your face, eyes, hands, personality, impatiences, indignations, love, I want."

Such were my thoughts as I walked alongside the artificial river created by Sir Hugh Myddleton to improve London's water supply when an incident occurred which provided a most unexpected bonus. I was struck by the passing resemblance of this scene to parts of Amsterdam when I heard the horrific shriek of an animal in pain. I looked up and saw a young girl – probably under sixteen – bending over a cat which had one of its paws imprisoned in a trap. She was desperately and hopelessly trying to tug it free.

"Wait a moment," I exclaimed. "You'll never free the cat that way." I knew very little about traps, but I did realise the girl was only making things worse for the animal. Putting my foot down hard on the trap, I hoped for the best. In a trice the cat was free and the girl was able to pick it up.

"Lucky she didn't get the trap across her back, or she would have had it," I said. "I'm afraid her paw may be damaged as she is obviously hurt."

" 'ow do yer know it's a she?"

"It's a tortoise-shell and they are invariably female."

"You like cats?"

"You could call me a cat person. Is she your cat?"

'No, I've only just found 'er like this. Why should anyone want to put a trap for 'er like this?"

"Probably for foxes."

"What, 'ere in this place?"

" 'fraid so. Foxes get into the cities these days."

"But surely it's beastly and wicked to put traps so close to where people exercise their pets."

"I agree, but not everyone thinks like you and I."

The cat was struggling in the girl's arms, plaintively mewing. "We'd better take her to a vet," I said. "Fortunately I happened to notice an animal hospital as I walked along here. It's not far away."

"Oh, would you really do this for me? She's such a lovely puss."

There was something oddly appealing about this gamine of a girl in her patched-up jeans, with her tangled mousey hair, perpetually pouting lips and button of a nose. She told me her name was Lucie Whitwell, that she lived with her stepmother a short distance away, but that, "My step-mum 'ates cats almost as much as she 'ates me." By the time we reached the veterinary surgery she had fired questions at me like machine-gun bursts with all the quick-witted intelligence of the Cockney. What was my name? Where did I live? Why did I live here – "You don't sound like 'oxton."

"What do yer do?"

"I'm a writer."

" 'ow exciting. Wot sort of things? The telly?"

"No. Actually at the moment I'm writing a novel."

"Wot sort of novel?"

"A romantic novel."

"That sounds sloppy. My step-mum reads all that romantic slush. It ain't real life, y'know. Not a bit of it."

At this point the veterinary surgeon intervened to examine the cat. He bandaged her up and suggested she would need further attention very soon. "Give her these antibiotics – two tablets a day for five days – and follow up with some vitamin B12 for a short period." As Lucie Whitwell's step-mum loathed cats, clearly the responsibility for what happened to this woebegone, bedraggled specimen whose paws and tail were tipped with snow-white fur, rested with me. I am in some ways a ruthless character – my work had made me that way – but I am a sucker where cats are concerned. It was a question either of letting the vet find a home for the animal, which he wasn't very keen on, putting her down, or my adopting her.

To Lucie's delight, I said I would look after the cat.

"Wot will you call 'er?"

"You tell me."

"What about Tortie?"

"That sounds as good as any."

"Then Tortie it is. I'll buy some milk for 'er as a christening present. Can I walk back 'ome with yer? Will yer wife mind?"

"I haven't got a wife. Yes, you can come along."

I pointed out that first of all I had to buy some tins of cat food, a large oblong plastic bowl and some cat litter. "No use letting her run wild in this area. She'll only lose herself, or someone will steal her, or, worse still, kill her. Besides, she needs rest. She's still fairly young and will have to be trained to use a scratch-pan and learn to live indoors. We don't want her getting into a trap again."

I was very glad of Lucie's aid in coping with these unanticipated shopping chores. She insisted on carrying the cat herself, leaving me to grapple with the various unwieldy packages. I had a hunch that I was bringing more trouble on myself by adopting Tortie, and possibly more than that when agreeing that Lucie should come up to my flat.

Lucie was surprisingly resourceful. Finding a recess at the far end of my small corridor she decided this was "just the right place" for the plastic bowl I had chosen for a scratch-pan. This she filled with cat litter and then decided that at one corner of the tiny kitchen I must keep a bowl of food and another filled with water for Tortie. In fact, she took complete charge of the operation of settling Tortie in. Then, to my surprise, she reverted to the subject of romantic novels.

"I'd like to see something quite different, not the soppy stuff my step-mum reads."

"Tell me more." I really was genuinely anxious to learn.

"Well, take Prince Charles."

"What about him?"

"It's silly to pretend that being married to the Prince of Wales is romantic. Most girls I know would 'ate it. We talked abaht this at school and nearly all of us agreed on it. Take Princess Di, now – she's always calling off all those boring old capers they think up for 'er. Bet she's so fed up with 'em, she gets in a bad space."

"Bad space? What do you mean?"

"Depressed like, 'aving a bad time. I mean, it's rather like being in prison. Can't do this, can't do that. Princess Di used to like chewing bubble-gum and buying it from a little shop near 'er 'ome. Now she can't."

"What's this got to do with a novel?"

"Why don't yer write a book abaht the Princess wot got away? Yes, you could make that the title. Tell the story of 'ow Princess Di (call 'er some other name, if yer like) gets miffed with the 'ole business. Married, yet watched all the time, never allowed out on 'er own, 'tecs following 'er everywhere. So she makes up 'er mind to escape. She can't do this easily because *they* are always watching 'er. So she 'as this Citizens' Band radio, the Open Channel stuff, you know wot

I mean. She can 'ide the transmitter and receiver in 'er private suite. She could take it to the loo wiv 'er if she wanted to be sure she wasn't caught.''

Lucie's story tumbled out of her mouth in sweet confusion, providing what was for me an enlightening education in the language of a precocious teenager. This was as splendid as it was unexpected and I begged her to tell me more.

"You like the idea? Well, she doesn't give away where or 'oo she is. She just gives a call-sign under a false name. So she chats up some bloke over the air. Maybe 'ees just lumping abaht. Or 'ee could be a stash-runner. This bloke suggests a plan for them getting together and they 'it it off and agree to meet. She escapes in the middle of the night while all the 'tecs are asleep and snoring . . .''

"What about the Prince?"

"Oh, 'ee ul be asleep in another room. I bet she and Charles 'ave separate bedrooms. Those types always do, that's why they don't 'ave the fun we do.''

"I doubt if everyone would appreciate this idea of yours."

"But you like it, don't yer? Oh, say you do. I'm quite excited abaht it myself. I'm sure it would make a real 'it and sell like 'amburgers.''

"What gave you this idea?"

"I've been reading a book called *Their Royal Highnesses* and it actually tells 'ow in the eighteenth century there was another Lady Di 'oo escaped from marrying another Prince of Wales. She was offered bags of lolly if she'd marry 'im, but she turned 'im down flat. That Prince of Wales was Freddy, son of George II. An awful little squirt – quite a 'orror. And the girl who got away, mister – you'll never believe it – she was Lady Di Spencer, the umpteenth great aunt or something of the present Lady Di.''

Lucie had offered to "tidy up a bit" and, as I had not so far found any kind of domestic help despite the rising unemployment, I somewhat lamely agreed. Soon, I could see, Lucie would be taking charge. "I'd like to come back and see Tortie now and again. Maybe I can 'elp you aht a bit more, once a week at least. And, 'oo knows, perhaps I can 'elp you wiv yer novel. After all, yer 'aven't done one before.''

What Lucie had suggested, of course, was *lèse majesté* and far from being "factional", though I could not help thinking that the theme she had hit upon would make a splendid melodramatic romance with sensational newspaper headlines and Scotland Yard mounting a massive search for a missing Princess. But what had suddenly struck me forcibly was the idea of using ham radio or Citizens' Band for seeking out not a hero, as Lucie had suggested, but a heroine. Might not chit-chat prove better than scribble-scrabble?

Not only was this an enthrallingly and seemingly original gambit – I was astonished that she should have thought it up – but it pointed the way to a sphere of operations in which I was fully qualified and experienced. I had passed the technical examination for a radio amateur and was also able to operate both as a Citizen Band user and a long-ranger. Better still, I knew how to build myself a transmission-receiver set. Here in fact I could combine research with recreation.

Lucie Whitwell had done me a good turn. While she could not be a model for my heroine, her forthright, imaginative fifteen-year-old mind might well be an asset in the task I had set myself. More important, her mind was freed from any inhibitions about saying exactly what she thought on any subject. There was no doubt that she owed much to her gift for engaging people in conversation than to the comprehensive school she attended. So when she called round on her way back from school the following day, bringing with her a tin of sardines for Tortie, I lost no time in explaining to her that if she really wanted to help me out, I would gladly pay her the adult rate for the hour. She agreed and it was decided that twice a week Lucie would come to the flat to help with my chores.

Both Lucie and the cat Tortie were in this period vital factors in helping me to come to terms with what amounted to my dismissal from the Service. I may have suggested a somewhat happy-go-lucky, indifferent outlook upon what had happened to me, but, deep down, I felt depressed by the collapse of a lengthy career. While in the Service, travelling around the world, being on my own had seemed to have many compensations. Now, alone in a flat in De Beauvoir Town, I seemed strangely isolated. If I had to live somewhere in which flats were relatively inexpensive, then this was a poor man's Bohemia, but nonetheless I needed Lucie and

Tortie. Not only was Tortie the bait to attract Lucie to the flat, but I became increasingly to rely on the animal as an affectionate, and comforting companion.

Tortie provided companionship of a soothing, yet totally uncomplicated kind as by day she curled up on the far end of my desk, softly purring, while at night she installed herself rolled up in a ball at the foot of my bed, nuzzling against my feet. It may seem a sign of a pathetic sort of loneliness (though this I would deny), but to feel wanted by a mere cat was a most effective tranquillizer. As the days passed by I began to hold occasional conversations with Tortie and she would reply with varying degrees of miaou, which ultimately I was able to translate.

Meanwhile I drafted out the following advertisement which I posted to carefully selected newspapers: "Author in quest of heroine. Seeks girl aged 18–23 to correspond with, answer questionnaires and exchange ideas for creation of factional contemporary novel. Prize for winner. Full details from Box No. H ."

FOUR

Just in case advertising in the Press might not produce the results I hoped for, I decided to make use of Lucie's bright idea by building my own transmitter-receiver. Not far from Englefield Road, where a blue plaque marks the house where a music-hall player known as Champagne Charlie lived and died, I came across one of those stores housed in a converted garage where almost everything from fishing-rods to radio spares is sold. Luckily, I had had to learn almost as much about the construction of a home-made transmitter-receiver apparatus – or "rig" as we call it in the world of radio amateurs – as about the idiosyncrasies of handwriting. Apart from having been a dedicated "ham" in my earlier days, knowledge of this kind was regarded as invaluable in the Service. At any time an agent might need to abandon and destroy his own rig to avoid discovery and then later be able to assemble a new set on his own without any aid from outside.

The cheapest way of doing this was to buy up parts from a radio receiver and use basic tools. My transmitter had to be something of a compromise, because if I used the valves from a radio receiver, they were not actually intended for this type of work. I had conducted some experiments and found out that most of the recent audio output pentode and beam tetrode valves would operate in a satisfactory manner. So I decided to make the transmitter crystal-controlled and this required fewer components and was much easier to build. Also, it did not require a mass of test instruments to be set up, and, above all, the crystal frequency was very accurate even with quite large variations in mains voltage.

Crystals for this kind of application are available in a wide variety of mounts, some no larger than a postage stamp and about one millimetre thick. This type had been very useful for agents in the field, as it was easy to conceal. I had kept various odds and ends of radio equipment in storage over the past ten years and most of the other materials I found in that store off Englefield Road. The circuit of the transmitter I kept as simple as possible so that it required only a soldering iron, screwdriver, pliers and wire-stretcher in order to build it. The morse key I constructed by simply using an ordinary table-knife, and by keeping the receiver and transmitter separate I avoided complicated switching. I was just starting on the construction work when there was a ring at the door. Hanson appeared with the declared intention of luring me out for a drink at the Duke of Wellington, a pub in the Balls Pond Road nearby noted for its backroom stage productions.

"Ah-ha! So you are now about to contact Moscow Centre," he chortled facetiously. I explained what I was doing and why, and his first reaction was, "I wonder what the Fluency Committee would say about *that*?"

I knew that Hanson would have to report back to his chief on all this, so I made it clear that I was quite happy he should do so. I didn't want him to feel guilty about telling tales on an old pal. "That should give Six quite a lot of fun," I added.

"Well, I've no doubt someone will listen in to your chit-chat in due course. Not me, alas. But I shall be eager to hear how you get along."

"Maybe that trick cyclist they employ at Cucking Manor will be asked for a report on my mental state once they hear about this."

"Oh, don't worry, old chap."

"I'm not. *They*'ll do the worrying. Talking of radio tapping, do you happen to know if Wetherby ever tried to tap Sean Bourke?"

'Sean who?"

"Sean Bourke, the Irishman who rescued George Blake from the Scrubs and then went off with him to Moscow. Remember, he communicated with Blake by walkie-talkie when George was in prison."

"Ah, yes, Bourke, I remember now. What a howl went up when Blake escaped. But what has Wetherby to do with it?"

"I never told the Fluency Committee about this because it didn't amount to evidence, only to hearsay, and in any case I could hardly betray a confidence. But some time ago I had it from a usually reliable American source that Wetherby actually employed Sean Bourke for certain inquiries about that time."

"Interesting, but again improbable. Like to tell me more?"

"Alas, I know no more than that. I didn't pay much attention at the time as I felt there was possibly a satisfactory explanation for such a report. But after what I saw in Paris . . ."

"Hm. I'll bear it in mind just in case something turns up. Bourke, as I now remember, is dead, so we can't ask him. But I think I know somebody who could provide an answer." He pencilled a note on the back of an envelope and then we went out to the Duke of Wellington.

Within the next few days I began to feel quite pleased with my efforts. It took me just under five and a half hours to build my circuit and this gave me a power output of 30 watts with a 6DQ6 valve. Under average conditions this would ensure fairly reliable contact up to 350 miles and possibly further in peak propagation periods. Then replies to my advertisement arrived all in one batch of post. There were seven in all and I decided that, while I should reply to four of them, the main hopes were centred on just two of the applicants. I could very easily have sent out questionnaires to all the girls who replied, but I found three of the letters unsatisfactory for various reasons and did not take them seriously.

Letter Number One ran as follows:

"Your advertisement was certainly original. To safeguard my reputation I hastily point out that I am not myself seeking a romance, but then nor, I think, are you. Anyway, I'll fill in with a few details about myself so that you can establish whether or not I am a likely candidate. I am 23, single and 'educated' in the conventional sense – i.e. I did a Lit. degree following numerous O and A levels. I probably fall into the category of archetypal student, mellowed a bit by a couple of years out at work. I'm probably the type *your* generation warned me about. I'm just playfully wicked and a bit rebellious. In short, I enjoy life and people and intend to see as much and experience as much as I can before I ever consider settling down. Briefly, that is me – or me in terms of what may interest you as a novelist.

"Should you wish to contact me I will be able to receive mail at the address I have given – it is my work address as I, too, am being cautious. I warn you that once I get your name I shall check you out in the Authors' *Who's Who* and other reference books just to make sure you do exist. You don't actually need a surname to contact me, so I will just sign off with the name – Jeannette.

"PS. Surname withheld until I can think up a suitable one."

Jeannette was certainly being cautious, but she projected herself as a promising candidate. I liked that bit about her being "playfully wicked."

Number Two was interesting in that she seemed to anticipate exactly what I wanted to know, as will be seen from this extract: "I'm not sure that I'll be much help, but I read a great deal and would like to give what help I can. I think it best to write rather than meet, at least for the time being. I'm afraid I'm younger that you want your heroine to be – only just sixteen – but if you don't mind that, I'll do my best to make useful suggestions. If, knowing that, you'd rather try someone else, fine. Anyway, if you do decide to reply, no doubt the questionnaire would include all that. I don't want to do this for a prize, or compete with anyone else. So a prize is out for me. If you think you need someone older, good luck anyway! The idea's sound.

"Yours sincerely,
                                  Tess."

Four questionnaires were duly dispatched and ultimately my first hunch was confirmed. In other words Jeannette and Tess were the only front-runners, though there was one dark mare who appeared to be very mixed up though she undoubtedly had something to contribute: she was Belle.

My accompanying letter was long-winded and very detailed, so I shall not waste time in quoting it all. The questionnaire probed quite deeply and was deliberately worded to encourage each girl to set out on an ego trip as well as to answer questions. They were invited to list their likes and dislikes not merely concerning themselves, but also about a prospective mate: "... for question number four, it might be useful if you pretended you were playing the role of a questor for a mate, setting out clearly some of the qualities you would *not* want him to have ... i.e. as regards habits, possessions, ideas, interests, pets, hobbies, clothes etc."

The aim was not simply to get numbered replies to the questions, but to inveigle the girls into exchanging genuine letters with me so that their personalities, ideas and fantasies came to the surface naturally and not self-consciously. I knew this would be a slow business and that it might take several letters before the right kind of author-heroine relationship was established. I had put an upper limit of twenty-three for the heroine because I visualized the development of this contemporary romance as being the story of a man old enough to have had an interesting past and a girl young enough to be excited about a golden, unclouded and romantic future. This was the reverse of the Oscar Wilde theme that the best combination was a woman with a past and a man with a future.

Unlike the correspondence emanating from a "Lonely Hearts" type of advertisement, which meant that either you met speedily, or you wrote to each other no more, this was a peculiar kind of challenge to girls and author. One of its attractions was that it was more a game than real life, and it left the parties involved totally free. There was no instant involvement, yet with each letter a positive relationship developed in a unique way. For example, one got to know the innermost mind of the correspondents in a manner which would probably not have been possible if one had actually met them. One hears a lot of talk today about "lack of communication" between one generation and another, between individuals and races. This was a first-class exercise in achieving a rapport and intimacy which was quite astonishing in this era of impoverished communication between human beings.

To keep the correspondence going the author needed to bring out every writing ploy in his armoury, while letting his correspondents have brief glimpses of his inner self and lifestyle – enough to establish confidence and shared interests, but not enough to dispel an atmosphere of mystery. Letters from Jeannette and Tess arrived by the same post and I thought it would be a good plan to take the unopened mail to a good restaurant and savour each over a bottle of wine and an *escalope de veau* cooked in Marsala. Somehow this mode of "consuming" the letters (this really was a more accurate word than reading) enhanced the whole business and made it somewhat of a ritual.

Jeannette's letter was handwritten and extended to some eleven pages! Tess's was typewritten and covered only one sheet, typed on each side. Clearly, Jeannette's work entailed the supervision of delinquent girls at a hostel which appeared to be privately run, though presumably with some aid from the State. This was not the kind of job I had visualized for my heroine, but I felt this was no reason for down-grading her markwise. I was not sure whether I wasn't being rather priggish and schoolmasterish in keeping up this marks system for heroines. Indeed, I soon discarded it.

Jeannette gave a long list of her likes which included "adventure – as long as it's not too risky . . . open country and especially the seashore . . . travel, cats, green leafy plants and talking to them – I like watching them grow . . . free-flowing clothes and . . . getting slightly drunk."

I paused, sipped some of my wine and savoured that last phrase. It appealed to me enormously, the more so because Jeannette had inserted the adverb "slightly". To be slightly drunk was half-way to abandoning oneself to the adventurous side of romance, that is to say the swift transition from formality to a rainbow-riding intimacy within the span of a few hours. Her dislikes indicated that she was very much an independent and self-determined, though not card-carrying feminist. "I always say that women who just want to be equal to men lack ambition!" was one comment.

"It's obviously a good letter, sir," remarked the waiter who knew me well. "Let me fill your glass to enjoy it better." I read on: "I may at times contradict myself or appear slightly bizarre. This is intentional as my aim is simply not to answer the questions in a literal, intellectual fashion, but to try to probe behind the mask of words and rationalize to give you insight into my whole being, rather than just a typical 'cultured' mind. I shall attempt to be as honest as possible, to provide you with information that specifically relates to me..."

There was so much more of Jeannette's philosophy and outlook on life that I decided to leave some of her letter until later and to study what Tess had to say.

"I have a very broad sense of humour on the whole, though I do sometimes a have a 'black phase'," she had typed with the professional skill one would expect from a seasoned secretary and not a sixteen-year-old still at school. "I enjoy most Monty Python-type humour and like *The Life of Brian* for instance... My job isn't much help [I had asked prospective heroines to say what work, if any, they did] – I'm doing A Levels at school, by the way. Hobbies? I ride, do sub aqua (with tanks, etc.). I quite often refuse invitations because I would rather be reading a book. I write poetry spasmodically, but am usually so disgusted with the result that it is a while before I am inclined to try again. I am a curious mixture of 'what does it matter' and philosophic idleness which is punctuated with outbursts of enthusiasm for something and the strong wish to put everything to rights – worldwide! I don't have much patience but a great deal of perseverance, if that is not too great a contradiction... I'm Aries. I am afraid to admit that I enjoy telling lies (if not too major) sometimes because I enjoy the ensuing confusion, or simply to make a story more interesting to tell."

Between courses I studied Tess's likes and dislikes. It was interesting to note that she recorded her dislikes first (quite often an Arien trait). These ranged from "most continuous loud noises" to "clinging friends and relations". Her likes were distinctly formal: "Books, acting, travel, fencing, archery, walking, history and historical discussions."

After I had finished the veal and was awaiting the zabaglione, I studied Tess's musical interest: "I don't like 'disco', only some reggae, no punk and a very little 'new wave'. I think it would give you more of an idea if I gave you a few examples of songs and bands." This she proceeded to do, saying she liked Elton John "when he's not screaming" and that the Boomtown Rats had made quite a few hits she liked. On the classical side her preferences were for Mendelssohn, Handel and some Mozart.

Even Belle, who was rather uncertain about life generally and obviously going through a somewhat traumatic period of her young life, was starkly honest about herself: "I have a problem with my self-control when it comes to cheque-books (which I can't relate to money) and having handed back my banker's card and Access card and being allowed a set amount of money each week to keep me in order, any chance I have to write a cheque without a card is only too tempting ... I have an enormous number of complexes which thankfully I am slowly overcoming with the help of a psychotherapist ... At this moment I am sitting amongst heaps of rubbish and washing in my horrible claustrophobic little bedsit, I am drinking grapefruit juice, smoking a Silk Cut cigarette and listening to 'Fur Elise' by Clair de Lune."

This gives some slight, if not altogether adequate picture of three girls. What impressed me most was the sheer quantity of well-constructed sentences which Jeannette poured out, despite the fact that her working hours seemed sometimes to be as long as twelve to fourteen a day. I guessed that much of this letter-writing must have been done during the long hours she was on night duty. Both she and Tess had shown an extraordinary desire to express their personalities and opinions and they had achieved this in a controlled and disciplined style. Even poor mixed-up Belle could explain why she disliked clothes: "... I am never satisfied with the way I look and hate the whole business and wish so much attention wasn't put on appearance. In fact I wish we were all just spirits without bodies – bodies are the biggest burden human beings have – it would be so much more interesting if we could just drift around and communicate to one another without all the superficial stuff which takes up most of our lives. However, on a good day, if I feel good and look reasonable, I do understand bodily pleasures and clothes."

I really wondered why they should take so much trouble to pour out their thoughts to me. Surely they were not lonely, unwanted, ugly girls? At least Jeannette was not, as she had enclosed a coloured snapshot of herself which revealed a tall, attractive girl with long brown hair, wearing a kaftan. It wasn't as though I had been advertising for a soul mate, or answering a "Lonely Hearts" advertisement. I had taken great care not to complicate the issue by almost going out of my way to stress that research for the novel was the sole purpose of the operation, even adding that it was not essential for author and prospective heroines to meet. I could understand girls of Tess's age answering a questionnaire like mine just for a lark, and I vaguely imagined her showing my letter around to all her schoolmates at her very exclusive boarding school. But what shone through in all these letters was not merely a genuine desire to keep up correspondence with a stranger (someone they might never meet), but a burning, almost intense sincerity and frankness which one rarely encountered in every-day conversation with the female sex.

One somehow sensed that these initial letters were but the tip of a whole iceberg of hidden thoughts. Certainly I approached Jeannette, Tess and Belle with a respect and admiration which I had never felt for my first, unplanned candidate for research – April. With April I was also in a holiday mood and in half a mind to have an affair with her. With the other girls this was not the case.

Lucie usually called at my flat every other day. Sometimes to clean up, or see if there was any shopping to do, at others just to chat and administer to Tortie. Obviously her stepmother knew nothing about this and I felt slightly guilty on the subject, even though our relationship, if unconventional, was platonic. It was chiefly unconventional in that I began to treat Lucie as an adult, which in many ways she was. Occasionally I wondered if some inquisitive neighbour would tell the police that there was "a dirty old man at Number Three", who appeared to be having it off with a schoolgirl. If the police should question Lucie, her sheer outrageousness might cause them to think there was some cause for complaint. She was as obsessed with the idea of my novel as Mr. Dick with King Charles's head. She was very disappointed that I had discarded her idea for a royal romance, but interested to know I might seek a heroine by radio. One couldn't hide the construction of the transmission-receiver rig from Lucie.

"Wot you've got to find out, if you want to make your book nice and juicy, is wot turns 'em on. Unless you get 'em to tell yer that, it'll be a waste of time. Now take me, I won't let any blokes mess abaht with me where they shouldn't. But there's one lovely boy I know 'oo can turn me on by just licking' my ear'ole. That fairly has me rockin' round the clock. It's surprisin' 'ow much fun yer can get that way."

"Lucie, you are quite a shocker. Never mind, if you go on like this perhaps one day you can get a job as research assistant to Anna Raeburn. But you have a point."

In many respects Lucie had begun to organize the flat. She was certainly versatile. She baked a cake at school and brought it to me. Sometimes she would do the washing-up. She was equally willing to run errands, do shopping and take clothes to the launderette. One of her talents was essential to my existence in the first few weeks of coping with the cat. Lucie had lived with cats all her life until the stepmother appeared on the scene, and was probably more devoted to them than to any human being. She had a marvellous knack of placing Tortie firmly across her knee, deftly opening the cat's mouth and popping a pill inside, and then closing the jaws and holding them shut until the pill was safely swallowed. When I tried to do this, the pill was usually ejected. It took me a long time and much perseverance to perform this chore competently. But for Lucie I should never have managed it.

Lucie exploited this talent of hers in an unforeseen way. One evening I asked her if she would give Tortie the pill and she folded her arms across her chest, tossed back her hair and said with a wicked gleam in her eye: "Tell you wot, I see you've got a bottle of rum on that shelf. Wot abaht a tot of rum and some Coca-Cola, if I give Tortie the pill?"

Previously I had given her nothing stronger than Coca-Cola, which I only kept in the flat in case I wanted to mix it with rum. "Lucie," I said. "You are under age for alcoholic drinks."

"I've 'ad it before. Oh, go on, mister, only a little drop. Do yer know wot my idea of 'eaven is? It's to drink rum and coke through a straw while someone tickles my feet." So saying, she kicked off her shoes.

Had anybody provided her with this taste of heaven? I don't know and I didn't ask. I compromised by giving her the rum and coke, but ignoring the invitation to tickle her feet. And she gave Tortie the pill.

FIVE

All this time I was persevering with the novel my mind kept turning back to the problem of Wetherby and the way in which, as I was now quite sure, he had helped to manipulate me out of the Service. Twice I telephoned Hanson, only to be told he was away on a mission. It crossed my mind that someone in MI6 might overhear some of my radio conversations. God forbid it should be Wetherby! It was partly for this reason that I hesitated quite a while before attempting to use my radio circuit for seeking a heroine. For one thing I visualized a fairly lengthy correspondence with Jeannette and Tess, even if Belle petered out. But it was fun just listening in once again.

Lucie was desperately anxious to see some action on my radio front. She picked up some haphazard information about Citizens' Band Radio, presumably from a schoolboy pal of hers who went under the CB name of "Hissing Harry", or " 'issing 'arry" as Lucie designated him.

Lucie wanted to know if she could be a radio ham. "You could be a CB user OK," I replied, "just by buying a Citizens' Band radio licence for ten pounds. That would mean you could only use a Home Office approved apparatus which transmits and receives in the 27Hz band in the frequency modulated mode. But that's only good for a range of up to twelve miles or so. To become a radio amateur you would need to pass an examination."

"But I could 'ave quite a lot of fun inside twelve miles, couldn't I?"

"Well, if you had any pals inside that area, yes."

"And if not, I could make pals."

"With luck."

"You sound doubtful. 'issing 'arry has plenty of CB pals."

"If you really want fun, then you want a rig like this."

Lucie interrogated me relentlessly. She wanted to know how she could find out more about "this radio ham biz". I told her there was the World QSL Bureau and the *73 Magazine*, published in the USA, and that in the latter one could find out all that was going on in the world of amateur radio. "You can get the names and addresses of all licensed radio amateurs and their call-signs from the *Callbook Magazine*, which comes out each year."

"So if I 'ad a bloke 'oo was a radio 'am, I could look up 'is call sign. Then all I does is to make a call on that gadget of yours."

"It's a rig, not a gadget. And don't call us hams. We don't like the phrase. We are radio amateurs. Yes, you might possibly make an accidental QSO, if you were lucky."

"What's that?"

"It's a contact. An accidental QSO is the real thrill of this game."

" 'ow do you set abaht makin' wot you calls an accidental contact? Say I know a bloke, but not 'is call sign."

"You make what we call a CQDX call, keep repeating it and hope for an answer from some operator. CQDX indicates the operator who is sending the call wants answers from long distance stations or countries other than his own."

"It all sounds a bit difficult, but I guess I get the drift of it. And there's a new lingo to learn, isn't there?"

"There certainly is, though it's much the same as CB talk. It's very colourful and amusing language. Look, I'll show you."

I broke off to operate my rig and let Lucie get an idea of both CB and amateur radio in operation. My call-sign, which had been duly registered, was G5ZUW. I concentrated on CB first of all and soon picked up the following intercepted message:

"Any breakers? Any breakers in the West End? Do you copy the Judge?"

Fairly soon afterwards came a female voice calling: "Hazel Eyes, Hazel Eyes. This is Hazel Eyes copying the Judge. What's your twenty, Judge?"

I explained to Lucie that the gist of this CB conversation

was that a caller using the name of "the Judge" was wanting to know if any other CB users were receiving him. Hazel Eyes wanted to know where the Judge was located (his "twenty"). As we continued to listen it became clear that Hazel Eyes would love to meet the Judge, who said he was "square wheels" (stationary) outside the Eyeball Club in Smokey City (London) and that, thank heavens, they no longer had to worry about "Smokey Bear" (the police). This was some time after legislation had been introduced enabling CB users to transmit as well as listen in.

Because of this new legislation the possibilities of utilizing amateur radio in my quest for a heroine were very much greater. On the other hand the odds were that this would be a speculative operation and might take months before any worthwhile contact was made. Lucie's idea had been a stroke of genius, but to bring it to fruition would need a lot of patience. I first became a radio amateur in my late teens, but after I entered the world of Intelligence I more or less ceased to pursue such communications as a hobby except to listen in occasionally, but never to transmit. You could say that on those occasions, relatively few and far between, when I transmitted I was only acting on strict instructions from London, sometimes illegally and secretly on foreign soil. Now that I could be a genuine radio amateur once again there was a whole new world to investigate, for by this time CB users were well over the three million mark and increasing rapidly.

Lucie was absolutely thrilled by all this, and, unless I had firmly discouraged it, would have spent much longer at the flat, clamouring to listen in. I needed to make a point of listening all round the clock to ascertain which hours I was most likely to pick up some promising female operators as well as trying to judge in which areas of the world the likeliest heroine would emerge. I spent hours studying the *Callbook* and *73 Magazine*.

Next day Hanson rang up and asked if he could see me urgently that evening. "Better make it away from our usual haunts," he suggested. "What about Vat's in Lamb's Conduit

Street? The house wines are excellent, especially the Sauvignon de Tourraine. Six-thirty OK with you?"

When I reached this wine bar in Bloomsbury, Hanson was already there. "Keep your eyes on the door," he said, "as it's just possible you have been followed and someone may come in here and try to listen to our conversation."

"What in hell's name is going on?"

Hanson had ordered a bottle of Sauvignon de Tourraine and he poured out a glass and handed it to me. "Drink up first and I'll tell you. Cheers!"

"Cheers. For the record, I don't think I've been followed. I'm still aware of the tricks of the trade and as I've been wandering slowly around the bookshops in the area I think I should have spotted, or sensed anyone tailing me."

"Well, keep your eyes about you from now on. You will be interested to hear that investigations into that affair in Paris have not been dropped. Somebody in the Office thought that the bomb scare in that cafe on the Île St-Louis was worth looking into. The French police had had a tip from one of their *agents provocateurs*. They were told that a well-known bomb-planter known as La Razzia was on his way to the Île St-Louis 'on a job'. That was why the gendarmes called in at the bar while you were there. La Razzia must have been in the bar for a short while, but he left without laying any bomb."

"So?"

"When the sheets of your bed were being changed after you left Paris an ingenious device was discovered under your bed. It was linked to a tiny clock and set to detonate at 4.30 a.m. In other words, if, as you had planned, you had stayed on in the hotel that night, you would have been blown to pieces. Someone must have slipped into your room before you left the hotel and there can be little doubt it was intended for you."

"Does that mean my story is now believed?"

"It's not quite as simple as that. It has cleared up any doubts that you were telling the truth about the search for a bomb in that bar. But it has not altered matters *vis-à-vis* Wetherby."

"Why ever not?" I asked him with an intense anger welling up.

"Because there is nothing to link Wetherby with what seems to have been an attempt on your life. He wouldn't have a key to your room and it is hardly likely that he would climb along the balconies and gain access through your window. Also he would have left the hotel *before* you left your room even for a few minutes. As to the name C. A. Walters in the hotel register, that has proved to be that of an Anglo-Argentinian with an Argentinian passport. He left Paris by plane for Brussels the same night that he booked out of the hotel. So the odds are that Wetherby and Walters are two different people, despite your evidence."

"That doesn't prove anything. Were they able to establish the exact identity of C. A. Walters with the Argentinian Embassy?"

"Oh, yes, they checked up as far as they could and all the answers suggested that Walters was a real person. The information they got was that Walters had indeed had an Argentinian passport for some years, but that he was an expatriate and had not registered with the Embassy in Paris and, as far as they know, lived mainly in South Africa. We are still trying to check, but it takes time. Especially as we want to carry out those inquiries on our own."

"Surely all this must boost my case to some extent?"

"It confirms a great deal of your testimony and that much is duly appreciated. But what the Office is now concerned about is not so much your reliability as the threat to your life."

"Are you convinced it's a real threat?"

"The Office feels you must now have some, er – slight protection. Mind you, I think this is not altogether a magnanimous attitude. Take a grip on your glass and don't raise your blood-pressure, but the fact that someone may wish to bump you off actually makes some at the Office more suspicious of you. In brief, they think you must know something they don't, if someone else wants to bump you off."

"Charming! The truth which their bloody, stupid parochial minds can't grasp, is, that I am an open book. If I hadn't been so crazily anxious to keep Six informed on everything, even when on leave, I should never have rung you up from Paris."

"I know, old boy, but that's life. Did you see the chap who

has taken a seat in the opposite corner to us? Well, he is under orders to follow you home. He will first of all try to find out if you are being shadowed, check up on the security of your flat and, most importantly, generally check you out for bugs or bombs at regular intervals."

"And I am supposed to be used as a bait for the bomb-planters?"

"Something like that, but, honestly, we do want to keep you alive. Also, with you alive, someone sooner or later may try to contact you. We shall be watching. And if things get too hot, then we'll think up a rescue plan."

"I might even do that myself."

"Well, of course, you're quite free to do so, but for God's sake in your own interest let us know if you do. Are you still sure you can think of no other reason why somebody should wish to bump you off?"

"None at all. If I said Wetherby, nobody would listen. And I must admit it seems ridiculously unnecessary for Wetherby to contemplate taking any such risk. By the way, isn't he bound to know what is happening and what's to stop him putting a spoke into your protection plan?"

Hanson grinned. "I rather thought you'd say something like that. Indeed, if you hadn't, I should have thought you were losing your grip. You are right, of course, in theory if not in practice, Wetherby could know all about this. Undoubtedly he already knows quite a lot. I have to admit he could know everything. That is why I warned you that you could have been followed here, though it would be a matter of guessing whether the shadower was working for Wetherby (as you suspect), or for the bomb-planting outfit (as we suspect). But for your private information it was 'C' himself who asked me to see you urgently, though I would have come on my own accord as a matter of course. And 'C' assured me he had arranged for you to be protected without anyone else in Six being told. I can only guess that Wetherby was not being given this information."

"So that means the chap in the corner is Special Branch. But, if so, how come you know who he is?"

"Good question, Richard. I know who he is because his orders are to contact me alone in an emergency. I am to be your sole link with Six. And you are not, repeat not, to attempt to contact any other member of the Service without seeing me first. This may sound arbitrary, but in the circumstances it's in your best interests."

"Fair enough. But what an awful bore this all is, just as I was beginning to enjoy myself."

"Ah, yes, how's the novel going?"

"It's been commissioned, that's the main thing. We have just enough time to split another bottle of wine, so I'll tell you all about it. But I mustn't be late as I want to operate my rig tonight. By the way, does your chap across the way know about my rig?"

"Yes, he has been thoroughly briefed on all your peculiar hobbies and habits."

"Such as?"

"Well, the fact that you are writing a book and researching heroines. Remember what the Old Duke of Cambridge once said, 'I always knew there was something wrong about that chap. Now we know for certain because it turns out he's a writer.'"

I forced myself to smile at Hanson's bantering comment and then told him about my activities to date, not omitting mention of Lucie and the picture of heaven as a place where one drank rum and coke while one's feet were tickled. Hanson had a macabre, sometimes even a black sense of humour. That was part of his charm. But, partly because of this, he was the easiest of colleagues with whom to string along.

We walked to the door together and then said goodnight. He dashed off in the direction of Theobalds Road to find a taxi and I made my way through the twists and turns of narrow thoroughfares to the Gray's Inn Road. I felt this was the easiest way of checking that the man who sat in the corner seat was actually shadowing me. Very discreet it was, but shadowing nonetheless. I caught a taxi in the Gray's Inn Road, knowing that he would follow on to my address in due course.

There wasn't one good reason I could come up with as to why anyone should want to kill me. It wasn't as though I was, or ever had been, in possession of any top secrets. The only reason Wetherby could have for wishing me dead would be because I had discovered his presence on the Île St-Louis on that fatal night.

I turned the key in the lock of my front door and opened it, curiously reassured by the miaou I had heard as I approached the flat. Tortie was there to greet me and the forlorn muted cry gave way to a slow, contented purr. I gave her some milk and then poured myself a fairly stiff pink gin in a large glass with the minimum of Malvern water. Shortly afterwards there was a knock at the door and the Special Branch man arrived.

He was a nice chap and I soon warmed to him. These SB officers are a much maligned species as they so often have to play the parlour-maid to MI5 when they could very well act more effectively on their own, and in turn are frequently frustrated and restricted by both the Home Office and the Foreign Office. He asked me all manner of questions about the inhabitants of the other flats (concerning whom I knew practially nothing) and then proceeded to check out the rooms for bombs and bugs. His search was a thorough one and he promised to send someone along to put a chain on my door, provide me with a spy-hole and carry out other security precautions.

"I'll almost certainly not be calling here myself in future," he said after we'd had a couple of drinks. "Two nights might alert the unknown watcher, if there is one. But here's a number at which you can reach me or safely leave a message if I'm out. We can, of course, always meet somewhere in town if necessary. Keep me informed of anything you think of, hear or see which strikes you as being useful to us."

By the time the Special Branch man had left it was just after nine o'clock and I decided to take my mind off the events of the evening by switching on my rig. Hell's bells, I thought, why not combine two ploys – the appeal for a heroine and the role of the spider luring in an enemy fly. It might well be that this could be a sound strategy from all points of view. So I sent out what was in effect a very brief, impromptu and informal paraphrase of my advertisement, indicating that any replies should come to G5ZUW. I was not anxious to be inundated with inquiries, some of which might merely be jokey and curious.

I repeated the operation an hour later and then prepared

myself a simple meal. After that I switched on the rig again and listened around. Finally, at about 11.45 I pressed down on the morse key and sent out a repeat. There was no response again.

Ten minutes later I called once more: "G5ZUW calling, listening on 3.622 megs. K please."

K is the signal for the end of transmission. Then, after a brief pause, came a terse warning from another amateur that someone was "ringing your bell" (calling me). I tried again. After a brief pause came this answer:

"G5ZUW this is EI5RP/MM." It was a girl's voice.

This was repeated twice before I acknowledged the signal. "Yes, your signals are 5 and 7 and the WX [weather] here is good. Did you get my message? G5ZUW standing by for EI5RP/MM. K please."

"Thanks for coming back to me. Your message intrigued me. I hope you are not beaver-hunting. If so, roger and out. Your signals are 5 and 9. How am I hitting you?"

A "beaver-hunt" is really CB language for looking for girls. This sounded very much like a message from a no-nonsense type. Still, she said she was intrigued. I said that I was not engaged on a beaver-hunt and that her signal was good and strong.

She replied: "My QTH is off Dalkey Island, which is 300 yards off Sorrento Point and three miles SE of Dun Laoghaire, Dublin Bay. Is that any good as Base Twenty [location] for a heroine? My rig is a home brew and I'm running 100 watts to the final. The RX is a DX300 with digital read-out. Please tell me about your rig."

"I'm running 150 watts on a home brew rig, too. My QTH is North London."

This may all sound highly unromantic, pedestrian stuff, but preliminary talk of this nature is fairly typical of two enthusiastic radio amateurs establishing contact for the first time. This is the basis on which a satisfactory over-the-air relationship is effectively initiated. I was beginning to recover some of my own youthful ardour for this pastime.

Then came this final message: "Got to cut the coax [switch off]. Can't explain now. Will co-operate as you suggest. Tomorrow night same time. My name is Zita repeat Zita. Many thinks for the QSO. Have to pull the big switch.

This is EI5RP/MM.K signing off and clear with G5ZUW and listening for any final over. K please."
    I briefly responded that I would call again the next night.

SIX

The *Callbook* revealed that Zita was registered as a radio amateur in the name of Zita Stanway and that her licence had been issued by the Irish Post Office. This did not necessarily mean that she was a resident of Eire. That country has a very easy-going policy towards radio amateurs and even foreigners are able to obtain a licence there very easily. Not only that, but a licence-holder in Eire could obtain an /M, /MM, or /A suffix for the call-sign, allowing the holder to work as a mobile, maritime mobile (that is, from a small vessel), or an alternative address. There were great advantages in being a radio amateur with an Irish licence. Not only could one be a national of almost any country, but one could operate from any vessel afloat from a tiny craft to a cargo ship. Quite a few radio amateurs held an /MM suffix, but they normally operated from small pleasure craft.

The name Zita appealed to me enormously. It had style, *élan* and a deliquescent quality as one tried it out. No name came off the tongue so easily. My thoughts raced madly ahead of me as I reached for Dr. Ebenezer Brewer's *Dictionary of Phrase and Fable*. I had a hunch that I should find this name somewhere tucked away among those of the female saints. Sure enough, Zita proved to be the patron saint of domestic servants.

The only female radio operators I had ever known were those working in Intelligence on one side or another. Some of them were amateurs, a few were "illegals", that is, operating without a licence. I assumed, indeed I fervently hoped, that Zita was not one of those. I could think of nothing more chilling than an ex-MI6 man finding himself chatting up a girl who was also in the Intelligence game. It was almost incestuous. At the same time I needed to be wary. It was just possible, even if improbable, that Zita could be used by my unknown enemies, whoever they might be, and told to listen for G5ZUW and make contact with me in this way. This would be perfectly feasible if anyone had checked out my call-sign.

I think my intense interest in Zita was aroused first by her voice, which was precise yet alluring, and secondly because she was a fellow radio amateur. But equally intriguing was her unusual situation. I wondered what she was doing "off Dalkey Island", as she put it. She had no trace of an Irish accent. The island itself seemed a romantic enough setting for any heroine. In one sense it was almost too good to be true, better than anything one would have thought up in fiction. She must be operating off some small craft. But why, I wondered, did she have to switch off so abruptly? Had her boy friend suddenly appeared on the scene without warning? Or was she in some kind of trouble?

Just in case there might be trouble and a "mayday" message was already buzzing over the air, I switched on my rig again and listened. I even sent out a call, but there was no response. I decided not to repeat my radio message about seeking a heroine. It was more than enough to cope with Jeannette, Tess, Belle and Zita as the four running candidates for an author's belletristic home help. Frankly, I was not surprised that there had been no further responses to my signal, for, while replies to advertisements in the press would be safely secret, those over the air were liable to be listened in to by many people. Also some Citizens' Band users had made chatting up by radio a somewhat dubious pursuit by substituting "toilet mouth" (obscene language) for heavy breathing and, in some instances in London and Southampton, by controlling "pavement princesses" (prostitutes) by this means. That was why Zita wanted to know whether I was beaver-hunting.

Next morning as I made myself some coffee and toast, I gradually turned away from my literary project and took a look at real life. It was a salutary change from the rose-tinted world in which I had been living for the past few days. Here was I, apparently the possible target for some cold-blooded bomber, spending my hours chasing phantom females I had never seen. No doubt by midday the situation would seem less serious. Nevertheless it required some attention. My former employers had at least been sufficiently alert to the dangers to give me a modicum of protection. But I was well aware that it was merely the minimum of protection so that they could keep a watching brief on events and not enough to deter a professional killer. All I could do was to carry on as usual and take more precautions.

A "well-known planter of bombs known as La Razzia", Hanson had mentioned. I tried to recall if I had heard of him, but the name did not mean a thing. Nor could I remember who, other than April, had come into that bar on the Île St-Louis while I was there. My mind had been on other things until April came in, and then, well, you know my story. To concentrate my thoughts I typed out in chronological order all the incidents and times at which they occurred on that day, hoping that this, when studied, would provide a clue.

I had to admit that Wetherby could have known I was in Paris from contacts in the Office. He could also have seen my entry in the register after I had left the hotel that first time, though somehow I doubted this. Possibly he had seen me in Square Barye seconds before I spotted him. Or he could very easily have seen me looking out of the hotel window. It was quite likely that there was no connection between La Razzia and Wetherby, or between Wetherby and the bomb in my hotel room. But I was still in my hotel and had no intention of leaving it when Wetherby himself left, so he could have presumed I would stay on. Similarly, if La Razzia had been shadowing me, he, too, would not know of my plan to return to London. For that bomb must have been planted in my room when I left the hotel for about an hour between nine and ten o'clock that morning. My room had been cleaned exceptionally early while I had gone out to get the morning newspapers.

Hanson had certainly given me the feeling that I had rather more allies in the Office now than a week previously. But this mystery was not going to be solved unless I could find out why someone had decided I must be maximally demoted, as the Service phraseology so cynically describes an ordered assassination. I was quite small fry as MI6 personnel rates.

My expertise ranged from checking on forgeries and handwriting analysis to clandestine radio operations and, so I was told, an ability to present detailed and logical reports in an objective manner. I posed no threat to anyone; nor was I in the process of unmasking a traitor in our ranks, or the villain of another power. I was simply going on leave. Indeed, the KGB, or any other secret service, might just as well have ordered the killing of any casual tourist for all the good my death would have done them. Or so it seemed.

I looked up the word *razzia* in my French dictionary, hoping this might provide a hint as to the nature of the assassin. "An incursion made by the military into enemy territory for the purpose of carrying off cattle or slaves, or for enforcing tribute," I read. "It is the French form of an Arabic word usually employed in connection with Algerian or North African affairs." So La Razzia could be an Algerian. I had had dealings with Algerians, but on no occasion could I recall having had trouble with them. Nor had I had any contact or trouble with the PLO, for whom La Razzia might be operating.

It occurred to me that it could be worthwhile making a few inquiries about the alleged C. A. Walters and his Argentinian and South African background. If I could prove that he did not exist, or rather that he was none other than Wetherby, then the whole situation would be changed and my own case upheld. I had a friend in the South African Embassy and I decided to contact him. I knew that any telephone calls I made from the flat were from now on almost certain to be bugged by my own people. (I was sure that this had already been done) so eventually I made my call from a kiosk in the nearest underground station. We made a date for lunch the following day.

I kept alert for any would-be shadowers, but the pavement artists were not in evidence anywhere. To know that one's career was in ruins was bad enough, but to be told one might be hunted down by a professional killer was pushing things to the ultimate point of endurance. For I had an uneasy feeling that, despite any precautions that might be taken, my life was regarded as relatively expendable. If I had been some defector from the Ukraine who had worked inside the GRU or KGB as a resident director, then I should have been given total protection at some place like Cucking Manor, or whisked away to that hide-out on the borders of Wales and Herefordshire. One of "C's" favourite sayings was that "So-and-So is hardly worth a mass", and I could well believe he would apply that verdict to me.

A leisured walk around De Beauvoir Town filled in an hour and gave me a better chance of assessing whether I was being followed. With its street stalls, Jacobean almshouses, flower market and the Cooke family's eel and pie shop in Kingsland High Street, this is certainly the most off-beat of London's villages. I slipped into the private bar of the Duke of Wellington, had one drink and then swiftly moved down the street for twenty yards, upon which I suddenly turned round and walked in the opposite direction.

For by this time I was almost certain that somebody had been keeping a discreet eye on me. As I left the public house I had noticed someone across the road, holding a newspaper while apparently watching the door of the saloon bar. When I turned round this same man was crossing the road hurriedly in my direction. For a moment he hesitated, as though taken completely by surprise at my turnabout. Then he walked straight past me, eyes bent low to the ground. Cloth cap, cigarette in the corner of his mouth, upturned raincoat (it was raining), he gave the impression of being one of those types who hang around a betting-shop for hours each day. It was vital to ensure that his face became etched in my memory and I noted he had bushy reddish sideboards. Only long practice enables one to take in a face at a glance because invariably the people chosen to shadow one are those whose faces are, once seen, never remembered.

I could not be absolutely sure at this stage that he was actually following me. But the odds on his being a shadow were something like two to one. I carried on without looking back, slowing my pace so that, if he wished, it would be relatively easy for him to catch up with me. Then I turned round a corner and positioned myself by a shop window containing dozens of those handwritten personal advertisements on postcards. High up just inside the shop was a mirror which would enable me to see who came by. There were not many people about.

Normally, a professional shadower would have taken

avoiding action, either by walking straight past me, or crossing the road, and certainly not stopping until he could observe me without my seeing him. But to my momentary surprise and horror this character suddenly stopped right beside me, began to read the advertisement cards and then, without warning, asked if I could give him a light.

It then flashed across my mind what had happened to Georgi Markov not so many years before. A Bulgarian defector, who had found work with the BBC in Bush House, London, Markov was waiting for a bus on the south side of Waterloo Bridge when he felt a jab in the back of his right thigh. He looked round and saw a man drop his umbrella, pick it up and apologize and then rush off to hail a taxi. Within a day or two Markov was dead and the inquest revealed that he had been killed by a metal pellet containing poison as deadly as cobra venom, ricin, which was derived from the seed of the castor oil plant. The pellet containing it was only slightly larger than a pinhead.

"Sorry," I said, turning quickly away. "But I don't smoke."

I lost no time in putting a considerable distance between myself and the intruder. This was not so much a question of instinctive training as of panic reaction. I realised I was in a classic situation for this type of silent assassination, for there was nobody else close enough to us to be an accurate witness of everything that might happen to me, while the man carried a rolled-up newspaper in his hand. This was a well-known ploy of Eastern bloc professional killers for disguising an attempted murder. To get the hell out of it at such times is prudent, not cowardly. But one also needs to plan one's next move, not just go away and hope for the best.

I needed time to think, to decide in my own mind whether the man was a mere shadower or a killer-shadower, or neither. I felt it was evens that he was at least a shadower and that, if so, he had possibly judged that I had rumbled him. I walked briskly on to the nearest bus stop, fully intending to get on the first bus that came along, providing the intruder did not catch up with me by then. Luckily a taxi crawled round a corner and I hailed it, asking to be taken to St. Paul's Cathedral. Once there I was confident of being able to throw off any shadower even if he had been lucky enough to find another taxi in which to follow me.

At St Paul's I hurried away to a telephone box and called my Special Branch officer. My luck was in, as he answered the phone personally. "Get a taxi, make sure you aren't being followed and meet me at the Polish Club in Kensington in half an hour. If you are followed, stop the taxi at Earls Court underground station and than make your way on foot to the Polish Club."

The Special Branch inspector had had no information about my being shadowed by anyone. This convinced me I was right when I hazarded a guess that my so-called protectors had not initiated any round-the-clock watch on me.

"It's a great pity you didn't offer him a light and let him think you didn't suspect him," was the unsympathetic response I had from the SB officer.

"I don't smoke and I don't carry lighter or matches. Even if I had been able to give him a light, remember Markov."

"Oh yes, I remember Markov all right. Those of us who were engaged on that case even have a Markov tie which we wear on occasions. But our problem is that we cannot be sure whether you are simply being shadowed by somebody, or whether there is a real attempt to kill you."

"Dammit all, there is supposed to have been a bomb attempt on my life in Paris," I commented with some degree of acerbity. "There is independent evidence of that."

"True, but we can't really be sure about that. We have to take in the possibility that this was an attempt to frighten or mislead rather than to kill. Interpol tells us that an anonymous phone call tipped off the French police about that bomb so that it could be defused before it went off. But if you have frightened that shadower away, we have less chance of finding out what the score is. However, you have given us an excellent description of your pavement artist, a really professional description, if I may so."

"Glad I've done something right."

"Not to take this to heart. No ill feelings, old chap. You say his accent was English. We'll carry out a saturation, round-the-clock watch on you for the next forty-eight hours. After that, we shall have to rely on you reporting anything untoward, I'm afraid. But my guess is you need not worry too much because if the chap asking you for a light *was* an assassin, you would have been totally demoted by now."

I didn't wish to argue with him, so changed the subject by praising the excellence of the Polish vodka we were drinking.

"Do you often come here?"

"Quite a lot. I have a few friends among the Polish exiles community. I need them professionally when checking up on some of the infiltrators the PZPR try to plant on us. Vetting phoney Poles who are seeking British passports takes up more of my time than I like. Recently there has been a big increase in their numbers. The consolation is that the genuine old school Poles are among my most reliable allies in the immigrant community and I do very much like them."

"And their vodka."

"The vodka, of course. It doesn't linger on the breath which, professionally speaking, is an asset."

"When I told you that my probable shadower spoke good English, that wasn't to say he himself must be English. He could have been Hungarian or Rumanian. Some of them speak perfect English."

"Well, you could be right. Possibly a Hungarian as I have a suspicion that either the Hungarians or the Poles are taking over from the Czechs as the Russkies' stooges in the UK. The KGB fairly got the wind up after Josef Frolik and Frantisek August spilt the beans to the Americans about how the Czech Secret Service in London had snared some of our MPs and trade union bosses into their network."

I returned to the flat realising that not much progress had been made. I was sufficient of a realist to know that the financial budget of our security services dictated that any prolonged watch over me could not be justified. In any event the necessary personnel could not be spared for such an operation. I should have to continue to fend for myself. When asked for that light, I must admit that momentarily I felt every muscle tense up and alarm bells ringing along every channel of my nervous system. But this was merely the body recording its own red alert, pumping up adrenalin and stimulating rather than frightening. But now I was glad to note that my chief concern was not to much my own personal safety as the fact that this distraction might prevent me from giving full attention to my novel.

So the novel had become more important to me than my own life? Was this because I did not really believe there was a plot to kill me off, or could there be a subtler reason? It was when I got back to the flat and found another letter from Tess awaiting me that I began to realise what the answer was. The letter started:

"Dear Richard,

I was quite thrilled to get another letter from you, chiefly because you took the trouble to burst into verse. If I may say so, it was very like you, or what I imagine you to be . . ."

Good God! Had I really done this, and I'm not even a poet? I then recollected that, in trying to respond to her interest in poetry, I had almost without further thought typed out a piece of nonsense verse. I turned back to Tess's letter: ". . . I have a pet turtle, a red-eared turtle, or terrapin, which I see when I go home weekends. I was wandering through Colchester Market one winter a few years back when a cat litter tray, filled with squirmy little green things caught my eye. On closer inspection they turned out to be a lot of immature (they're brown when they're mature) little turtles, tier upon tier. At the very top sat one little lady gazing disdainfully at the writhing mass below. I bought her. She is a she, by the way, because she hisses when annoyed. Males only grunt, and then rarely. She spent the weekend in my pocket, and was transferred during the term to my locker in the dormitory at school and she flatly refused to eat until she was comfortably settled in a small heated tank in my bedroom at home. Since then she has become quite tame and the best way to put her in a good mood is to delve around in the garden ponds for wriggly insects and snails which she will eat very messily."

After I had put the letter down the truth dawned on me at last. I was engrossed in this novel project not just because it had been commissioned and offered me the chance of a new career, but because the actual research involved had become a way of life. When I advertised for a heroine my whole concern had been whether this form of research would succeed. Now it had not merely succeeded beyond all expectations, but I knew that I awaited each post with all the anticipatory thrills of the starry-eyed romantic of my youthful past. What had started out as a literary exercise had become something quite different. It was no longer just a model for a contemporary heroine I was seeking, but a soul mate for myself. Well, perhaps soul mate sounds rather too much like Edgar Allan Poe in his darkest moments, but it was certainly something rating higher than a mere paramour.

This realization of the truth should have boosted my hopes for contacting Zita that night. Instead it filled me with doubts and apprehension. I had the feeling of being disembodied from my fingers as I switched on my rig and listened in. Writing letters and getting replies constitute an uncomplicated, cosy relationship between two people, but establishing a relationship over the air is totally different. There is no time to think up witticisms or elegant phrases whether in making one's own approaches, or answering back. This applies as much to talking over the air as to communicating by morse. Any hint of romance is strictly conditioned by atmospherics, reception and all manner of other technicalities.

My first two attempts at contact drew a blank, but then I sensed some kind of interference on the rig. I tried again, having boomed off an interloper who had picked up my message of yesterday and was listening in out of sheer mischievousness or a warped sense of humour. The intruder was one of the very few rogue elephants of amateur radio who misuse our code of international goodwill to all rig operators. Then I tensed myself to catch the gist of a rather faint transmission: "G5ZUW this is EI5RP/MM. I'm working from my boat. QRL. [Are you busy?]"

Somehow Zita must have detected the attempts of the interloper to gatecrash our respective transmissions. I replied, "EI5RP/MM. Delighted to hear from you. I am free to receive, so go ahead. QRO [Shall I increase power]?"

Zita replied in the affirmative and also asked if I would "send more slowly". This I did, at the same time enquiring whether she had any queries on my message of the previous night.

"Not really," came the response, "except that I am somewhat chary of continuing this transmission if any others are joining in. If that is so, I see problems for both of us."

"Nobody else so far and I suspect there is only one earwig [listener-in to conversation]. Intend to talk to you only."

"Might be more helpful if we wrote as well as talked, if

you wish, that is. If you want to send me a questionnaire, please do. Then, if we lose contact for any reason, we are safeguarded by having each other's addresses. Sorry I've no Base Twenty [home] except for the boat at the moment. Shall be on the move soon. Meanwhile you can write to me care of GPO, Dun Laoghaire, County Dublin. Make it poste restante."

"Will do. How long will you be there?"

"Not more than five days, so you had better write fast."

I assured her I would, and gave my London address. "What happened last night? I thought you might be in trouble."

"I just had to pull the big switch. Someone was howling at me to move my boat from the moorings. I had bagged someone else's by mistake."

So it wasn't the intrusion of a boy friend. "Are you on holiday?" I asked.

"Sort of. I'm looking after a girl friend's boat while she's in the UK. It's a very tiny one-cabin craft, the kind you see on rivers. I live aboard and save the cost of a hotel or digs. It's great fun because it is marvellous territory for painting and I simply adore seascapes."

"That gives us something in common. I very nearly bought myself a small craft so that I could live on the Thames."

"Why didn't you?"

"Finding the right moorings isn't easy these days."

"What makes you want to write a romantic novel?"

Nobody else, except my publisher, had actually asked me this question. And I was not sure I knew the answer. Oh, yes, I knew what I gave for an answer but as from that particular night I was no longer sure this was the truth. "Chiefly because I don't like the so-called modern romantic novels that I read."

"I don't read any, so I wouldn't know. Spy thrillers are more me."

At this remark the author in me registered a slight depression. If she didn't read romantic novels, was she really likely to be much help answering the questionnaire? Then I suddenly remembered that my novel was already threatening to become, if not a spy thriller, then thirty per cent a kind of spy story. It hadn't started that way exactly, but that seemed damned likely how it could finish. At this stage there was further interference which seemed to make conversation almost too difficult. Luckily I was chatting to a competent amateur who kept her cool.

"More breakers [interrupters], I fear," advised Zita. "Will await your letter. The mush [interference] is dreadful. Have to pull the big switch now. Seventy-threes. This is EI5RP/MM signing off and clear with G5ZUW and listening for any final over. K please."

I could think of nothing else to say but *"Hasta la vista,"* which, though Spanish, is internationally accepted as an abbreviation for "See you later." Not perhaps a highly satisfactory chat, but at least it provided a glimmer of hope and addresses had been exchanged. I had a hunch that Zita might be quite a strong runner in the Heroine Stakes. I felt that somehow we had a strong, invisible force working to bring us together simply through the camaraderie of radio amateurs. Love of the sea was another. It might seem very little, far, far less than I already knew about Jeannette, Tess and even Belle, but it added up to something quite potent.

On the other hand there was much yet to learn about Zita and that was a challenge. It was like the Kipling adage that "the more that you think of the other, the less that you think of the one". What did she look like? How old was she? Why had she not given me a home address as well as the poste restante at Dun Laoghaire? What did she do? Was she an amateur or a professional painter? Why was she a radio amateur? While there are plenty of female radio operators in the amateur game, to find one in Eire of all places was somewhat rare.

SEVEN

My friend from the South African Embassy was not able to help very much, but he promised to make some inquiries about the mysterious "C. A. Walters." Naturally, I did not tell him why I was interested, or my suspicions about Wetherby. Nor was he inquisitive.

"I doubt whether I shall find out much," he told me. "But my guess is that this chap Walters could be an Argentinian arms purchaser, as we do have dealings with one or two of them, some being Anglo-Argentines. Slippery customers who keep a very low profile."

There were no further signs of anyone shadowing me and I began to hope that I might have been mistaken after all. I returned to the flat to write to Zita. For some reason I funked the task and so tapped out on the typewriter this stilted, unfunny and wholly artificial beginning:

"Dear Zeta, [oh yes, I got the spelling wrong]

Zetetic Zeta: It's an unusual, but marvellously euphonious adjective when linked to your name. Zetetic means a seeker, someone who proceeds by enquiry, which is just how I see you."

I stopped, read what I had written and groaned. Was I trying to show how bloody clever I was and, in the process, making a statement that didn't really make sense? The question is apt because it is salutory that we writers should sometimes admit we are capable of producing unmitigated crap.

So the first page of this letter was tossed into the wastepaper basket and I started again:

"Dear Zeta,

You will only be in Ireland for a few more days, so this is a brief letter, enclosing the questionnaire. I hope you will be able to give me a permanent address soon, though I appreciate you may wish to be wary of a strange author with unusual ideas of research for romantic fiction. Really it amounts to this: I need guidance and direction so that I keep my book firmly on the rails of modernity. However, I think you will find the questionnaire straightforward and sensible. The answers need not be too terse, or rather, I should say that if you feel like expanding wildly on any particular question, this will be doubly appreciated. The object is to bring this author up-to-date on contemporary thinking of a modern girl aged eighteen to twenty-two and on her recreations, ideas, tastes, likes and dislikes and, if romantically inclined, what she is looking for. Equally perhaps what she is *not* looking for . . ."

The rest of the letter was not important. Nor was it a particularly inspiring screed. I began to think that Zita had unnerved me. I couldn't understand why I found it so much more difficult to write to her than to Jeannette, Tess or Belle. Partly the reason was that the other three girls had all written to me before I had written to them. Once they had poured out their thoughts, it was easy for me to come forward with my own. It was some measure of how seriously I was beginning to regard Zita that I walked nearly a mile to the local post office rather than put the letter into the nearest pillar-box.

That night I tried to get in touch with her again by radio, but she was off the air. Meanwhile I tinkered around with the rig, made a few changes in it and soon discovered that, while I could be sure of excellent reception most times on a radius of up to 400 miles, I was occasionally able to extend my range effectively to as far afield as 1,500 miles. I also made full use of my rig for establishing contact with one or two old pals in the amateur radio game.

By this time Lucie, a wily one for worming out the truth, had pestered me into admitting that I had advertised for a heroine over the air. This may seem incredible stupidity on the part of an ex-Secret Service agent. All I can say is, "You don't know Lucie."

Next day Lucie called round at the flat to do her usual stint of cleaning. With a triumphantly impish grin on her face, she waved a copy of the *News of the World* at me. "Blimey, mister, you ain't 'arf going to get into trouble if yer don't watch yer step. Just look at these 'ere." She pointed to two news stories side by side on a single page and I must say they made me exceedingly glad that I had not tried to seek a heroine by means of CB radio.

One story told how a CB radio fan with the improbable code-name of Big Sardine had been jailed for six months because he had seduced a thirteen-year-old schoolgirl after having chatted her up by CB radio. The girl's father, also a CB fan, had listened in to their chatter and reported the affair to the police. The second story was about another female CB fan who became outraged when her neighbours spread malicious gossip about after listening in to her late night prittle-prattle with a male CB user. So she drove around the neighbouring streets in her car, with her CB pal beside her, and, flicking on the public address switch of the rig, announced loudly and clearly who she and her companion were, adding: "I know you have been gossiping about us for ages, and I thought now you have eyeballed us, it would stop the gossip."

I must admit these two news items made me realise that using radio to seek a heroine could create problems if one was at all careless. "You're quite right, Lucie," I told her. "Both stories are a warning. But I'm not chatting up thirteen-year-olds and I don't use a CB rig. That's the difference."

"But somebody could still listen to you, couldn't they?"

"Too true. But the risks are less and anyhow I have nothing to hide."

In fact the stories rather depressed me because I wondered whether Zita might read them and decide not to reply to my letter. There was a fair chance that the Big Sardine story might even get into all the Sunday papers.

Lucie was exceptionally inquisitive that morning. She had spotted the extra lock put on the door, the chain and the installation of the sentrycom.

"Wot you 'ad these put in for, mister?"

"Just a precaution, Lucie. There have been some strange types around here lately."

"Wot kind of types?"

"Dubious characters, people trying to pick locks," I lied.

"Sure you ain't in trouble and some girl's pa isn't after yer?"

When Lucie was just chatting generally, she could be amusing and enlightening. But once she started asking questions, her charm began to vanish. Her questioning could be relentless and wearing. In some ways it was more intelligent and perceptive than the kind of queries put to one in what is so inaptly called positive vetting. Maybe the Lucies of this world could do a better job of positive vetting than the arrogant barristers and so-called professional interrogators who often miss all the vital points and let the clever villain slip through the net. If Lucie was quick to draw all the right conclusions, she also had the imagination to fill in the gaps and to process those conclusions into something more sensational that the exact truth. In my case I felt sure she suspected I was not telling her the real reason for the security precautions.

"You won't change Tortie for a dog, will yer?"

"Certainly not, Lucie. I've become very attached to Tortie. She purrs away on my desk while I type."

"Think I'd better check you've got enough food in for 'er."

It then dawned on me what Lucie was doing. Hanson had rung up to ask if he could call and see me. Lucie must have overheard this and I guessed that she was trying to find various excuses for staying on until he arrived. It was somewhat of a nuisance, but I was sure Lucie would be highly suspicious if I asked her to go.

Hanson had not seen Lucie before and, when he arrived, he gave me a very quizzical look. I then handed Lucie her usual pocket-money and a list of things to buy for me the next time she called. Soon after she left.

"Well, well, well," smiled Hanson as he sat down for a drink. "I knew some of the Foreign Office types had a penchant for paedophilia, but I didn't know that our brothers of Six had succumbed to this recreation. Is she part of your quest for a heroine?"

I had to tell Hanson the whole story about Lucie. "Now I'm out of the Service it really doesn't matter a damn what I do. Maybe six months ago I would have kept Lucie discreetly at a distance. But she happens to be quite useful and is a good-hearted kid."

"I'm sure you're dead right. Can't help a bit of leg-pulling, old chap."

"And what have you got to tell me?"

"Remember you asked me about a connection between Sean Bourke and Wetherby?"

"Yes. Have you discovered anything?"

"Not exactly. But by a curious coincidence the Special Branch have told us that an Irishman known to have been an associate of Sean Bourke has been seen loitering in the vicinity of this street on at least three occasions in the last few days. He could have been shadowing you, but the police aren't sure. I assume this man couldn't be the chap who accosted you for a light as he doesn't really answer your description and had a marked Irish accent. If I remember correctly, the chap you described spoke good English, according to the SB."

"That's right. Not a trace of accent, just classless English."

"Well, take a look at this photograph. Have you seen him before?"

"Not to my knowledge."

"Well, he's the chap you need to look out for and his name is Seamus O'Donovan. Better keep that picture in your wallet."

"Thanks for telling me. I must say life has become more complicated since I left the Service than when I was in it. And that's saying a lot. But, frankly, where do we go from here? I have been trying to to convince myself, not very successfully, that I could have been mistaken about the shadower. But I'm pretty sure I was being tailed. I should prefer to carry on as though nothing had happened. But is that possible any longer? How sure are you about Seamus O'Donovan?"

"Nothing is for sure. If the Specials get an excuse, they might pull O'Donovan in for questioning. But they haven't got the vestige of an excuse for doing that as yet, and they don't want to frighten him off. They have tabs on him, know where he lives and, of course, they always expect you to come up with something which might help them further."

"It is rather disturbing that I haven't actually spotted him. It suggests I haven't been particularly vigilant. Yet I've been on the look-out all the time. If the Specials have spotted him, then so should I."

"Not necessarily. He may not actually be shadowing you, but just keeping watch on who goes in and out of this flat."

"If Wetherby had dealings with Sean Bourke, isn't it probable that he knows all about O'Donovan?"

"What you mean is: why don't we ask Wetherby?"

"In effect, yes. Why not give Wetherby some of the treatment that was given to me?"

"My dear Richard, have patience. If something turns up that I can show is in your favour and could clear you in the eyes of the firm, I'm only too anxious to act on it. But you must see that I can't tell you all we may be doing about Wetherby, or indeed what we are doing at all. There is no doubt he has protectors in high places, Cabinet Ministers and ex-Cabinet Ministers. Any indiscretion on my part could equally lead to my being booted out of the Sevice, or transferred to some other inauspicious territory which would mean disgrace in disguise. I'm afraid you've just got to believe me when I say I'm on your side."

"Yes, I do know that and I do very much appreciate your keeping me in the picture. Apart from which, as you should know by now, it's like a treble shot of vodka on the rocks seeing you now and again. Half an hour with Hanson is a guarantee of at least one *bon mot*, if not two."

"Thank you. Getting back to business, O'Donovan must know by now just who calls on you. I'm not trying to pry, but it would be useful to know – if only to safeguard you, and possibly others – who your callers are. I'm sure you see what I mean. Should any of your callers pose a threat to your unknown enemies, you would need to take much greater precautions."

"I've nothing to hide. I should say that the only person who comes into the category you have just mentioned would be yourself. Oh yes, and the Special Branch man, but then he's only been here once. Except for Lucie there have been no callers at all. I haven't even attempted to lead any kind of social life in the past few weeks. I've just concentrated on settling into the flat and writing my novel. Oh, and making amateur radio chats the substitute for a social life. I haven't as yet even been in touch with any old friends."

"Good. But, as you say, you have been visited by the SB man and myself. And tradespeople?"

"No. I've done my own shopping with the sole aid of Lucie. All the security arrangements were put in by someone approved by the Specials."

"You might discreetly use Lucie to do a bit of spying for you. She seems an intelligent girl."

"I should hardly call Lucie discreet. Her sense of melodrama would prove too much for her discretion. But I suppose she might be useful in some way."

"By the way, your reported shadower was not detected by the Specials. You could have frightened him off, or it could be that whoever is behind all this is changing the shadowers every few days. It is absolutely baffling why this should be the case because there is no real reason why so much attention should be paid to you."

"I agree it's totally mystifying. I'll keep you posted about what I see or discover. But this Irish connection is puzzling. I really don't see . . ."

Suddenly I checked myself and I suppose a look of shock must have crossed my face because Hanson wanted to know what was wrong.

"Nothing, just a thought. It couldn't be."

"Try me."

So I told him about Zita and her living in a boat off the Isle of Dalkey.

"You do cast your net wide in your search for a heroine."

"I'm sure there is no connection between Zita Stanway and Seamus O'Donovan."

"You mean you bloody well hope there isn't. How many other radio contacts have you made in your quest for a heroine?"

"None. I haven't even attempted to make any more."

"Well, watch it and be on your guard! I only hope you are right about the Stanway girl because O'Donovan's birthplace is Dun Laoghaire, the very place your radio pal collects her mail. And why hasn't she given you her permanent address?"

"I dare say she wants to be cautious. After all, she knows nothing about me."

"My dear Richard, you are becoming accident-prone. You need to be very vigilant indeed. I shall be very interested to see how this radio romance develops. What is more, can we be kept in the picture as to what transpires? It is in your interests, you know."

"I suppose so. But I'm not exactly enthusiastic."

"Well, look at it this way, old chap. Suppose your Zita is an enemy posing as a potential heroine. Couldn't that give a marvellous twist to your novel?"

"It could, I suppose. And yet I should feel slightly sick, if it did."

EIGHT

Zita now tells her own story, picking up the thread from shortly before my first contact with her.

I suppose the idea of a do-it-yourself romance was first mooted during a drink with my two flatmates after supper one evening at our home in Ifield Road, Fulham.

Julie and Sandra, aged twenty-three and twenty-four respectively, were both secretaries in the City while I was the youngest of the trio at nineteen and very much the odd girl out. I was a kind of freelance helper-out rather on the basis of "you name it and I'll do it". I waited until the agency rang me with an offer and then dashed off to wherever they told me. Sometimes it was to go down to Richmond and cook for a house party. Then it was baby-sitting, or meeting a child off a plane and taking her home, or it might be taking people to view houses they might, or might not wish to buy. What I really wanted to do was to paint, but painting doesn't pay for bed and breakfast.

Sandra suddenly drew our attention to an advertisement in *Time Out* which stated: "Scorpio male would like an attractive lady for lasting relationship. I'm 23, five feet nine inches tall, slim with blond hair, blue eyes and steel-rimmed glasses (they make me look intelligent) but working unsocial hours. Sense of humour essential (I'm mildly crazy). Photo appreciated, returned. Please write to Paul, Box No. . . ."

"Typical male chauvinist pig. *He* wants a photo, but doesn't want to send one in return," I replied.

"I rather like this one," said Sandra. "It says 'Warm and cuddly, tall, good-looking blue-eyed company director, thirty-four, seeks bubbly, attractive girl, aged twenty to forty, for fun, friendship. Write with photo, if possible.'"

"Yuk! He sounds positively revolting," commented Julie. "I have no desire for a company director anyhow."

It had been Sandra's turn to produce the meal that evening (usually I was pressed into doing the cooking). She hated working in a kitchen and had brought back a Chinese take-away package from a restaurant in the Fulham Road. It was one of those rare occasions when we were all in for a meal together. While we were finishing off the wine which Sandra had bought as a special treat, someone, I forget who, suggested that for a lark we should each write a different advertisement in quest of a male.

The idea was that we should compare notes once we had received responses to our respective letters. I don't think any of us really took it seriously. But Julie and Sandra were both somewhat bored with their various boyfriends at that time so they may have half hoped something would come of it. We continued discussing our idea for ages.

"Why don't we line up the men in our lives scientifically?" I ventured. "Finding the ideal mate is such a hit-and-miss game that we need to approach it much more seriously..."

"Like what sign of the zodiac he's born under?"

"Yes, that, and of course what planets were positioned where at the time of his birth. And then a full list of his likes and dislikes, especially those he would be likely to hide from me."

"Zita, you really are a hopeless romantic and so hard to please."

Sandra thought that maybe in the future we should all use some form of computer-dating. Although that sounded pretty grim to me, I had to agree there was an element of adventure in this approach to finding a Highly Desirable Date. So we each agreed (Sandra with enthusiasm, Julie in rather a flippant mood and myself, reluctantly) to try a different system for seeking our HDD. We also agreed that after giving each method a fair trial, we would swop information and compare experiences.

Sandra was given the task of answering advertisements in the various weekly and monthly magazines, but she concentrated mainly on *Time Out* and *Private Eye*. Julie promised to explore the possibilities of marriage bureaux and computer-dating.

"I wonder if a computer can really match people up effectively?" pondered Sandra. "What if the computer has on its books the sexual failures of the world?"

Until then I hadn't made any suggestion as to what I should do and suddenly my flatmates noticed it. "Come on, Zita, what's your method going to be?"

"Obvious, isn't it?" Julie broke in. "She'll seek her bloke out by radio."

"I certainly shan't," I replied rather indignantly. "That would be asking for trouble."

"Why?"

"For very many reasons. Now that Citizens' Band radio is permitted, all and sundry are using it to chat up and spy on one another. It is also being used by pimps to control prostitutes."

"Surely not?"

"Just look at this glossary of CB and radio jargon. You see 'Pavement Princess' – it means a prostitute."

"Yes, but that's only local, isn't it. Couldn't you discreetly chat up someone from a distance. Do say you'll try."

Reluctantly, I agreed to try. Amateur radio had long been a passion of mine. But though I kept a diary of contacts made, I had never used my rig for seeking out dates. Not that I was in any way priggish, but, frankly, the idea of doing this just hadn't occurred to me. I tended to get bored with boys of my own age and I was not madly keen on any kind of dating. Up to that time I preferred going out in a foursome, just making up a party for the theatre or late night cinema with either Sandra or Julie and some of their male friends.

My parents had been killed in a car accident when I was only twelve-years-old. Since then I had been brought up by an aunt who, being a spinster, was inclined to be over-protective. But I was by no means cossetted and had, from my eighteenth birthday, managed to live my own life in my own way in London. I had my own room and whenever I was bored I used to switch on my rig and focus around the world. I suppose this passion for radio was in one sense my subconscious urge to hold a torch for my dead father. I had adored him and until his death he was the most exciting man in my life. A naval officer who specialized in radio, he taught me all I knew about it. It was he who built my rig and I had cherished it ever since.

During the next few weeks Sandra and Julie would tell me what progress they had made and ask what I was doing in seeking a man. I carefully explained that, while I myself would not try to find a man over the air, I would listen in to any requests for female companionship which might not sound too dangerous. I think they thought I was both a spoilsport and a coward, but I had had one or two nasty moments on my rig when I got tangled up with some of the ratchet jaws (non-stop talkers) of the radio world. And I had no intention of getting tangled up with some CB lunatic's squawk-box.

I was learning rather more from the girls than they did from me when I was given an unusual assignment. I was to meet a seven-year-old girl off a plane from Switzerland, take her over to Ireland and spend six months as her governess at a house in the hills overlooking Dublin Bay. I hadn't been to Ireland before and I was delighted about it because an old school chum of mine spent the summer months living aboard her small single-cabin, outboard motor-craft off Dalkey Island in Dublin Bay. It was one of those islands close to the mainland, which are normally only inhabited on a part-time or seasonal basis. I love boats, but, not knowing much about them, I thought it could give me a splendid chance to learn, especially as I was promised two whole days off every fortnight.

When I arrived at Dalkey on my first weekend off, Cathleen announced, "There's just about room for two of us as long as we don't quarrel. We can cook, eat and sleep aboard, if you don't mind some slight discomfort."

I didn't. It was fun and I loved every moment of those first two days on Dalkey Island. To be in Ireland is somehow to feel romantic. Dubliners made frequent picnic trips to Dalkey in summer and there was a centuries-old custom of crowning a King of Dalkey when a local man was elected King and the latter appointed Ambassadors to various non-existent realms. A jolly day was had by all. It was the kind of nonsense I liked.

"If only I had my paints with me," I told Cathleen. "This is paradise for anyone who paints."

Cathleen then made me a proposition. "When do you finish your job here?"

"The end of July."

"That's just when I am supposed to pay my duty visit to my parents in Cork. I shall only be away for ten days. Look, if you really like it here so much and would like to do some painting at leisure, you would be helping me out if you lived aboard for that period. Normally I take the boat over to the mainland and have it towed into a boat shed to be stored until my return. I should save all that expense and trouble if you looked after the craft for me."

I accepted Cathleen's invitation with alacrity. I used to look forward to those weekends aboard her boat. Though she was very much a loner, passionately fond of the sea, of fishing and bird-watching, I found her a very easy companion. What I really missed more than anything else was my rig. I was bored stiff at night after the child had been put to bed. So I decided to follow my father's instructions and build a home-made rig for myself which I could easily operate from Cathleen's boat. I knew that Eire had a very easy-going policy towards radio amateurs and that even foreigners were able to obtain a licence with the minimum of trouble and, even better, could have an /MM suffix to their call-signs which allowed them to operate from a boat. So there was no problem. To obtain a new call-sign with the /MM suffix was just what I wanted as the people for whom I was working wouldn't allow me to operate from their premises. They were British tax exiles living in Eire and I think they would imagine I was up to all manner of skullduggery, if I operated a rig in their home. But I bought parts in Dublin and, with some help from Cathleen, actually built the rig in her boat. I was enormously proud of the achievement.

Eventually I finished my job and spent ten days aboard Cathleen's boat. It was wonderful just to have escaped from the rather claustrophobic atmosphere of the Vanstones' mansion. Though the cabin on the boat was tiny, it seemed spacious in comparison. It was glorious weather and I loved pottering around the island on my own, sketching and painting. My ambition had always been to illustrate children's books and make a living that way – a forlorn hope, I fear. At nights it was rather lonely and I whiled away my time listening in on my rig and making a few contacts, twice with my London agency to see what jobs they might have lined up for me when I returned to London, and three or four times with other radio amateurs just exchanging information rather haphazardly.

Maybe I then sounded rather blah about the other sex. I was deep down a romantic and it was fear that I wouldn't get what I was seeking which held me back from a lot of dating. I had this thing that if it happened to me, I would recognize it, but that otherwise I wasn't much interested. Perhaps the fantasies I felt so deeply when I was alone held me back from casual contacts.

Then things happened in a *blitzkreig* kind of way. I happened to pick up Richard's radio appeal for "an author in quest of a heroine". If it hadn't been for the agreement I had reluctantly made with Sandra and Julie, I would probably have ignored his plea. But I could hardly let them down on this occasion as I knew it was just the sort of crazy ploy that would intrigue them.

I was, of course, well aware of the menace of the CB chauvinist pig, but Richard was a genuine amateur and not a CB user; and, as he was a long way off, I felt this was an advantage on my side.

That is how it all started. I must admit I never realised what I was letting myself in for when I set off for the post office at Dun Laoghaire to see whether he had written to me.

It was a straightforward, rather formal, but quite sensible letter from Richard that I found awaiting me at the post office in Dun Laoghaire. But it was the questionnaire which fascinated me most because I suddenly became aware that what he was seeking was just the kind of information which Sandra, Julie and I had been discussing in our own purely hypothetical quest for a Highly Desirable Date.

A quick reply was out of the question. I had to return to the boat, prepare a meal for Cathleen's return, do my packing and be ready to depart at the first whisper of dawn. Nor did I want to call him on my rig. Writing was much safer. So it was not until I had been back in London for two days that I replied in the following terms:

"Dear Richard,

I got your letter the day before I left Dalkey Island and

here is my permanent address – in London, as you will see, like yourself, though nowhere near you. I think it would be best if we just exchanged letters as you suggest. Whether I really can help you in trying to build up a picture of a heroine remains to be seen. I shall try. I suppose others will also be trying so that you will have a fairly wide selection of prospective heroines to choose from!

"However, your letter has cast some doubt in my mind that I am purely a project and you do not relate to me or see me as a fellow human being."

I took a deep breath. Maybe I had become too stuffy. But I didn't want to be used in some remote control way. However, as I continued with the letter I mellowed somewhat:

"By the way, you addressed me as Zeta, so I guess you must have taken the spelling from the call-sign book, as they have got it wrong. It's Zita with an 'i'. Zeta is, of course, the Greek letter, but I see in my dictionary that it's also 'a little closet or chamber with pipes running along the wall to convey fresh air into it'.

"Before I answer your questionnaire I think I ought to say a little about myself. And so, I hope, will you about yourself. Unless we each know what kind of person the other is, this exercise becomes somewhat unreal. I am a Libran so you will need to consider the characteristics of a Libran in adapting my answers to your heroine. Perhaps you don't believe in all this. We shall soon see. I read a very great deal, whenever possible out of doors, and this is perhaps one reason why I am interested in your proposed romantic novel. I hope it will be very different from what is supposed to pass for romantic fiction today. That is why I think your plan of researching your own heroine has something to commend it.

"As I think I told you when we talked, I don't read romantic novels. Spy thrillers are much more in my line. I suppose that is because there is something romantic about a spy. So you may be sure that I probably won't appear as a conventional model for a heroine.

"I am nineteen and live in a Chelsea flat (well, strictly speaking, it's Fulham, but Chelsea sounds more heroine-like) with two other girls. We all work very hard and share the flat chores. My job takes me all over the place, as I'm one of those Girls for all Seasons who picks children off planes and sometimes cooks for a special party (oh, yes, I did a *Tante Marie* cooking course.). Not to mention being a governess – that's what took me to Ireland.

"I dislike routine, love travelling almost anywhere, and would rather be a painter than anything else. I spent my days on Dalkey Island painting seascapes and the plant life. Radio and painting are my two great passions. I feel I get some kind of tranquillizing effect from painting and I'm even vain enough to hope my pictures have a similar effect upon people. I like to think they do. People don't realise the effect colour has on their everyday lives. Colours can wash unpleasant things out of one's mind. There are days when one wants to paint just to pacify one's feelings – greens, blues and perhaps a hint of subliminal yellow. Then again there are days when one paints in red and gold to build up one's energy. This isn't quite as mad as it might sound.

"I'm not a loner, however. I love working in partnership and adore parties, especially the sort one can plan oneself as surprises for one's guests. I love discovering exciting little coves tucked away on an unexpected stretch of coast where I can sit in a windcheater and paint. Afterwards I find it fun to meet up with some friends for a few drinks and some laughs.

"I'm writing this letter sitting in the basement garden patio which belongs to our flat. The sun is quite hot even here under the laburnum tree, which is dropping a confetti of crinkly yellow-white petals on my head. See, I have stuck one of them on this paper . . ."

And so I babbled on. Although Richard was still very much a stranger, it seemed quite easy to tell him a little about myself, how I loved bicycling along leafy lanes, how I learned about the fun of being a radio amateur from my father. But I warned him: "You may probably decide that a radio amateur is not the ideal heroine for a romantic novel. Just imagine your hero sitting alone and despondent by the fireside while his mate is fiddling with the dials and knobs of a rig! Not very romantic, is it? On the other hand I suppose there is an element of romance in chatting up someone you've never seen. Not that I have ever attempted this with romance in mind. But I'm not a fanatic like some amateurs.

"I'm not going to answer the whole of your questionnaire

this time. But I promise to send you the rest soon. It will be easier to do this after I have heard something about you and any of your supplementary questions. I will just add now that I attach some importance to astrology – not in the sense that it predicts the future (that's a load of rubbish), but it does give one an insight into the various types of human characters and one can learn from studying one's own strengths and weaknesses. One learns with whom one can have a rapport and with whom one would inevitably clash. That is why I should love to know your sign of the zodiac because I shall then be able to assess your likely reactions. For example, the verdict of the Stars is that any liaison between a Libran and a Virgo simply won't work unless the Libran can accept the Virgoan's self-sacrificial nature as a virtue instead of the exasperating defect it so often is.

"Having been born on 7 October, I am a moderately typical Libran. If I differ at all from the identikit of Libra, it is probably because I have rather more staying power than the average Libran . . ."

I paused for a few moments and read through what I had written. "My God!" I said to myself involuntarily. "I hope he isn't a Virgo, and because if so, bang goes any further contact. A Virgoan would never say 'Yes I am a Virgo and I promise to prove you are wrong.' " It had always struck me as odd that male Virgos tended to be rather wet, whereas female Virgoans had much greater strength of character even if they also went in for self-sacrifice like Elizabeth the First never getting married. But somehow I had a hunch that Richard was not a Virgoan, so I let that sentence stand.

Sandra and Julie were both surprised and amused that I had actually played my part in their rather pointless little game. At least I thought it was pointless because it didn't seem to be telling us anything worthwhile. The HDD was as elusive as ever for both the other girls. But, as Sandra commented, "At least *your* man has style and originality. Actually to advertise for a heroine, that's really something."

NINE

Zita continues her story.

I must admit I was secretly rather flattered by what Sandra had said. Also I had a feeling I had scored one over both her and Julie. But then I realised that other girls would be writing to Richard and that they would be more likely to give him the kind of answers he wanted. But the next few days gave me two assignments in quick succession. First of all cooking for a dinner-party in Putney and then conducting an American family to places of American interest in London. I had to do a lot of swotting up at midnight to make a list of churches, taverns, buildings and graveyards associated with celebrated Americans of the past who had visited or lived in the metropolis.

Feeling quite exhausted after all this, I was greatly cheered to find a letter from Richard awaiting me. It was typed, but he explained that he could "only think on a typewriter". Then he went on, "Maybe you have a point, when you suggest that it is easier to build up a picture of a heroine simply in informal, off-the-cuff letters than in dead pan replies to a questionnaire. You haven't positively said that, but I feel you mean it. I can also see that an exchange of letters, ideas and views, with each of us contributing, is by far the most constructive way of setting about this.

"I'll try to take your letter point by point, as that, I feel, is how you would like me to tackle it. Radio directness, eh?

Point One: I'll come clean to the extent that there are three other prospective heroine-creators, none of whom I have met, incidentally. I think part of the magic of this exercise is that there is something rather exciting about writing to someone one has never met.

"Point Two and this applies to all: none is regarded purely

as a project. I do feel very strongly that it isn't just the questionnaire that counts, but the exchange of letters over a period. In other words, the idea isn't just to fill in a questionnaire and that's that. I hope this explains that I do regard you as a fellow human being and somehow, some way, I might even be able to help you as you are helping me. It would be fun to meet, but for the present let's keep up the magic of the unknown.

"Point Three: I have now spelt your name correctly. Curiously enough, when I sent you my first letter I nearly addressed you as 'Zetetic Zeta', meaning that you were an enquiring person. But I decided that sounded as though I was trying to be clever.

"Point Four: I am a Sagittarian, born at 3.30 p.m. on 9 December. I am not a student of astrology, but I do know a little about it and think there is something in it. After all, that French scientist, Michel Gauquelin, set out to collect statistics to disprove astrological theory and found that, far from achieving this, facts and figures showed it actually worked. Anyhow, I'm glad not to be a Virgoan from what you tell me.

"Point Five (I hope this doesn't sound too much like a company report!) my idea of writing a romantic novel is somehow to make it realistic (which may sound like a contradiction) and at the same time to escape from what I call the dull-dirty novel of today to the joyous erotic. Not nearly as easy as it may sound. Hence the theme of the book is the author researching his own heroine.

"Your job sounds both exacting and calling for great versatility. I should like to feel I could call you up again by radio. But did you bring your Dalkey Bay rig back with you, or will you use a different call-sign from London? Would it be possible for you to call me on Tuesday night between, say, seven and eight and, if that's not convenient, then between ten o'clock and midnight? It would help just to have a chat, though I'd like letters too.

"About me? Well, I'm old enough to be your father, forty-two in fact. That's why I need to research what your generation thinks. I had a divorce several years ago and I live by myself in a flat in De Beauvoir Town. You've probably never heard of it as it's the seedier side of Islington. But I have travelled a lot, all over Europe and the Middle East, North Africa and some places behind the Iron Curtain.

"I should welcome a longer list of the things you like. It would also help from the viewpoint of my book, if you could paint me a picture – in words, not one of your canvasses – of the type of man you would like as a husband, mate, what-have-you and what you would like him to be – job, looks perhaps, hobbies, quirks etc. You see, it isn't just the heroine which is going to be the problem, but the hero, too. It would be easy to get the girl right and the man all wrong. One of my correspondents opted for her hero to be a man on an oil rig. But somehow I don't see myself spending days aboard an oil rig to research such a character.

"I see you have a sense of the artistic in the way in which you so neatly attached the flake of laburnum blossom to your letter. It instantly gave me a picture of a girl sitting under a tree in a basement patio, writing a letter, while a cat slumbered at her feet. I somehow feel there are always cats in garden patios, and if not, there ought to be. I am a Cat Person, by the way, and my cat is my sole companion.

"Yours ever,
   Richard."

Naturally my flatmates wanted to see the letter and wouldn't rest until I showed it to them.

"Are you going to have it off over the air with him?" enquired Sandra, always the crudest of the three of us.

"I might try to make contact on Tuesday."

"Are you smitten?"

"Of course not. I still don't know an awful lot about him. Sounds as though he's holding something back. I don't quite know what, but Sagittarians are most elusive characters."

"An old man with a cat."

"I like cats," I replied indignantly, not realising I was automatically springing to Richard's defence. "And forty-two is not old."

Julie was more thoughtful. "You, know, Zita, I'm beginning to think you are quite a bit ahead of all of us in a quiet kind of way. This is rapidly coming near to being a Highly Desirable Date."

"But he has indicated fairly plainly that it is writing he wants, not a meeting."

"Ah, yes, but he's probably playing hard to get. Want to bet he doesn't ask for a date?"

"No, I wouldn't want to bet on this one way or another. But it is rather fun. I think I shall go on writing, drawing him out, finding what makes him tick. It will be some sort of recreational therapy."

"You've got it all sussed out, haven't you, Zita?"

I radioed Richard that Tuesday night, but deliberately waited until ten, partly because Sandra and Julie were going out to a party and the flat would then be empty.

"This is G5ZUW. Delighted to hear you again. I assume you got my message. Can you talk freely?"

"Oh, yes," I replied. "Why do you ask?"

"I didn't want to create problems for you in any way."

"You haven't. My flatmates are out. Thank you for the letter. You reassured me on some points, though I still feel you are rather a mystery man."

"Oh dear, I don't intend to be."

"I just wondered what you really did."

"I'm a writer. I thought you realised that. I travel to get background for my work."

I didn't quite believe him. I felt sure there was more he could tell me. But I switched the conversation to what I had been doing since I returned from Ireland. I told him that I was a "cat person", though I did not possess one at present, and I enquired after his own moggie. He seemed quite happy to talk about his cat, said her name was Tortie and, as I guessed, that she was a tortoise-shell stray he had rescued.

"Look, I had better explain why I asked you to call me," said Richard. "I think from now on it would be wiser if we simply corresponded and only called one another up in an emergency. Otherwise I do foresee trouble for you from the breakers. But before asking you to agree to this, I felt it would help to have a chat."

"In what way?"

"I think it might clear the air, remove any misapprehensions and so help us to correspond better. Also, just to hear the voice of someone who is writing to one is helpful. Your own voice, if I may so, admirably matches your letters. It is like the tinkle of an *étude* by Albéniz."

This compliment, if that was what he intended, left me momentarily speechless.

"Are you still there?" he enquired.

"Yes, I'm not sure how to take that as I don't know anything about Albéniz."

"Pity, otherwise you would have got the point. To listen to Albéniz being played on the piano is rather like listening to the music of the Sirens."

"Are you suggesting my voice is like that of Ligea – intent on luring Ulysses on to the rocks, and with some kind of menace?"

"Not quite. I see you know the legend, but I would remind you that Ligea was no Mata Hari. It was simply that her voice was so sweet that the seamen listening to it forgot everything and just died of hunger."

"I hope you have already eaten."

"A long time ago. Never mind, I don't think I'll die of hunger. Eating to me is one of the delights of life."

"For me, too. What do you like?"

"Anything that is colourfully and artistically presented whether it's a pizza, a vegetarian dish, or some exotic Chinese concoction. And you?"

"I am happiest when eating in exotic surroundings and plush places. This may sound bad, but it's best to be honest. I have a passion for colourful puddings, pancakes filled with honey and liqueur – that sort of thing. Otherwise I'm happy with quite simple food.

"And drink?"

"Lots of dry white wine, suitably iced. Oh yes, and Pimms cups of all kinds. And you?"

"Any drink almost except canned beer and Kümmel. I like experimenting with mixtures of drinks. This exchange of tastes is quite amusing. If and when we meet, we shall at least know something of one another."

"But you said letters only."

"I know I did. But it might be fun to meet sometime."

"Aren't you afraid it might break what you call 'the unknown magic'?"

"Not really. At heart I think it might help."

"You or me?"

"Both, I should hope."

"Do you dance?"

"Well, I do my own thing, as it were. It isn't really dancing, but swinging around in the mood of the moment – my mood not anyone else's. Let's say I dance to some tunes better than others. I like New Orleans jazz, Stravinsky's 'Ragtime for Eleven Solo Instruments'. On the classical side, I like almost all Greig. I hate opera, but love ballet. I detest bridge, tennis and golf, but am a soccer addict."

"That is some breath-taking information for me to absorb. I think I'd better pull the big switch now."

"Understood. And do please write soon."

"I will."

"I'm signing off and listening for any final over. K please."

For a moment I was flustered. I wanted desperately to send some final message that wasn't just banal, but I couldn't think of one. Previously we had not used the number code and in fact had kept all code down to a minimum in our conversations. I wanted to say something special and yet still to leave him guessing. Then inspiration came in a flash:

"Eighty-eights," I called. "Eighty-eights to Tortie."

In the Telegraphers' Abbreviations in Current Use "eighty-eight" means "love and kisses."

All this may seem to add up to little more than a will-o'-the-wisp relationship with a vague promise of something better to come. Yet though these chats on the radio and the letters contained little more than an exchange of pleasantries and ideas, there was something about them and Richard which lit a lamp in my heart. True, it was a faint glimmer, but at least a recurring twinkle. Previously I had given men low priority in my life. I tended to shirk getting involved with them, while being secretly an incorrigible romantic. What I found myself liking about Richard was that he was himself a romantic in a quiet sort of way. There was something special about him and I found myself wondering what he looked like. His voice was pleasantly self-mocking at times.

There is something strangely satisfying about someone

saying nice things about one's voice. It might have been blatant flattery on Richard's part, but I had fallen for it. Being a Libran, I possessed the romantic impulsiveness, or perhaps the impulse romanticism associated with this sign of the zodiac. Deep down I knew that I could never have an affair, live with, or marry any man who was not a genuine romantic. And I thought that Richard, by what he said in his casual remarks as well as in his letters, was a kindred romantic spirit, one who liked to give a boost to a male/female relationship rather than just opt for a casual affair.

As Richard had not merely given me the date, but also the the time of his birth (data which the British rarely record, but much of the rest of the world does), I determined to get his horoscope cast. I immediately sent off details to an astrologer friend of mine and she came up with following answers:

"This is a man who must never be made to feel he is hedged in, or kept under restraint. He is not the type who likes to lose his freedom. If he should have any suspicion that he is about to be trapped into something he doesn't want – possibly even marriage – then he will quickly disappear from your life. On the credit side, he is strongly romantic; for this he can be given the highest rating. He appreciates a grand romantic gesture both of his own accord and by others. If he feels that his romantic conception of life is shared by a woman, then he will be loyal. But he does not fall in love easily and there tends to be more than one woman in his life."

Here was a distinct warning. I had to bring my Libran mind to bear on this. Until now it was he who needed me, if only to help with his book. But suddenly I had become the one who began to feel I needed him. The hints of his elusiveness made me aware of this. The horoscope also advised: "Always be ready to pack and travel at short notice with this man . . . he reveals a strong streak of optimism, even when this is against the odds. The result is that he will seem a luckier man than he really is. In short, he will create his own luck . . . Sagittarians are born flirts and women often misunderstand this and imagine any relationship with December's men is more serious than it actually is."

But it wasn't all dire warnings. The horoscope ended up with the comment that Richard appeared to be "fundamentally honest and dependable, easy-going and kind". I turned to my bookshelf for consolation and took down Liz Greene's *Star Signs for Lovers*, and read her assessment of Sagittarian Man, "He can arm himself with a stunning array of quips, jokes and nasty asides which make you think he has no heart. But inside he's a child. Don't fall for it. Sagittarius has a heart of gold."

And my friend delivered this bonus at the end of her horoscope, "Between Librans and Sagittarians there is a mutual affinity and a need for independence on the part of both individuals augurs well for a deeply satisfying and harmonious relationship in the context of an open marriage."

But Sandra's typical warning was, "Don't say you haven't been shown the danger signals. There seem to be more hidden minefields around your Richard than any man I've ever heard of."

"He may be elusive," I replied. "But at least he sounds interesting."

"Do you really believe he is genuinely seeking a model for a heroine?" asked Julie. "It's certainly more of an original ploy for dating than 'come back to my flat and see my stereo.'"

"I don't know and strangely I don't care. From now on I'm going to try to play things my way."

TEN

Richard takes up the story again.

So much happened in the latter part of July that year that I didn't have any time to forge ahead with my novel. There were weeks of almost incessant activity, with both pleasant and unpleasant interludes.

I kept a sharp look-out for Seamus O'Donovan, but failed to see anyone who resembled his photograph. For once I was cautious. I decided not to make use of Lucie in this connection, despite Hanson's suggestion. My contact in the South African Embassy rang up to suggest a meeting. We had agreed he should use a code-name when telephoning me and also a code-name for a meeting place. Each of us was wary of telephone-tapping. We met in the naval and military books section at Foyles and then adjourned to a nearby wine bar.

"You wouldn't like to tell me why you are interested in C. A. Walters?" parried my friend. "I know that normally we don't ask such questions of one another, and this is breaking an unwritten rule. But it might help, if you did."

"Sorry. You will appreciate I am not in a position to tell you much. However, I think I can say this – there is a strong possibility that C. A. Walters is a cover name and that he is really someone quite different from the man he claims to be."

"That's fair enough. What is more, it begins to fit into the jig-saw puzzle of this mysterious chap. Not that I personally am acquainted with him, but my people are. I haven't found out much, but it would seem that he has been of some marginal help to the National Security people. But he doesn't live mainly in South Africa, as you suggested. Nor is there evidence that he ever has done. He has undertaken some undercover work for us as an intermediary for arms deals for the Argentinians, but his entire contacts have been through the South African Embassy in Paris. I gather that he rings up when he has something to tell us and arranges a meeting with one man only at some secret place. Obviously, he takes great care that these meetings are very hush-hush."

"That's interesting. And I suppose your people find it equally interesting that I am on his trail?"

"Of course. 'Find out more,' they urge me."

We both laughed. My contact had known me for many years and we had had some good times together, especially when we were on the same station for two years.

"I can't honestly tell you much more now, though it is just possible I might be able to barter some information once I've made the usual inquiries," I ventured. "But I think I can safely say that if your C. A. Walters is the same chap as mine, then both your people and mine could be in deep trouble. But if your people wish to probe further, I suggest you warn them that they will need to go very softly indeed, because if Walters is the man I think he is, he's a wily bird."

My friend added that "we haven't had a peek out of Walters since early last May."

Although this did not add up to much information, it did not dispel my theory. The question that intrigued me was: what had happened to the original C. A. Walters?

A sudden and unexpected chance to meet Tess caused me to be active in another direction. I had decided the previous week that I must now eliminate the remaining heroines and make a final choice. This may sound ruthless in view of the fact that all the girls had been splendidly co-operative, but if I had kept up a correspondence with all four, I should certainly never get the novel written. Even then I was behind schedule with the book. The research had proved more enjoyable than the writing! So I reduced the four to two – Tess and Zita. To Jeannette I sent two rather lovely plants with a note suggesting she talked to them each night, while watching them grow. To Belle I sent a box of her favourite cigarettes.

Zita was my odds on favourite, but I suppose I kept Tess "in with a chance" to become the ultimate heroine as some kind of a precaution. In one of my letters to Tess I had casually mentioned that I had lunched at the Inn on the Lake at Shorne which was not far from her home. This rendezvous was in a wooded setting beside two lakes, just off the main road between Gravesend and Rochester. Then came a note from Tess to the effect that she would be free the following Sunday because she was a weekly boarder . . . "so what about one o'clock at the Inn on the Lake? My mother has promised to give me a lift. I'd like to ask her in for a quick drink if that's all right. You would find it difficult to miss me, as I have blonde hair, blue eyes and shall wear black."

This was not exactly the kind of meeting I had envisaged, but I replied that I would be waiting for her. Tess was right: I could hardly miss her. The light blonde hair and the blue eyes were perhaps not exceptional, but the black blouse, black skirt and black stockings gave her the air of a mourner. She was pretty, rather more serious than I had imagined and drank cider throughout lunch and ate heartily. Mother, who was actually a couple of years my junior, stayed for one gin-and-tonic and then left us alone. It was a pleasant afternoon and we walked for a whole hour while wandering around the lake paths. But by the time I returned to my flat I knew that there remained only one heroine from whom I had much to glean – my radio amateur contact, Zita.

Whereas only weeks ago the quest for a heroine was more important than any of the prospective heroines, now Zita herself acquired a positive priority in my thoughts. Not only was she my final model for a heroine, but she had become of more consequence than the novel itself. I was anxious to meet her. It is true at the back of mind was the possibility that she might in some way be linked with the obscure Sean O'Donovan. But this seemed less and less likely. Moreover, because I had held back on much information about myself when talking or writing to Zita, she had more reason to be suspicious of me than I had of her. I had avoided any references to my former work. She, on the other hand, had even named the agency for which she worked and given me her telephone number. I also felt a deep sense of guilt in that I had asked Hanson to carry out a check on her. His report was that, while they had no time or excuse to conduct any major investigation of Zita Stanway, a "quickie cross-check" had shown there was nothing against her as far as was known, which suggested she was "clean". I think it was the appalling Service jargon of "clean" which made me feel guilty.

Then came a long handwritten letter from Zita, quite her best effort yet. I decided to study the handwriting for some clues as to Zita's character. Graphology had originally been merely one of my minor hobbies, but I had been encouraged to develop this interest in connection with my Intelligence work. I was convinced that Zita was sincere because of the apparent speed of her writing. This could be deduced from the formation of her rounded letters, suggesting a lively mind and thought processes. Many people who write quickly completely neglect the basic forms and change the slope of their writing. This always suggests someone who is rash and over-hasty. Zita's speed was not like that.

"This is partly in reply to your last letter and partly a follow-up to our radio talk," she wrote. "I think you are absolutely right that we should keep to letters rather than expose ourselves to the outside world with too much radio communication. But we might arrange to listen in to one another one particular night of the week – say each Sunday night between 21.00 and 22.00 hours. Generally speaking, I'm in the flat at this time on a Sunday. If you should fail to get me, you will know I'm away on a job and without my rig."

I had been touched that Zita should send "eighty-eights" to Tortie. The cat and I had become increasingly devoted to one another. One had the pleasantly surprising feeling that Tortie was making me a rather nicer human being than I actually was. I can't quite explain this except to say that in some esoteric manner the cat, too, played a part in my novel and brought me closer to my heroine. This was swiftly borne out when Zita went on to say, "I can't keep a cat because of my work. Sometimes a job like that which took me to Ireland turns up and it would hardly be fair to ask Sandra and Julie to look after a cat while I was away for so long. So maybe, because of this I'll take a special interest in yours. I think I told you that I love painting seascapes and plant life. But I also love painting cats. I have painted quite a few of my friends' cats.

"It was nice to get some more of your likes and dislikes over the air," Zita continued. "My list could go on and on and I could easily get carried away thinking about them. My musical tastes may not be quite yours, though I love Greig's

"Peer Gynt Suite" and some jazz. Otherwise I know very little about Greig. My scene is somewhat different. I tend to divide music into two categories – what you listen to and what you dance to. I like such singers as the Grateful Dead, Jefferson Airplane/Starship (they changed names in case you didn't know) and Bob Dylan. But only in certain moods. Reggae and New Wave are good dance music. Discos I hate as they are full of bad commercial crap and irresponsible teenagers hell-bent on getting high. I loathe the cattle-market aspect of discos. There's more fun in open-air dancing, gigs in parks and in the country and especially the kind of open-air dancing one gets in some parts of France.

"Sporting interests? Well, I share your dislike of golf and am bored with tennis. I love roaming the countryside, long walks in really remote areas – the North Downs, for example, especially those hills in Berkshire, and the woods in the Kentish Weald. I adore the Thames Valley, every little nook and cranny of the river. I think I am what you call a psychic romantic, but it's hard to explain. When I arrive in certain new places I get the feeling I have been there before rather like that character in the Priestley play which had a title like that. Then I know at once that *this place is me,* that I belong there and that it holds some kind of romance for me. But romance means so many different things, doesn't it? Really, it is a way of life. When I went to Haworth to take a stroll up to Wuthering Heights, I got a special thrill; it was like living a book one has read and loved.

"Thus, if it helps you, I personally would find it romantic if the man of my choice selected for our meeting somewhere that would stir that feeling in me – the feeling that I had been there before in another life and that there was some aura of romance surrounding it. What kind of a place? I can't tell you because it would have to be somewhere I was least expecting, somewhere I had never heard of. But it would not be a claustrophobic place. It would be high up rather than low down, possibly near the sea, and it would need to have something special about it even if it was somewhat remote. Is this rather scatterbrained idea of mine of any use for your heroine?

"You have asked me to give you a picture of the type of man I should like as 'husband, mate, what-have-you' and what I should like him to be. I haven't really thought about this very much mainly because I prefer to have a lot of purely friendly relationships rather than a single intense liaison. I suppose it is because, as a Libran, I tend to suppress my emotions and rely on reason and commonsense. So you see, as far as I am concerned, only a truly romantic male could change this. He would need to know and anticipate what would give me a lift, to stir my sense of adventure.

"I am trying to be both honest and logical in telling you all this, and you must understand that although it may in some ways sound contradictory, it's me. I can see arguments for and against. I can sum up and, when it comes to a stirring of the emotions, probably be more logical than a man. The theory that the feminine is governed solely by emotions in human relationships is just another male chauvinist myth. But, at the same time, I am romantic, I like seeing dreams come true. Perhaps I am rather like a butterfly, or, as I used to call it as a child, flutterby. Possibly 'flutterby' describes me rather better than 'butterfly'. I do flutter around.

"What should your hero be? He would need to be something special not only as far as I am concerned, but as far as the readers of your book were concerned. You talk about the 'joyous erotic'. Well, I don't think a stockbroker or a man on an oil rig is going to provide much romance. I should want a man who was reasonably tall with rather special eyes. He needn't even be handsome as long as the eyes were right. They should be pleasingly wicked, but not in the sense that the man himself was wicked. Rather eyes with a sublimated romantic urge. Or, as Byron put it, '. . . his eyes were his heart, and that was far away.' There would have to be something romantic, or at least unusual, about his job. As I prefer spy stories to romances, I would rather like him to be a Secret Service agent . . ."

This quest for a heroine was becoming an increasingly incredible personal adventure. At times like this a man becomes hopelessly clouded in his judgement. By clouded I mean by the euphoria induced by cloud nine, not the fog of misapprehension. I was even blinded by Zita's last suggestion. My training, my instincts should have told me to beware of this. Alarm bells should have rung in my head. Was this a trap? I should have been asking myself. Instead I was bemused and flattered, almost preening myself that I complied with her portrait of a hero, even though I was a sacked agent.

Hanson rang up to say that he was going to be away from London for a couple of weeks, but that if I had anything urgent to tell him, I was to use a certain telephone number for making contact. We met briefly at a prearranged rendezvous and I passed on the information I had received from my South African contact. "Rest assured,' said Hanson. "Someone will work on this." It was mildly encouraging to feel someone in Six was trying to substantiate my case.

Meanwhile an unpleasant development – more so because it was intangible – was that Tortie had not only lost her appetite, but was behaving in a peculiar manner. Obviously something was wrong with her, but I somehow felt it wasn't a matter for the vet. Then one evening, she emitted the most unnatural and alarming shrieks at intervals and crouched under chairs. Nothing seemed to appease her, not even the offer of a saucer of milk on my knees. It was as though she was not so much sick as terrified of some unknown thing.

Cats are probably the most psychic of all domestic animals. In dealing with them, in nursing them when sick, one cannot proceed on the basis of ratiocination alone. An old school friend of mine had told me of an extraordinary cat story of the Second World War. When Captain R. S. Gwatkin-Williams, master of the *Tara*, was about to leave Malta, the ship's mascot leaped into the sea and swam ashore. A boat was launched, the cat pursued and, though it fought desperately, was taken back and locked in a cabin. A week later the *Tara* was torpedoed and sank, taking the cat with her. It was a story I had always remembered and now it seemed to have new significance. Here was Tortie repeatedly giving the impression that she wanted to escape from the flat where hitherto she had been perfectly happy. Each time I pulled her back from an open door she protested vigorously. I felt she was anticipating, or telepathically warning me that there was an external threat to both of us and that it centred directly on the flat.

I recalled that Zita had more than once expressed a keen interest in Tortie. Still avoiding radio contact, I decided to telephone her not from my flat, but from a call-box near by.

Briefly I told her my problem. There was a long pause before Zita replied. "I understand how you feel. Maybe I could help if I could see Tortie. But for the next few days I'm flat out on a new job, helping to move an aged couple from Bicester to Hastings. I've never been to Hastings before, or to any part of Sussex east of Eastbourne. By Thursday midday I should be free until the following Monday. Have you a cat basket in which you could carry your Tortie around?"

"Oh, yes, she normally sleeps in it except when she chooses the foot of my bed, or my desk."

"If you could fix a convenient meeting place and bring Tortie along, I could take her back to my flat for two or three days and see if I could do the healing trick. But I don't promise miracles."

"That's asking an awful lot."

"I did make the offer in the first place."

She had just given me her Hastings address, asking me to drop her a line to reach her by Thursday, adding that the telephone had not yet been installed there, when the pips went. I had no more small change, so could only promise I would write and suggest a date and rendezvous.

It was about a quarter to ten on the Sunday night when I returned to the flat. I had an ill-defined hunch that something was about to happen to me that very night. I was fairly certain that any Special Branch watch on me was very low key indeed by now, if not entirely negligible. I did not blame them for this. Faced with the many daily problems posed by the IRA, the PLO and various other terrorist groups, they had far more important chores to perform than looking after an ex-MI6 man.

Tortie seemed even more agitated that night. Yet far from distracting me from my overriding problem of personal safety, this concentrated the mind wonderfully. I felt instinctively that the cat's behaviour and the possibility of a threat to my life were somehow linked. What puzzled me most was Tortie's change of demeanour since I returned to the flat from the telephone kiosk. Prior to this she had been crouching abjectly beneath chairs, desk or bed, while refusing all food. Now she was ambling towards the kitchen periodically, then suddenly stopping, making hissing noises before retreating, sometimes backwards, until she reached the front door. There she remained, hunched up on the mat, but facing the rear of the flat.

To allow imagination to colour one's thoughts extravagantly can either induce fear or stimulate one's sense of self-preservation. It struck me that the cat's behaviour was not something that could be cured by a vet, but indicated some deeply felt fear. Something at the rear of the flat. The story of the *Tara*'s cat kept coming back to me. I looked round the rooms overlooking the back of the flat to see if there was any possible clue. Though the flat was situated on the second floor and with no back door, or rear staircase in the block, there was an outside iron-ladder fire escape. This would provide an access to the flat if I left any windows open.

My main study window was wide open and the door closed. Provided it was left like this, it would be relatively easy for an intruder using the fire escape to get into the flat, particularly as the ladder was on the side of the building outside my range of vision, but curving round towards my study window at the approach to the second floor. However, knowing something about the various techniques for professional assassination, the odds against making at attempt on my life by this means seemed to me to be about 200-to-one against. It was only because of my knowledge of the telepathic talents of some cats that I argued that Tortie's behaviour somehow reduced those odds to at least twenty-to-one against.

Perturbed about the continuing threat to my life by unknown persons and excited at the prospect of actually meeting Zita within the next few days, I did not feel in the least like sleep. So I crept into my study without putting on the light, left the window open for the night and sat in a far corner to read a book by torchlight. I made this decision vaguely without thinking out what I should do if somebody popped his head around the corner of the wall and climbed to my window.

I was engrossed in one of Harry Keating's books about the astute Indian detective, Inspector Ghote, when Tortie emitted a terrifying wail, then instantly became silent. For a moment I wondered whether danger might threaten from the front door rather than the back of the flat. I went to the hall and saw that the cat was still crouched with her back to the front door, so I returned to the study and took up a position close to the side of the window. Then my tongue went suddenly dry and the blood raced through my muscles as I saw a blurred form crawl around the side of the house alongside my window.

My mind was astonishingly clear and alert. A few seconds previously I had no idea what action I should take if an intruder appeared. Now I knew instinctively that the threat was a direct one towards my person. This was no burglarious attempt because there was nothing worth burgling at so great a risk as climbing a fire escape. If this intruder were a killer, he would strike instantaneously because he would have been trained to do so. Therefore I must attack him first. The vital question was: what was his weapon?

It took the man several seconds to ease himself up to the top of the ladder and edge himself towards the window. I had deliberately switched off the alarm system while staying up in the dark, intending to put it on again when I finally went to bed. I should perhaps explain that the alarm system installed for me was purely an internal one and had no telltale external red box on the wall to warn off those seeking illegal entry.

I pounced, seizing the intruder's right arm as he thrust it through the window. He let out a muffled cry. Something dropped on to the floor, then he recovered and lashed out at me with his left arm. His punch doubled me up with pain and I let go his right arm. He tried once again to crawl through the window. I kicked the object on the floor to the far end of the study and then feebly lurched with a fist at his body half inside the window. There was no real chance of my stopping his entry because I was still suffering an acute pain. Luckily, he panicked first and retreated down the ladder.

Sick as I felt with the pain in my solar plexus, I managed to shut the window and then flashed my torch around the floor as I felt sure that the object he had dropped was the weapon he intended to use on me. Yet at first glance it did not look like any known weapon. I went down on my knees to examine it cautiously. It was a metal tube about seven inches long, with what appeared to be three sections screwed into one another; and in the bottom section was a firing-pin.

Luckily I had had training in the development of terrorist weapons and, although this was almost certainly the latest of its kind, it bore a distinct resemblance to diagrams of the type of weapon which had been used by the KGB for the murder of Ukranian Nationalists in Germany and elsewhere.

This KGB weapon operated by means of the firing-pin igniting a powder charge which caused a metal lever in the middle section of the tube to move. This in turn crushed a glass ampoule in the orifice of the tube, releasing a deadly poison in the form of vapour. If fired at a person's face from a distance of about ten feet, it not only caused death within half a minute, but the vapour left no traces. For that reason I made no attempt to touch the weapon. I switched on the internal alarm system and rang my Special Branch contact to tell him what had happened.

"We'll be around fast," said a sleepy voice. "Meanwhile don't inform anyone else, not even the local police; and don't touch anything."

ELEVEN

I was somewhat disgusted with myself for failing to trap the intruder. Yet I had to admit that, if I had delayed tackling him until he got right through the window, I might now be dead. Although it looked innocuous, that seven-inch tube could have been so sure, silent and deadly a weapon.

Now the pain began to ease and I poured myself a neat malt whisky. Then I gave Tortie her first meal for a very long time; it was astonishing how she had resumed her normal behaviour and appetite the moment danger had receded. I vowed I should always remember this debt I owed her, for I was sure that she had helped keep me alive by telepathically instilling her fear into me. From now on she would be treated as a very privileged animal.

The Special Branch inspector came within the hour. He cross-examined me in great detail and seemed annoyed that I had not alerted him before the intruder arrived. But, as I pointed out, I had no positive indication that anyone was going to try to break into my flat, and the testimony of a cat would hardly have counted. After examining the metal tube he confirmed my worst fears. "No question about it, this is a very deadly instrument. It probably contains cyanide with some nicotine extract, but it could be a new poison that is almost impossible to detect in a post mortem."

Once one's mind has grown accustomed to danger, it becomes wonderfully concentrated so that swift decisions are that much more easily arrived at. While awaiting the inspector I had made up my mind to disappear for a few days without telling the Special Branch or MI6 where I was going. After an interval of a few days, or maybe a week, I would keep them informed, once I had made plans for my future. I was also determined to see Zita and not let anything interfere with this.

If the Special Branch knew my whereabouts after any move, MI6 would also know, and certainly MI5. Too many people would know exactly where I was, including Wetherby. I just did not believe there was any sure means of keeping my enemies totally in the dark other than by my acting entirely independently for the present. While it was unlikely that there would be another attempt on my life in the immediate future, it would have been crass stupidity to stay on in the flat indefinitely. Even the inspector gloomily admitted, "Whoever it is will know he's left his weapon behind and that you will have called us in. For that reason he is unlikely to show himself in the vicinity for some time yet. So you are safe here for a while. But, clearly, your life is in danger and you should make plans to go to a secret address, always letting us know, of course. Just in case my hunch is wrong and some villain is still lurking around, I'll see that a watch is kept until morning comes."

When the inspector left I did not attempt to go to bed. There was too much planning to do. Zita's suggestion had been that I should bring Tortie along to her somewhere in London and that she might look after the cat for a few days. This seemed a most inauspicious way of planning a first meeting. It was certainly not my own idea for a romantic rendezvous either in a novel or real life. Nor, when I came to re-read Zita's letter, would it be her conception of romance ("... I personally would find it romantic if the man of my choice selected for our meeting somewhere that would stir that feeling in me – the feeling that I had been there before in another life and that there was some aura of romance surrounding it ...")

I searched her letter over and over again for some clues as to what sort of a place would appeal to her. It had to be somewhere she had not been to before, somewhere "high up ... possibly near the sea ..." That was what she had said. My first impulse was to select a small place within easy reach with an unusual and romantic name. I opened my gazetteer in a quest for the most delightfully named places in the British Isles. There was the highly evocatively named hamlet of New Delight near Halifax, Stay-a-Little and Red Roses in distant

Wales, Paradise in Gloucestershire and Love's Green in Essex. But while the names were appealing, I had never visited these places myself and they might prove less charming than one would imagine them to be.

It was now five o'clock in the morning. I had packed a bag with essentials for a journey into the unknown and made myself some coffee. After a few sips, inspiration came to me. Zita had stressed in her letter that the meeting place should be somewhere she had never been to. Then I recalled that on the telephone she had told me apropos her visit to Hastings that she had never been there before, or any other part of Sussex east of Eastbourne. Why not somewhere in Sussex? Somewhere near Hastings, so that she could easily get there.

I got out my ordnance survey maps of the British Isles and studied those of the Sussex coast from Eastbourne to Rye. Pevensey Bay, Cooden, Bexhill – none of these was either suitable or original and she would have heard of each even if she hadn't been there. I ran my finger along the map east of Hastings, covering that attractive stretch of cliffs belonging to the National Trust . . . Ore, Covehurst Bay, Fairlight Glen. *Fairlight Glen*! Somewhere in the recesses of my memory that touched a chord. I knew the area and the fact that there were splendid, unspoilt stretches of cliff-lined coast between Hastings and Rye. Zita had asked for somewhere that wasn't claustrophobic, somewhere "high up . . . possibly near the sea." That fitted Fairlight Glen. But she added, "it would need to have something special about it." And I felt sure there was something very special and even romantic about the Fairlight area, if only I could remember it.

Such romanticising may seem pathetic folly when my very existence was threatened. In fact it was the perfect antidote to any possible unpleasant side effects of the dicing with death which I had been experiencing over the past twelve hours. I then spotted on the map the clue to what lay hidden in my memory: Lovers' Seat. Hastily looking up an old guide to Sussex I read, "A gentleman from Hawkhurst, Mr. Samuel Boys, had an only daughter, Elizabeth, whose health was very delicate. It was thought that she might benefit from sea air and so the family came to Fairlight Place, or a farmhouse nearby. There the young lady met Charles Lamb, an officer commanding the *Stag* revenue cutter and they fell in love. But the match was not welcomed by her parents and they had to meet by stealth. The place they chose is now known as the Lovers' Seat on the cliffs at Fairlight. In the end, as there seemed no prospect of her father relenting, they eloped to London and were married at St. Clement Danes on 16 January 1786. Her father never forgave her, but Lieutenant Lamb gave up the sea and they settled at Salehurst and had one daughter."

Eureka! Eureka! This was it – surely as convenient and happily named a rendezvous for seeing Zita as could be conjured up in so short a time. I would write to her, make a date and then find my way down to Hastings and stay somewhere in the vicinity.

"Rather than meeting for the first time in London," I tapped out furiously, "wouldn't it be much more fun to get to know each other in the kind of remote, high up rendezvous, near the sea, which you indicated in one of your letters? Naturally, I should not suggest going to such extremes as proposing anywhere in the Outer Hebrides. Somewhere close at hand is what I have in mind and, since you will be in Hastings on Thursday next, I think I know a really splendid meeting place, provided you don't feel this is carrying play-acting a bit too far.

"You very kindly said on the phone, 'I will meet you anywhere, any time between noon Thursday and Monday.' So will you please meet me at the Lovers' Seat, Fairlight Glen, at any time from two o'clock onwards on Thursday next? I promise to wait until you arrive even if this means a wait of up to an hour. I really do hope you can make it, but if plans 'gang agley', as Bobbie Burns has it, then send me a note care of Poste Restante, GPO, Hastings.

"Lovers' Seat is a place with a story but I'll keep it until we meet. There is no direct transport, but if you take a car or bus from Hastings to Fairlight village, you can get within a mile of Lovers' Seat before having to walk. You take the footpath to Fairlight Glen. Lovers' Seat is a ledge of rock at the head of the Glen.

"This may sound a mad escapade. But it is the closest I can get to the description of the meeting place you envisaged. If it pours with rain? Well, let's be optimistic. Fortune is said to favour the brave. And I will be there, come hell, high tide, thunder, lightning and a torrential downpour. Then we'll eat and drink."

There was no time to say more, nor even to re-read the letter. I posted it before eight o'clock in the morning, somewhat afraid that if I delayed doing so I might be tempted to tear it up. I could visualize its being rejected as some sort of male menopausal lunacy. What I had embarked on was very much of an ego trip, however romantic might have been the original intention. I was like Don Quixote without Rosinante, Romeo clinging to Juliet's balcony by the tips of his fingers and Humbert Humbert trying to make a date with Lolita in the Catskill Mountains in a winter blizzard. Bearing in mind the uncertainties of the English climate, there was every prospect of disaster with this madcap scheme of mine. What had seemed a bright idea at dawn had turned into an ill-conceived prank after I returned to the flat.

Even if Zita was crazy enough to turn up in a deluge, things would be almost as bad. This was not so much a recipe for romance as an exercise in how to destroy it in a single afternoon. I tried to cheer myself up by dialling the Weatherline number for Sussex and the South Kent coast; the forecast for the next twenty-four hours was good, though there were hints of showers afterwards. But it was pointless to waste time on self-recrimination. There were too many other things which called for instant decision.

Tortie presented one problem. Most people in my predicament would have set about boarding out the animal at a cattery. But that would have wasted valuable time in ringing up cats' homes and then trying to find a suitable one. In any case, after what she must have suffered, I couldn't bring myself to board her out. Tortie would go with me. In any event, if I ever managed to see Zita, she had said "bring the cat".

I decided to make only one telephone call from the flat and that was to ask the vet to call round. Fortunately, one can nearly always get a vet to call more speedily than a doctor. It was no use going away with a sick cat and, though Tortie seemed much better, I thought a check-up desirable. But my real ploy in asking the vet to call was to use him as part of my cover for a getaway. He came round within an hour and readily agreed to take me with the cat to his surgery, give her an injection and some tranqullizers for travelling. I wrote a brief note for Lucie, telling her I was going away with the cat for a few days, and pinned it on the front door. Then the vet took my travelling bag while I carried the cat's basket so that nobody watching the premises would think I was going far.

Once Tortie had had her injection I left the surgery, looked round the corridor to make sure nobody was about and then walked briskly through a swing door out into the yard, through a side gate into the narrow passage, with cat basket in one hand, travelling bag in the other. Within two minutes I was in a side road, at the other end of which was a hire-car service. I managed to find a driver to take me to Charing Cross. From time to time I looked over my shoulder through the rear window, but could not see anyone following me. It looked as though I had succeeded in giving everyone the slip.

At Charing Cross I made a number of telephone calls. Three of them were to hotels seeking not merely a bed for myself, but accommodation for the cat. Finally I fixed myself up at a hotel in Rye, which was rather further away from Fairlight than I had hoped to be. My last call was to my Special Branch inspector.

"Where the hell have you got to?" he asked. "I've been trying to get you on the phone for the last hour."

"Sorry, I can't tell you. I'm safe and it's best, if, for at least a few days, I keep my whereabouts known only to myself. I can't give you all my reasons for this, but I want you to know it is no reflection on you or the Special Branch."

"That's all very well, but how can we be expected to look after you, if we don't know where you are? And what are your colleagues going to say?"

"I can only stress that it's best if nobody knows. You can tell my ex-colleagues that, if they stop to think, they should be able to appreciate the point of this. If not, they are pretty dim. Anyhow, if anything should happen to suggest I was being shadowed again, then I promise I'll let you know at once. But just give me a break for a few days."

I cut the call short while he was still pleading with me to change my mind and say where I was. I guessed he was playing for time while he beckoned to a colleague to try to trace the call. Not wishing to have it traced, I put down the receiver and went to buy a ticket for Hastings, as there was a train leaving in about ten minutes. Once aboard, I suddenly felt blissfully free from the external pressures which had been harassing me in recent weeks and chuckled at the thought that my disappearance must have caused consternation in certain places.

Arriving at Hastings, I took a taxi all the way to Rye, registering at the hotel under a false name and address. Once in my room I let Tortie out of her basket, gave her some food and milk and flung myself on the bed. Soon I was fast asleep, but having disturbing dreams. In one of them I was parachuting out of a plane over Fairlight and slowly descending towards someone I imagined to be Zita. As I finally landed on Lovers' Seat, the female figure threw off a cloak and revealed one of my would-be assassins pointing a gun at me.

Next day I awoke fully refreshed and able to make plans more leisurely and logically. I still felt very angry with officialdom for their unconcealed mistrust of me and my motives and their continuing reluctance to clear me and concentrate on Wetherby. This made me more determined to root out my enemies and not leave things to the Establishment as I had done, in the so far misplaced hope that they would come round to my way of thinking.

Wetherby must have been able to concoct and plant some evidence against me which had swayed the Fluency Committee. If I wanted to counter-attack I must somehow find out what this evidence was and why I had been given no chance to refute it. It was, of course, possible that the mysterious threat to my life had nothing whatsoever to do with Wetherby, but if there was a link, as seemed likely, this hazard would remain as long as the enigma of my forced resignation from the Service was unsolved. Pondering on all this, I came to the conclusion that one possible short cut to finding a solution was to get in touch with my old CIA contact, Bram Stoppard. This I decided to do as soon as the weekend was over.

Meantime I prepared for my meeting with Zita. If we were really going to hit it off in a romantic kind of way, there must be something worthwhile to round off the trip to Lovers' Seat.

Rather more than tea and scones after a hike on the Downs was called for. I recalled that Zita herself had told me she was "happiest when eating in exotic surroundings and plush places". This in itself presented quite a challenge. But obviously the first move must be to hire a car for a few days and for this purpose I decided to go to Hastings.

I am not exactly enthusiastic about either cars or driving and I hadn't driven in the United Kingdom for some years, though I had kept up my driving licence. So I wasted very little time in hiring a type of car I had driven before, a brown and gold striped Mini 1000, rather than anything more glamorous and modern. I then returned to Rye, parked the car and explored the little town and its narrow, cobbled streets on foot. At the end of Watchbell Street I stopped at the Look-Out to admire the superb view it offers of Romney Marsh and Camber Sands. Down below at the base of the cliff on which Rye stands I noticed a narrow channel of water alongside which were various boat sheds. A closer look revealed that here was a boat-building yard.

Already an idea had formed in my mind, one which might satisfy a long held ambition of mine and, at the same time, help solve the problem of somewhere to take Zita. I turned back into Traders Passage and then downhill by Wish Street to the Quay. Both Zita and I were passionately drawn to boats, so why not try and hire one and use it as a temporary residence? One problem was that the time for our meeting – two o'clock in the afternoon – was just about the worst possible hour for a romantic first time rendezvous. It was too late for lunch and nowhere near dinner-time, and by three o'clock all the bars would be closed.

But if I could manage to rent a modest cabin boat, somewhere in the area (never mind if it was unseaworthy and had no engine), or a house-boat, then I could solve two problems at one go. I could fix a meal for Zita and also some booze. I could also move my things into the boat from the hotel and plan my own next moves in this rather more relaxed atmosphere.

The yard on the banks of Rock Channel at Rye had been used for boat-building for centuries. The craft turned out were mainly sturdy clinker-built fishing craft, specially designed for longshore fishing and beach hauling. It was a delight to see and hear from the workers about their craftsmanship. For the boats here were constructed entirely by eye and the keels cut from trees specially chosen so that their wood could be used for the curving bow. Clearly, however, none of these were suitable either for hiring, or for shacking down.

Then, just as I was beginning to think I was out of luck, one of the men on the quay enquired, "Perhaps, if you could tell me just what you are really looking for, I might be able to help."

"I want a small cabin-craft that I can use as a temporary home. It doesn't matter if it has no engine and is unseaworthy, as long as I can shack down in it. Not a full-scale house-boat, but something in which one or two people can live reasonably comfortably. Enough space to cook, eat and sleep in."

"I think I know just what would suit you, but it's out near Rye Harbour. It's definitely not seaworthy. In fact really it's an old river barge, long since discarded. But it has been lived in by the owner. Now he's going away for the next few months and I don't think he would be averse to letting it."

I lost no time in meeting the owner and drove out with him to inspect the craft. The barge was, if not what I had visualized, still possible to convert into the mini-houseboat of my dreams, and in some ways even better than I had expected. There were two cabins, one quite small, the other quite a bit larger and there was also a sizeable space below decks in which Tortie could both rest and roam around. Better still there was a variety of splendid views, extending seawards to the English Channel, east to the vast expanse of Camber Sands, and astern to the red-bricked town of Rye, crowned by its ancient church, perched on a sandstone hill. There was a minimum of furniture, but it was adequate: an Elsan lavatory, calor gas and pots, pans, china and bed linen. I paid a deposit on the spot and, to avoid any question of references, offered to pay two months' rental in advance. I think that clinched the deal there and then.

By Wednesday night I was installed in the boat, having taken with me some food and booze as well as some potted plants and flowers to liven up the cabins. I soon managed to make the barge look reasonably attractive inboard even if the exterior could have done with a coat of paint. True, there was no fridge into which to pop the bottle of the Widow

Cliquot's champagne that I had bought for Zita. But that was a minor detail. All I now had to do was to plan carefully for the rest of the day. After Lovers' Seat, what?

What indeed! Ideally, I should like to have whisked Zita straight back to the barge, planned a cosy little dinner at the famous Mermaid Hotel in Mermaid Street, Rye, and then persuaded her to stay the night aboard, carefully pointing out that there were two cabins and one would be for her alone. This was not a ploy to seduce her on the first night of our meeting. After all I had no idea what she looked like, but merely a hunch that her looks could be as delicious as her voice. But I felt that it would help if we could be together for a couple of days. But I turned down the idea of inviting her to stay aboard because I was quite certain any such proposal would be rebuffed.

My intuition was that Zita planned to go back to London that night. So my first task must be to look up all railway timetables and be absolutely certain of the times of the last trains back to London, not only from Hastings, but with connections from Rye as well. True, I had the car, but many women have a thing about being clued up on timetables. Trains give them more confidence. Then there was the question about how to spend the rest of the day. When one is meeting a rather special girl for the first time and wishes to maintain a romantic momentum, whisking her off to a succession of parties where you can show off your friends can sometimes work better than trying to keep the girl to oneself. But Zita was not a Sloane Ranger and unlikely to be impressed by these tactics. She lived on the wrong side of the Fulham Road. In any event none of my friends were in the district.

With Zita, I discerned a preference for two people being alone. Now the tactics in such a case are easy enough if bed in one is the target for both. With someone like Zita, or what I imagined Zita to be, the solution was much more difficult. It called for a day of surprises, with each little surprise dropped like a time-bomb at regular intervals. But the problem in using this strategy was that there must be a careful balance between not pushing one's luck and still suggesting a certain sublimated wickedness on one's own part. Not enough to alarm, but certainly to charm. What women really want is a bit of mystery.

I hadn't got it worked out exactly when I set out to meet Zita, but I more or less thought I knew the drill. So it was in a somewhat smug frame of mind that I set off by car for Fairlight and stopped at the Fairlight Cove Hotel. I ordered a large pink gin and sat down at the bar, drawing from my pocket an ordnance survey map of the area just to make sure I knew which path to take across the greensward to Lovers' Seat. I noticed some odd names on the map such as the uninviting Wet Wood, the intriguingly named Pook Hole Shaw and that somewhat obscenely titled Low Flash.

"How far is Lovers' Seat?" I asked the barman.

"Lovers' Seat? It's not there any more. Washed into the sea in a landslide some five years or more ago."

"Are you absolutely sure?"

"Sure as can be. Mind you, maybe there's a signpost to show you where it was. But that's all."

TWELVE

The shock I sustained at hearing what the barman said can only be compared to the momentary paralysis I felt when I saw that dark figure crawling towards my window. Now I really was in a dilemma.

I ordered another pink gin. It was the only thing to do to restore some semblance of normality.

"From time to time," ventured the barman sympathetically, "we get people in here asking for Lovers' Seat and they do go away quite disappointed." So I must have shown something of the way I felt.

But I pulled myself together and suggested, "Surely there's no reason why they should go away disappointed. After all Lovers' Seat was a ledge of rock. There must still be something there, if only the ledge beneath the ledge."

"Perhaps so, sir."

"And you say there are sign posts?"

"Well, one at any rate. But there's nothing to see. There isn't really a seat there."

"Maybe not, but there's a splendid view; and there's an awful lot in a name even if it's of something that doesn't exist. Now, you may find this somewhat eccentric, but I have made a date today with a young lady for Lovers' Seat. It's just possible she might call in here to ask the way. If she were told that Lovers' Seat no longer existed she might, well, be more than a little choked. Either she would think I was making a fool of her, or that I was totally incompetent. So, if she should turn up, that is to say if she should ask the way to Lovers' Seat, could you just say nothing but send her in that direction."

"I'll do better than that, sir. I'll say you've been in here and that you're on your way. Perhaps I could explain that there isn't exactly a seat for her to look out for, but . . ."

"That's fine. That's about just right. Anything more and I'm sure she would be confused."

"Anything to oblige. And the very best of luck."

I left the hotel and realised it was too late to try to send a message to Zita. But there was ample time to reach our rendezvous and the route there is so spangled with an unexpected pageantry of colours that in ordinary circumstances it would have been a sheer joy just to have made the walk. To the east are the Firehills, so called because of the extensive blaze of gorse which covers the cliffs at this point. It is the kind of coastline that deserves to be consecrated as an open space in perpetuity. Luckily it is. I turned off the main road into some fields towards a path known as Brakey Bank which is thickly wooded on both sides, occasionally enlivened with a tapestry of wild flowers. Quite suddenly, out of the woods, one emerges towards Fairlight Glen, at the head of which is the Dripping Well, shaded by an enormous beech tree and lit up with the stars of golden saxifrage.

From the Glen woods one emerges on to the cliff walks, chalk intermingled with broad stretches of green, but on that August afternoon there was nobody in sight to tell one where Lovers' Seat had been before it collapsed into the sea. It could have been at almost any point on the cliffs within a quarter of a mile's walk. What I really needed was a huge banner on which the name Lovers' Seat was inscribed in foot-high letters, or a giant balloon bearing the same motto.

The shock at learning that Lovers' Seat no longer existed had made me forget all about the weather, which, until then, had been the chief hazard on my horizon. Now it seemed a disastrous obstacle to our meeting. I tried to cheer myself up with the knowledge that slowly, yet seemingly surely, the clouds were drifting seawards. But the fog was only lifting a little, though in one break in the clouds there was a tiny patch of blue sky.

A minute past two o'clock! Zero hour had just passed and I climbed off the path up the cliff face to the next ledge, hoping that the higher up I was the more likely I should be seen. I was rather glad that I had put on a somewhat flamboyant, orange-hued sweater. It would certainly shine like a bush fire from a considerable distance. There was nobody was in sight, but that was hardly surprising. People didn't normally take walks along steep cliffs when fog is about.

Visibility had at one time been as low as twenty yards. For this reason I shouted out Zita's name every few minutes. But by a quarter past two there was still no sign of her. By now I was frantically chasing around first in one direction, then another, sometimes climbing upwards, then going down again. Once I thought I saw a female figure high up and I waved my arms wildly, but whoever it was either did not see me, or ignored me.

My mouth was dry and I was somewhat breathless. Then at half past two, when I was beginning to give up all hope of finding Zita, the fog seemed rapidly to evaporate and the sky overhead and inland became both cloudless and blue. It was an astonishing transformation within the span of a few minutes. At exactly twenty-five minutes to three a slim silhouette appeared over the top of the cliff. I held out both arms like a windmill and started to wave them madly. It was several seconds before I obtained a response. Then there was a brief wave of one arm. It could be, it must be Zita, I told myself.

And so at long last it was. Tripping down the cliffside in my direction with the grace of a young gazelle was a girl wearing a cassata-coloured floral outfit, with a nipped-in waist and fine shoulder straps, which she wore with a chiffon scarf, possibly taking the view that a scarf was softer and prettier than a belt. She blended perfectly into the cliff scenery and gave the impression of being just as at home dodging the boulders and tufts of coarse grass as she would be walking in Kensington Gardens.

"Hi!" She spoke first.

My first impression was that she looked younger than she actually was. It was her smile that dazzled me most; it was a child's smile that warmed both heart and mind and it lit up her whole face. This was the heroine of my dreams.

"Hi! So glad you've actually found the place."

"I began to think I should never find it. I must have missed the right path. I don't think I should have got here unless

111

you had waved. When I saw that fog over the cliffs I nearly turned back."

"It's all my fault and it was very nearly a total disaster."

"Why? The sun is peeking through now."

"Did you ask anybody the way?"

"No. I just asked for directions in Hastings and hoped for the best."

"Well, I hate to tell you this, but on the way here I stopped at the Fairlight Cove Hotel and learned to my horror that Lovers' Seat collapsed into the sea some few years ago."

Zita threw back her head and laughed until her shoulders shook. "I'm sorry, but I do find that rather hilarious. Anyhow, we can afford to laugh because we did meet – we could have gone wandering round and round all afternoon and never caught up with each other!"

"I do apologize."

"Rubbish. It's been fun making, the er, pilgrimage."

She pronounced the last word in a slow, mischievous kind of way, accompanied by a grin. We neither of us smoked, so there wasn't that always perfect opening gambit for when two people meet for the first time. I almost regretted that I had kicked the habit some years previously. I was now able to form a more appreciative impression of Zita and, looking back even now, I can still say that, despite many views to the contrary, first impressions are best.

Zita was of average height, but with long, slim arms that were somehow intensively expressive in a subtle way. Her auburn tresses, slightly streaked with red, tumbled casually over her shoulders. Her eyes were large and green and whenever she smiled they sparkled like smoky emeralds. She was not a beauty in the conventional sense of the word, but in all truth she was better for not being. Great beauties do not often have fascinating smiles. Zita had tiny features, a pert little nose and ears curling out of her hair like miniature shells. A merry sprite in short, of a kind born to frolic in the countryside. But that smile . . .

We talked in monosyllables, as Zita seemed content just to absorb the scene around her. "It is a splendid afternoon," she said, "so let's just sit here and sniff the sea breeze for a while. If we wait a little longer we might actually be able to see the Channel and way out."

After a while, she asked me to tell her the story of Lovers' Seat, which I did. I was beginning to think I should make some move, but Zita kept on pointing out objects of interest as the fog cleared on the seaward side, inshore sailing boats heading for Hastings or Piddinghoe. I noted that she was extremely knowledgeable about ships generally.

Suddenly she turned and faced me with a look of serious intent, "What have you done with Tortie?"

It was the first time I had noticed an authoritative note in her voice; it was almost as though she had accused me of abandoning the animal.

"Tortie isn't very far away. I hope you'll come to see her."

"Is she better?"

"Much better. But I still think you might do her some good."

"Where are you hiding her?"

"You'll see. It's supposed to be a surprise."

"You love springing surprises, don't you?"

"I think creating surprises is great fun. I wish more people did it."

"Oh, so do I. I wish right now some magic fairy could drop an easel, a canvas and some paints beside me. I could happily paint here all day."

I bit my lip. I had actually thought of bringing some painting tackle along with me, but decided that this might seem a little too zany. Back at the boat, however, I had some sketching materials . . .

"Let's walk along the cliff, shall we?" said Zita, springing to her feet.

"Of course. By the way, I've left my car not so very far away. I thought you might like a trip into Rye."

"Does that mean we shall see Tortie?"

"That's part of the plan."

"I'd better warn you that I must get back to London tonight. So I must leave Hastings in reasonable time as I've got to pick up my luggage."

Problem – this gave Zita the perfect excuse for a quick getaway just in case I didn't come up to her expectations, as obviously the left-luggage office closed relatively early. "In that case," I countered, "we'd better go to Hastings station now and pick up your luggage. That will give us more time."

113

"But that's an awful bore for you. It also means I've still got to make another journey to Hastings later on."

"Not necessarily. I could drive you to Hastings, or you could catch a train from Rye to Hastings. As a matter of fact Rye station links up two ways to London – via Hastings and Ashford as well. The last train from Rye to Hastings is eight minutes past eleven tonight." (Thank heavens I had done my homework!)

"Well, if it's not a bore for you."

"Not at all. Let's go. You will have dinner with me tonight, won't you? I thought we might go to the Mermaid at Rye."

"I've heard of it. Hasn't it got a rather splendid inn sign and a bedroom named after Dr. Syn?"

"That's right. Better still it's in one of the loveliest streets in Rye."

Our conversation to date had not been exactly sparkling, but it was moderately successful in that neither of us had boobed or jarred in any way. It had been rather like verbal fencing. Clearly, with Zita's emphasis on seeing Tortie, my next move after picking up her luggage at Hastings was the long journey back to Rye Harbour. I had gleaned from our casual chatter that she took a romantic interest in history, that is to say, she positively loved taking day-dreams into the past. So, partly to make a break in a lengthy journey, and also in the hope of pleasing her, I made a detour to Winchelsea on the way to Rye. Here was a marvellously peaceful village on a flat hill-top which, from a distance, looked rather like an island of trees jutting out of the flat, marsh-like countryside. It is meticulously planned in ten squares with its church and centuries-old Court Hall, now a museum, as the majestic centre-pieces.

"What a really lovely place to live in,' said Zita. "Each single house is different and they are all entrancing. And how peaceful."

We did not stop there more than a few minutes, though we walked around two of the squares while Zita took some pictures with her camera. But as we approached the converted barge I became somewhat worried as to how she would react to this ploy of mine. She might become suspicious that I was setting her up for a seduction. I recalled that from the very first of our radio chats she had ruled "no beaver-hunting". I must play things very cool indeed and utilize Tortie as a kind of chaperone. I also sensed from our radio talks that she regarded me as somewhat of a man of mystery who declined to tell her what his various jobs had been. The irony of it all was that she had nominated a spy, or secret agent, as her fictitious hero's job, while I was an ex-secret agent and couldn't tell her. And even if I could, she would probably not believe me.

Zita noticed that I turned away from the town of Rye and headed for the harbour instead. "You are taking me to the sea again?" she said. "It couldn't be a boat, could it?"

She had the most deliciously wicked smile on her face when she posed questions like this.

"You'll see in a few minutes. We're just coming to the point where three small rivers link up together before they go into the sea, the Rother, the Brede and the Tillingham."

Just afterwards we drew up alongside the barge's moorings which were not too far from a public house known as the William the Conqueror. I had almost forgotten to mention that the name of the barge was *Amanda*.

"Take a deep breath," I told Zita. "This is my temporary home."

She stayed silent for a few moments, then turned to me and said, "Somehow I can picture you living here much more than in North London. The boat is you. Is Amanda the name of your prospective heroine?"

"No, the barge had the name when I took it over. It's a name with a local link apparently. There's a passage in Rye known as Turkey Cock Lane. The story is that one of the brothers in a local friary fell in love with a girl named Amanda. They eloped but were captured and the brother was condemned to die by being bricked up alive in a wall. His ghost is said still to haunt the passage, gobbling like a turkey cock – hence the name of the lane."

"I want to see Tortie."

So together we went aboard. I showed her into the large cabin while I went below decks to bring up the cat. Tortie made a leap on to Zita's lap and started to purr. What a blessed ally a pet can be on occasions! From that moment

Zita took off, as it were. She emerged from her protective mental chrysalis and became an easy-going, enchanting companion.

"I like it," she said, looking around the cabin. "And you've even managed some flowers."

"Oh this, is only the start. There is much to be done as I only got here yesterday. But before we do anything else, you must be famished. I have a bottle of champers and some sandwiches."

"You do do things in style."

"Well, let's say the style is to compensate for the surroundings. I'm afraid the barge's owner hadn't bothered much about painting or comfort."

"Have you got your rig here?"

"No. You see, I only discovered the barge a few days ago. I'm renting it for a few months. I also have an option to buy."

"What fun. Will you give up your flat?"

"I might sell the flat and spend some money in doing up the barge, if I can clinch a sale. I find living in the country or near the sea so much pleasanter. It was a sudden whim, if you like."

I opened the bottle and poured out two glasses of bubbly. "Cheers!"

"Cheers, and here's to your novel! The very best of luck. By the way, I haven't mentioned the novel before because I just wondered whether our meeting was some kind of rehearsal of your hero and heroine getting together."

"Rehearsal? I hadn't thought of it quite like that, and yet, I suppose, at the back of my mind it was."

"If you hadn't been writing a romantic novel, where would you have suggested meeting me?"

"I still think I should have tried to choose some place that fitted your own description of a romantic meeting place."

"But you wouldn't have known that, if you hadn't been writing a novel and had put the question to me."

"True. But you don't mean that the type of rendezvous you suggested was a false picture and that you would have preferred somewhere else?"

"Oh, no, it wasn't a false picture. But it was you who made me think out what I'd like. And I love surprises and the barge is fun. Perhaps more fun than Lovers' Seat. Just think, it might have been pouring with rain out there."

"I know. I had an agonizing time, praying that the weather would hold. Did you think my suggestion very mad?"

"A bit. But nicely mad. By the way, I actually like walking in the rain, provided I'm clad for it. I may seem fairly commonsensical, but I assure you I love doing mad things on the spur of the moment. Can I see over your barge?"

I showed her around, apologizing for the lack of furniture. "I can see great possibilities here. I can appreciate them after living aboard Cathleen's craft. She was my girl friend at Dalkey Island. You have far more space here than I had and I should absolutely adore trying to furnish the barge and painting it up. There are so many things one could do – tubs of lovely flowers, a whole splash of colour on the boat, perhaps one arm chair and a bookcase – that's a 'must' – and quite a lot could be done to improve the galley. Now there I could really help you get organized. If you'd like, of course."

"I'd welcome it."

"Just one point, though. Tortie. Do you think she'll be safe aboard, that she won't find some means of escaping, or, worse still, falling into the water?"

"I was slightly worried about that myself at first, but not too much so as she is house-trained and fastidiously clean in her habits. And, of course, she's used to being shut up in a flat. Right now I imagine she's absorbed in just exploring the barge."

"Does she like being on or near water? Some cats don't."

"She seems to have settled OK. Don't forget that many ships have cats as mascots."

"Certainly she seems in good nick," said Zita, picking up Tortie and hugging her. "Those adorable white paws and that white chin of hers are really rather special."

Time passed happily and rapidly. The conversation flowed naturally and easily. Zita and Tortie established a quite astonishing rapport quite quickly. She insisted on making a couple of pencil sketches of the cat when she heard I had sketch-pad and pencils. Then she set about tidying up the galley for me, throwing out various practical hints for me to act upon in future. She didn't ask any more questions as to what jobs I might have had in the past. For that I was grateful. She went up on deck and made a pencil and crayon sketch of the distant ruins of Camber Castle and the outline of Rye on the horizon. It was not the sort of late afternoon and early evening that I had envisaged, yet somehow it seemed to be just what Zita enjoyed. "This is the next best thing to being on a desert island," she quipped, adding, "with no Roy Plomley to ask one questions."

"Sorry I've nothing to provide any music with except my pocket radio. But the time has come to head towards Rye and dinner at the Mermaid."

Dusk was approaching as we drove off to Rye, but Zita insisted on our making a quick tour of the little town on foot. In many respects the winding passages of Rye and its twisting lanes reminded me of an Arab kasbah. It is the sort of place in which, provided one sets out to absorb facts, the whole history of a nation unwinds itself in one's mind within an hour. I once met an enquiring American from Rye Patch in Nevada who felt he must explore Rye in England and afterwards declared that "it's just one long heaven of a history book". The watch towers, the Gungarden, Jeakes' house, the parish church with its eight inscribed bells and famous quarter boys which strike the quarters of the hour, but not the hour, and the Mermaid Inn, were, he said, "a sheer delight", adding that, in his opinion, Mermaid Passage, where the Mermaid Inn was situated, was "one of the five loveliest streets in the world".

"It really is a fairy-tale town," said Zita. "You couldn't have chosen a nicer place to visit. Do please put Rye into your novel. It's half like wandering around something out of the *Arabian Nights*."

"Funny you should say that. I always felt it's a bit like the Kasbah of Algiers, especially if one half closes one's eyes of a night and wanders along narrow cobbled lanes like Mermaid Passage."

By this time we had reached the Mermaid Inn at which I had already carefully planned dinner, having made a mental note of Zita's culinary likes and dislikes. I recalled that she liked Pimms, so I had secretly asked the barman to bring us two Pimms Number One before dinner, insisting that he added a small measure of Benedictine to each. A good Pimms, even if a modicum of Benedictine has been popped into it, can always be enhanced by this top-up.

"You actually remembered," said Zita.

"I've done better than that. I've even tried to work out a special dinner for a Libran."

She clapped her hands delightedly. "Oh, how exciting. Do tell me about it."

"It took quite a lot of homework, if you must know. But I found it rather fun. Did you know that each sign of the zodiac has its own birth salt, according to one homeopathic doctor who also believes in astrology? Well, a Libran's birth salt is sodium phosphate, which you could take in a tablet form . . ."

"You're not giving me a tablet dinner!"

"No, but this doctor chappy has worked out what foods are beneficial to your sign and those to which you are supposed to be allergic. It would seem that Librans don't have many allergies, except for tomatoes and shellfish."

"Well, yes, some shellfish I never touch. Tomatoes I do eat, but, come to think of it, I'm not wildly keen on them. How very fascinating!"

We went into the panelled dining-room where the whole atmosphere seemed to swing one back into a nostalgic past, subdued lighting, candles on our table, the ancient fireplace, a faint suggestion of the eighteenth century and the scent of pot-pourri. I hoped that this was a useful contrast to the rigours of the barge.

A bottle of Le Pontet-Canet Bordeaux was produced in an ice-bucket. We started off on whitebait with thin slices of brown bread and butter. "Candle-light makes all the difference," said Zita as she sipped the wine. "It makes the food seem much more glamorous." The next course was *Veau Normandie*, which is cutlet of veal with apple garnish and a Calvados sauce, served with green beans and sweet corn.

"Do you think this gimmick would work in my novel?" I asked Zita.

She thought for some seconds, took a long drink of wine and then said, "I think it's the kind of thing that would be a splendid surprise for anyone's birthday dinner. It just shows that someone is prepared to make the effort to be different. And that's what matters in life. And, of course, I am loving jit. But I just wonder whether for a first-time meeting it might seem a bit . . ."

"Taking things for granted? Piling it on?"

"Not quite that. But suppose it didn't come off? It might not work in all cases. There is an element of chance with anything astrological."

"Maybe you are right."

To round off the dinner we had pancakes filled with ice cream and served with almonds in a Tia Maria sauce, followed by coffee and that romantically named liqueur, Parfait Amour.

"This is a splendid end to a perfect day. I do hope you know that *I* have loved every minute of it. And I take back my criticism for the novel. If it worked for your prospective heroine like it has for me, then of course you should use the gimmick, as you call it, for your book."

I was sure that Zita meant what she said, but her earlier comment caused me to be cautious. We had not drunk an awful lot, but my own consumption had tempted me to suggest to Zita that, if she liked, there was a spare cabin aboard the barge and she could stay the night and we could then do more exploring tomorrow. But I felt this would be a blunder. Things had gone so well, it would be a pity to spoil them. Much better to adopt a nonchalant attitude. If there was one thing many women couldn't stand, it was a man who tried too hard.

"I must be going. Sorry, but it will take time to get to Hastings."

"Not to worry, I'll drive you over."

"But you said there was a connection from Rye."

"There is, but . . ."

"No, I wouldn't dream of asking you to drive all that way. If you could see me off at Rye Station, that would be fine."

"If you are absolutely sure, I'll do that. When shall I see you again?"

"You really want to?"

"Of course."

"For research?" Again that wicked smile and the tinkling laugh.

"No, just because I should like to see you. Look, if you could manage to come down tomorrow or Saturday, I might be able to fix up some sand-yachting for us on Camber Sands."

"Sand-yachting? That would be marvellous. I'd love to try it. Are you an expert? Ring me up tomorrow morning between nine and ten. Then I'll give you the answer. With luck it will be 'yes'."

I carried Zita's hand-luggage to Rye Station and saw her on to the train. She wouldn't let me buy her ticket. As she opened the door of the train she turned swiftly and gave me a gentle kiss before saying good-bye.

THIRTEEN

I drove back to the barge that night highly elated. I felt I was riding on a rainbow of psychedelic proportions. It was something more than exhilaration, rather like a powerful muscular injection of methylemphetamine which I had once tried as a recommended cure for smoking. The effect could perhaps best be described as becoming high on one's own dreams.

Those hours with Zita had been a marvellous tonic even though we had barely got to know one another. For more than an hour I lay awake thinking about her, trying to recapture her looks, her movements and, above all, to remember first the smile and then the voice. Zita's sense of humour lay in the inflections of her voice, or a pause before she uttered a certain word which often could convey a wealth of humour very economically. In this drowsy never-never-land half-way between being awake and asleep my mind drifted along prinked and prismatic paths, a dream world of that kind of transcendental ecstasy which is best summed up in those lines of Shelley:

> "Life, like a dome of many-coloured glass,
> Stains the white radiance of eternity."

I awoke as early as 5.30 a.m. and went on deck to see how the weather was. Swift disillusionment followed; there was a steady downpour of rain and it seemed likely to continue. The early morning radio forecast was not encouraging. Any hope of sand-yachting appeared quite impossible as there was hardly any wind whatsoever. Maybe I should have suggested going up to London for the day to see Zita there.

Just after nine o'clock I went to the nearest telephone box

on the quay and I dialled Zita's number. She picked up the phone, almost instantly, as though she was waiting for my call.

"I'm so glad you rang," she said, "because I was beginning to get worried about you."

"Why? Did you think I'd forgotten my promise to ring?"

"No, not that. Someone has been asking for you, wanting to know where you were."

That sounded really ominous and my mouth went dry, not so much because of any possible new threat to myself, but because what had happened might cause Zita to have the gravest misgivings about me.

"Who was it?"

"I rather think it was the police. It happened while I was away."

Oh God, I thought, here goes a hoped-for romance. "Tell me what happened."

"When I got back last night the girls were still up, waiting for me. Apparently on Tuesday night, while I was away, a plain-clothes officer called at the flat to ask for me. Julie was out, but Sandra asked him in, thinking something serious must have happened. It was all very mysterious, according to Sandra. He wanted to know when I should be back and where I had gone. Sandra didn't know exactly where I was, so that was all she told him. But then he mentioned your name and wanted to know if Sandra knew you, or where you were. Of course Sandra didn't know then that you had gone to Rye. But she did tell him that you lived in North London in the Hoxton area, and though she hadn't the exact address, I should imagine that it wouldn't be difficult for them to trace you either through your telephone number or some other records. Anyhow he telephoned twice for me after that and has said he will telephone again this morning. That's why I wanted to speak to you first."

"Did he give a name?"

"No, but he said he was from the Special Branch and I should think he must have been genuine, as he showed Sandra some kind of official card. What worries me is that Sandra got the impression that he desperately wants to see you and that he is concerned about your safety, whatever that might mean."

"Zita, do you trust me?"

"I think so."

"Are you still free today?"

"Yes, except that I have to telephone my agency. They have another job lined up for me. It doesn't start before Monday, but I might have to travel on Sunday, so there will be quite a lot to do."

"It's a heavy downpour of rain down here and no wind at all. So, sad to say, sand-yachting is out and a trip down to Rye would not be very attractive. In view of what you've told me I must return to London today. So could we meet?"

"Yes, of course. Why don't you come to the flat? My mates will be out until tonight and then they will probably not be here for long. I could cook you a meal."

"Right. Many thanks. I'll come along and explain all then. By the way, if the Special Police chap should ring up, or call, you can say I shall be in touch with him by telephone. I'll try and phone him meanwhile."

"What are you going to do about Tortie?"

"I haven't thought that one out yet. My movements for the next few days are problematical."

"Richard, if it is any help, I'll gladly have Tortie here. True, I am occasionally away on jobs, but I think I could persuade Sandra and Julie to agree to look after her in my absence. Sandra isn't madly keen on cats, but Julie is. Also I'd love the chance of painting her. A tortoise-shell cat presents quite a challenge."

"That's terribly kind of you. It would help enormously for a while."

"Bring her up then. And I'll expect you when I see you. I shall probably do some shopping this morning, but I'll be in from 12.30 onwards."

I hurried out of the telephone box, went back to the barge and started to pack a few things into a bag. Fate seemed to be dealing me a rotten hand whenever the chance of a romance was on the horizon. On the Île St-Louis the bomb scare had separated me from April, and then Wetherby turned up and I was recalled to London. Now even the Special Branch was threatening my chances with Zita. The fact that the SB inspector had sought out Zita surprised me. It was the one possibility I had overlooked. Hanson knew about Zita, of course, and he had even made some cursory checks on her. He must have passed the information of her whereabouts on to the Special Branch as soon as he heard I had disappeared. Maybe he was genuinely worried that my life was still in danger. There now seemed nothing for it but for me to emerge and let the authorities know where I was. If I didn't, Zita would be pestered again and would begin to lose any trust in me, and they would certainly catch up with me very soon. If Zita's telephone had been tapped, they would possibly now know that I was in the Rye area. A false name wouldn't protect me for long.

Having packed my bag, put Tortie into her travelling basket and locked up aboard the barge, I made my way to the car. I had paid to hire it until Monday morning, so there was no reason why I shouldn't take it up to London. But before setting off I rang first my Special Branch inspector and then Hanson, who was now back in the Office. In each case I explained where I had been staying, what I had done and that I was coming back to London that day and would keep in touch.

"I hope so," said Hanson, "because the top brass here are now sitting up and taking quite a lot of notice. It could spoil your chances if you do any more disappearing tricks."

"It could also spoil my chances if I don't."

"We have plans to ensure it doesn't. What are you going to do in London? Back to your flat?"

"I don't know. I'm going to Zita's place first of all."

"You really were rather irresponsible, buggering off like you did without telling us. If your enemies had discovered you were living in a barge at Rye Harbour, totally unprotected, they could have wiped you out quite easily. Remember, you are up against professionals. I'll get in touch with the SB and ask them to be more discreet in future. I must say they might have got in touch with me before blundering into chats with your girl friend's flatmates. Ring me when you get to London."

I then set off for London and tried to think out some plans for myself. My hunch was to put the London flat on the market and to return to the barge, making any arrangements for my furniture to be stored until I could actually buy the barge. I didn't bother to stop for lunch en route, but, noticing some superb roses for sale on a street stall in the environs of Tunbridge Wells, I pulled up and bought a large bunch for Zita. After that I headed straight for her flat in Ifield Road. It was a great relief to know that she was willing to look after my cat for a while, as I rather anticipated having to do quite a bit of travelling between London and Rye in the near future. Nonetheless I was worried as to how Zita would have reacted to the Special Branch enquiries about me.

Zita opened the door to me and her smile was as warming as a hot Calvados toddy on a wet day. "Have you had any lunch?" she enquired. "I hope not."

"No, I came straight down here."

"Well, I took a chance and remembered some of the things you once told me you liked eating. So, not knowing quite what time you would arrive, or if you would have eaten meanwhile, I made a pizza. It is rather a colourful one, too."

"Marvellous! I really am famished. I thought you might like these," I said, pointing to the roses.

"Oh, lovely! Red ones, too."

The flat was much as I had pictured it, reflecting the mixed tastes of three girls rather than those of any particular one. There were masses of potted plants, some almost sprouting to the ceiling, others in the basement patio. I noticed two paintings which I guessed were Zita's handiwork and a guitar which probably belonged to Sandra. In one corner of the patio Zita had set up an easel and laid out her paints – "all ready to get to work on Tortie."

We sat down on the patio to enjoy a rather exceptionally good home-made pizza, artistically decorated with anchovies, almonds, olives and red peppers. "You once told me you liked pizzas and anything that was colourfully and artistically presented, so here you are. There's a bottle of plonk to go with it."

"Plonk? I would hardly call this particular Muscadet plonk."

"I've some news for you. Guess where my next assignment takes me?"

"Not a clue. Surely not Dalkey Island, or Ireland again?"

"New York. I leave on Sunday."

This was an unexpected blow. "For how long?"

"That's the rub. I just don't know. A short while ago I

was asked to take an American family round London, just a day out. Now they have enquired of the agency whether I could help them locate some missing relatives of theirs in the UK and at the same time trace their ancestry. It's quite a challenge really. They want me to spend some days in New York going through their family records as a preliminary to making the search."

"You do undertake a variety of chores."

"Too true I do. But, anyway, enough of that for the moment. When are you going to tell me what all this cloak-and-dagger stuff is all about?"

"The story I have to tell is a long one. It is too long for all of it to be told in every detail at this stage. One day I will tell you everything, but today it must be simply the basic essentials. If I hide anything from you, it is purely for security reasons. But, first of all, take a deep breath. While I am now a writer by profession, I was until a few months ago working in a branch of Intelligence."

"You mean you were a spy, secret agent, or whatever, just like I said I'd like your hero to be?"

"Something like that. But please don't ask me any more questions on that, or tell anyone else. I shouldn't be telling you."

"But what an absolute giggle. How very thrilling. This makes my day."

Zita was bubbling over with mirthful excitement.

"It may seem a bit of a giggle to you, but it can hardly be called that from my viewpoint."

"Sorry, but it seemed such an astonishing coincidence after what I'd said. I'm rather relieved more than anything else. I wondered whether you might be mixed up in something peculiar, though my instincts told me to trust you. But, rest assured, I won't tell a soul."

"All else I can tell you is that the powers-that-be have told me that there is an unknown person, or maybe persons, threatening me in some way. I decided of my own accord to disappear for a few days to a secret hide-out and not even tell the authorities. Frankly, I wanted a break, I wanted to see you, and I was afraid they might put restrictions on my movements. Legally, they couldn't force me to do exactly as they want, as I've left the Service, but they could put pressure on me in other ways. Anyhow, they must have found out about you – probably our radio chats were monitored. So they tracked you down. That's about all I can tell you now."

I didn't dare tell Zita any more. She seemed to accept my version of events as the truth. It was a great relief at last to be able, if only partially, to discuss my personal problems with someone other than an ex-colleague like Hugo Hanson.

"Have you been in touch with the Special Branch since we spoke on the phone?"

"Oh, yes. Not only on my own account, but yours, too. But what are you going to tell your flatmates?"

"You tell me. It would be so easy to drop a clanger. If they knew the truth, they would want to live out on the story at every party for the next month."

At that moment Hanson rang. He couldn't have been more tactful. He deliberately set out to charm Zita, who answered the phone. So sorry she had been troubled by all those rather heavy-handed enquiries, but if by any chance Richard was there, could he speak to him. "Things are moving a bit," Hanson told me, "but very slowly. We can, of course, fix up some kind of security for you down at Rye, but this had better be arranged entirely through me and not via our friends in the Special Branch. If you want to put the flat on the market, we can probably handle that for you. I won't waste your time now, but give me a call tonight."

"Zita is anxious to know what she can tell her flatmates in the way of an explanation about the SB and myself."

"Oh, just say you're on the IRA hit list. That will do."

I told Zita what he had said, but she still seemed doubtful. "Sandra would love to tell that story."

"It doesn't matter if she does. It isn't true."

"You mean you are not really in any kind of danger?"

"No, I'm in danger all right, but not from the IRA. So that story doesn't matter."

Over coffee I told Zita rather more about myself. I did not want to be a total mystery to her. I mentioned my brief marriage (it only lasted four years) and the fact that most of my adult life had been spent without a home, just moving from one city to another. She in turn gave me a summary of her own life. I think we were both equally in the mood for confessions.

"Why did your marriage break down?"

"Nobody's fault really. But let me try to be honest. It was mine in that, always tending to be an optimist, I thought marriage would work without weighing up all the pros and cons. I was too young and my wife, Auriol, hated my work just as you seem to find it rather fun. I was away a lot and that really precipitated the break-up. Sometimes it would not have been desirable for Auriol to have been with me when I was overseas. And when she could have been with me, she didn't want to come."

"How does all that make you feel about marriage?"

"Well, being an incorrigible romantic, I still believe in it as a way of life. Not just because of a piece of paper, or a solemn marital vow, but because it means a personal commitment to an ideal. It may not always work, but it's much better to go into marriage believing in it as something for keeps than just thinking, oh well if it doesn't work one can always get divorced."

"I think that's what my father felt. You see, because he was killed when I was quite young, he's still my hero. I tend to measure the men I meet by him, or by his standards. I know they aren't necessarily my standards, but they are a useful guide."

"By the way, doesn't this trip to New York make it impossible for you to have Tortie at the flat?"

"I'm sure I can fix it with Sandra and Julie. After all I can point to the fact that I once looked after a dog for Julie for a whole five days while she was away and that meant taking it for walks, too. They won't have to take Tortie for walks and you have trained her to be admirably clean and domesticated."

"I shall move back to the barge as soon as I've made certain arrangements and then, of course, I'll take her back. It shouldn't be long before I get things fixed – a mere few days."

"I think I'd like to start painting Tortie now, if you don't mind. She's such a colourful cat that she makes a challenge for any artist. But she's also excessively lovable and that's quite a difficult quality to catch. After all, it's rare to see a lovable face in most human portraits, let alone with a cat."

"While you do that I'm going out to buy some wine –

partly to replace what I've drunk of yours, and also, it might be a good idea to pass on a couple of bottles to your flatmates as a gesture of gratitude for their agreeing to have Tortie. If they do, that is."

"Perhaps you'd like to have a look at my rig first of all. Let me know what you think of it."

She showed me into her bed-sitter which consisted of a divan bed suitably disguised with gaily coloured cushions and an enormous model of a pierrot, a long built-in wardrobe, a dressing-table, minute desk and, taking up all one corner, her rig. On the walls, as I might have expected, were some of Zita's pictures which I thought showed remarkable talent, though she herself said, "They are the experimental ones, those I don't as a rule show to my friends."

"The rig is most impressive," I said.

"Would it pass muster for one of your, er, agents in the field? I suppose you have other reasons for being interested in amateur radio."

"It would indeed pass muster. You are very wise, as I see, by keeping the receiver and transmitter separate, avoiding complicated switching."

Glancing casually around Zita's room, I noted that there was only one photograph; and from what she had told me, I felt sure the photograph was of her father. In front of it was a tiny glass of South African violets. Then I went down to the Fulham Road while Zita started her painting. I also wanted time to think: I was in a hell of a mess and a lot of things needed sorting out. I felt rather sad that Zita should be going away so soon.

When I returned to Ifield Road, she hadn't actually completed her picture of Tortie, but it was sufficiently advanced to show that she had captured the colours of a tortoise-shell cat remarkably well and the animal's somewhat wistful expression. At the same time she had given Tortie a faint, yet distinct halo of light. Zita tried to explain, "While painting her, I left my easel every now and then and went over to Tortie to get a close-up impression. I don't pretend to understand this involuntary gesture, but the sense of an aura of light and a conscious desire to make the cat feel at home were curiously related. I sensed that Tortie had had a real shock recently and that she needed healing. I just placed my hand over her and, as you will now notice, she is purring non-stop. Do you know anything about orgone therapy?"

"Isn't that what Wilhelm Reich invented and is also known as Reichian therapy?"

"Something like that. The underlying principle is that body energies are blocked by areas of muscular tension and that memories are stored in the body. Therefore massage can release both energy and memories and the anxieties they have caused can be discharged. Sometimes the holding of a hand above the body is as effective as massage. This is shown by the fact that the cat then begins to purr."

At that moment there was the sound of a latch-key at the front door. "Oh God, no!" exclaimed Zita. "Sandra and Julie must have come back sooner than usual. Do you mind? I must warn you that they are dreadful jokers and very, very flippant."

A short while afterwards Zita's two flatmates joined us in the patio. Julie was the taller and more serious while fair-haired Sandra was the smiling one. It was a stuffy day, despite the rain, and the patio was partially sheltered by a glass roof. After introductions I suggested opening the bottles of wine which had been placed in the fridge. That would ease the tension, I thought, for I was under no misapprehension as to what would happen in the next half hour or so. I should be subjected to a very close scrutiny. That was what Zita had meant when she said that Sandra and Julie were a couple of jokers. To try to avoid this trial by flatmates by making excuses to leave quickly would do me no good at all.

Zita picked up Tortie to show her to the girls, told them about her New York trip and asked if they would look after the cat. That hurdle seemed to be satisfactorily cleared when Sandra enquired, "Have you two been talking radio stuff?"

"Not all the time," I replied. "As a matter of fact, just as you arrived we were having a fascinating conversation about Reichian therapy."

"Good grief! Is that something Zita's taken up, or is it one of your hobbies?"

Zita came to the rescue. "Actually I started off talking about orgone therapy and Richard mentioned that it was invented by a man named Wilhelm Reich."

"What is it all about?" asked Julie.

"If I remember rightly, Reich believed that human energy could be stored in a little black box," I said.

"In fact it's called an accumulator and various forms of orgone therapy have been developed since Reich's time," chipped in Zita. "For example, there is electro-crystal therapy which involves the electrical stimulation of crystals and gives a boost to energy transmission. Nobody knows how it works, but it has helped to cure all kinds of ailments in a high percentage of cases."

"It all sounds rather kinky to me," commented Sandra. "But who is Wilhelm Reich?"

An awkward pause. The situation could easily develop into Sandra and Julie becoming convinced I was some kind of nut-case. But fortunately I was able to say something. Part of my professional work had always been to try to understand the stupidities of the Communist mind. "Reich was a member of the Austrian Communist Party in the thirties," I said, "and was actually expelled from it because he expressed the heresy to Communist ears that fascism was the outcome of sexual repression rather than economic forces. The Commies didn't like that idea at all."

I was working on the principle that to baffle is often better than to explain. But the very phrase "sexual repression" made the flatmates all agog.

"Ah," said Julie, "so that is why in the Lonely Hearts advertisements one sees more men advertising themselves as of left-wing persuasion and hardly any right-wing types."

"Aren't you writing a romantic novel?" asked Sandra. "How would orgone therapy go down in that?" I saw poor Zita lose her composure for a moment. Sandra was hitting below the belt.

"A few months ago I should possibly have agreed that it would sound unconvincing in a novel. Right now I feel sure it could possibly fit in if one mulled things over for a bit. Romance, energy and life force are all mixed up. I suppose one could say it is heading in the direction of alternative romance. Maybe by telepathy, or some therapy, one learns how to make love without talking about it."

"Love as a form of reassurance," said Zita.

"Love on an intellectual plane."

"The counter-sexual revolution?"

"Isn't that already taking place?"

"Have you heard of SCUM?" Sandra asked me.

"I fear not."

"It means the Society for the Cutting Up of Men. It's an American Women's Lib organization. It announced the destruction of the male sex as part of its manifesto."

"Not so much a revolution as a total war on men," I ventured.

"How much research have you done on your romantic novel?" asked Julie.

"Julie, don't be so bloody inquisitive," said an indignant Zita, suddenly showing her teeth. I felt sorrier for her than for myself regarding this inquisition. At least the two other girls seemed interested in the subject, though I realised there was an undercurrent of leg-pulling.

"But he wants to know what makes girls tick," replied Julie. "Don't you, Richard?"

"Well, let's put it this way. The aim of the book is to create a factional romance, one that bears some resemblance to reality, not something dreamed up in the mind."

"What are you going to do with your hero and heroine once you get them together? Isn't that the trickiest part of the book?"

"In many ways, yes. One American publisher advises authors not to let them make love too early in the plot."

"But then you have to keep the reader waiting. Isn't that a bore?"

"In some ways, yes." I was beginning to fall on the defensive. Then Sandra cut in, "You would spell out specific details of the love-making, wouldn't you?"

"Here again that American publisher has some advice. He says, if I remember the exact phrase, 'explicit details will be used only in foreplay and the fadeout should occur . . .' "

"After they've had it off!"

"Exactly."

"Do you think he's right? Isn't that just going to leave the reader feeling she's been cheated?"

"I hope not. I didn't say I was necessarily going to follow the American publisher's advice."

"But what sort of a romantic novel will it be? Not Barbara

Cartland, I gather. Nor Beryl Bainbridge. What about Anais Nin?"

"None of those. Nothing like any of them."

"What sort of a heroine? Will she be a virgin? Or will she be wildly and daringly experienced?"

"I'll have to see how it works out," I said diplomatically, but not very convincingly. "But of course I'm open to any ideas as to actual love scenes."

I thought that by now the wine was beginning to have an effect. We had finished two bottles and were half-way into the third. Sandra and Julie were drinking much faster than Zita who was obviously finding the conversation somewhat of a strain. Unusual for Zita, I felt, but I understood how she must feel. I began to think it would be sound tactics if I made my departure.

"We will all try and think up some really original love scenes for you," said Sandra. "Won't we, Zita?"

Zita's reply was a cushion hurled at Sandra.

"Thank you for all the proffered co-operation," I said. "And now I had really better be on my way. But before I go I do want to say how sorry I am that you have been bothered by all those calls from the Special Branch. You must have wondered what was going on. I am frightfully sorry. But I think Zita will be able to explain things to you."

FOURTEEN

Back in De Beauvoir Town I had plenty to do. I rang Hanson to say I was back at base and he suggested coming round to see me more or less straight away. Meanwhile I tried to clarify my own mind as to what exactly I wanted to do. Then it came to me in a flash that one tidy solution to all problems might be if I followed Zita to New York and joined her there. If I did that, I could look up my old CIA pal, Bram Stoppard, who might very well be able to help me clear my name and pinpoint the villains. It was a long shot, but worth trying. Edmund Burke was a bit of a berk himself when he made that sweeping statement that "to love and be wise is not given to men". In my case love had pointed the way to wisdom.

A discreet call to my CIA contact's home revealed that he was in Washington, but would be back on the following day. I left a message that I was planning to come to America within the next few days and that I would stay at the Barbizon Plaza Hotel, which I knew of old and was pleasantly situated close to Central Park.

Hanson arrived fairly speedily and told me: "We have checked on your hide-out in Rye Harbour and we think it's viable for the immediate future. You may be reassured to know that the address of this new abode of yours is known only to me in the Office and the SB outside it. Now, on balance, you can trust the SB, now that we have sorted out the problem of their indiscretions, whereas I still wouldn't like to say you could entirely trust MI5. Not on their track record. Too much questioning back to Century House, despite any verbal promises. The Fivers have cleaned their stables, no doubt, but they are still much concerned with their petty squabbles and internal wars and that can spell trouble for us on occasions."

"Zita's going to America on Sunday. Just an idea, but I thought if I can get the flat put on the market tomorrow, leaving you to keep an eye on things and make arrangements for moving out of furniture, I could happily push off to America myself and look up my old CIA pal. This way I might be able to straighten out my own problems and do Six a good turn."

"You really are exoceted by this girl, aren't you? But it's a jolly good idea all round. It would give us time to organize security for you this end and you might even pick up a few clues for us. You're on your own there, but if you need any aid, we'll be on hand. Unofficially the angels will be ministering unto you. But give us your addresses."

Hanson was one of those MI6 executive officers who will probably never get promotion because of the first class job they do. As a key figure behind the scenes, dealing with all manner of problems, Hanson was indispensable.

The next few days were go, go, go. On the Saturday I put the flat on the market with local estate agents and then started packing up my books and rig ready for the removal people. There wasn't a lot to do other than ensure my rig was secure against clumsy handlers and to prepare a list to hand on to Hanson. Later I drove down to Hastings to return the car, going back by train the same night. I then rang Zita because I was just a little worried that the Sandra – Julie banter might have spoiled our relationship. We didn't say much, but she gave me an address at New Haven, Connecticut, where I could write to her. At that stage I didn't mention my idea of going to the USA, as I couldn't be absolutely sure I could make it. Only one thing worried me after our telephone conversation: Zita said that Sandra and Julie were going to give her a memoranda on the subject of the romantic novel. That, I felt, could turn our relationship into a complete joke.

On Sunday morning Lucie called round. I felt very sorry for her because she was not only hurt about my abrupt departure without telling her, but she seemed distressed that I was going to leave the flat. What was going to happen to Tortie? As I had no adequate explanation, it made matters rather worse. But I did have a conscience as far as Lucie was concerned because I felt I owed her a lot. I made her some toasted cheese sandwiches and coffee and we sat and talked for a while. I decided to give her two weeks' pay in lieu of notice, not that she had hinted at any money being due to her – maybe it was a question of my being in love that made me feel kinder. I don't know, but I rather detect that real love works that way. Lucie cheered up, especially when I assured her that in due course she could come and see Tortie in my new home. I purposely had to refrain from giving her an address, but promised I would write. After that she offered to help me pack and this I gladly accepted.

I made some telephone calls, one to New York to the Barbizon Plaza Hotel and another to book a flight to New York. Then on the Tuesday I flew into Kennedy airport.

Once installed at the Barbizon Plaza Hotel I lost no time in telephoning my CIA colleague, Bram Stoppard, and arranged to see him.

"I had heard a whisper on the grapevine that you were either on your way out or definitely out," he said, "and I did wonder why. If you have much to tell me, maybe it would be wiser to meet at some inconspicuous place. What about the Tavern on the Green at Sixty-Seventh Street, just inside Central Park. It should be easy for you to get to. Lunch tomorrow at 13.00 hours. There's a welcome heat-wave so maybe we can eat outside."

Zita hadn't supplied a telephone number where she could be contacted, but I had no difficulty in tracing one from the addresses she had given me. I rang her up and announced that I was in New York.

"I can hardly believe it," she replied. "What a really lovely surprise. But how, why and what?"

"Well, you will remember that I love springing surprises and you said you liked them, too. Apart from all that, however, I should tell you that the one man who can solve the mystery of my unknown enemies is here in New York. At least I hope he can solve it. What chances are there of my seeing you?"

"I'm delighted you rang now because tomorrow I have to go into New York to do some research at the Genealogical and Biographical Library, so maybe we could meet some time after three o'clock. I shall be staying in the city overnight, going back to New Haven the next day."

"That's splendid. So is the weather. After that terrible day last Friday this late summer heat-wave in New York is like a touch of magic. Would you like to risk another romantic rendezvous with me?"

"Where is it this time?"

"I suggest 3.30 p.m. at the bottom of the right-hand steps facing the Bethesda Fountain in Central Park. It's in quite one of the most attractive parts of the Park and we couldn't miss each other there."

"Bethesda Fountain, what is it?"

"Well, the first Bethesda Fountain was, according to the Apostle John, 'a pool with five porches' where people went to be cured of all manner of ailments by the so-called Angel of the Fountain. The fountain in Central Park is at the centre of a small plaza which is close to a lake. It has a sculpted angel on its roof."

"You do love outdoor meeting places, don't you?"

"It's fun to watch someone arriving from a distance, just to say 'is it she?' or 'it can't be'. The agony is prolonged, but in the end it's much more worthwhile. I remember wondering whether it really was you in the distance at Fairlight Glen . . ."

We each had business to attend to, so we didn't talk for long. But the date was clinched. It fitted in perfectly with my meeting with Bram, also in Central Park.

Bram was one of those forthright, outgoing and hospitable Americans who really do make one feel that the special relationship of the English-speaking nations is worthwhile and that, even if all else should collapse, this really should survive. With Bram one more or less took off from when one had been chatting previously. "The last words I heard you say were that the dames in Beirut left much to be desired. I never did quite click on to that observation. Tell me now, is it a dame who brings you over here?"

"In a way it is."

"You goddam Brits do love the understatement, don't you? In a way it is. You bloody well know it's the most important thing."

"It's the pleasantest reason for my coming over here, but

not the most important by a long shot. To match your forthrightness I'll just say for a start that my life has actually been threatened by unknown enemies."

"Ye Gods, that's a one-thousand-dollar answer! Sorry if I seemed frivolous. You'd better have one of the first Daquiris of the season and so had I for that matter."

So far I had maintained a total silence with everyone on my resignation from the Service. But now I had to choose between keeping to the rules and obtaining the information I sought. But with Hanson's implied blessing, it now seemed worth the risk. Bram Stoppard knew I had been in trouble; that much was clear. What he called his grapevine was one of the most extensive networks of one-man intelligence I have ever known. It included all manner of snippets on foreign secret services from the KGB to the SIS and the Mossad to the South African Directorate of National Security. He stored it all on his personal computer (at least that was what he claimed). So, using my judgement in this instance, bearing in mind that the astute Hanson had actually encouraged me to talk to Stoppard, I told him everything.

"I'd always taken a keen interest in you because of the skilled manner in which you operated, and I thought it was all wrong you hadn't got yourself more promotion. So I kept my ears open for news of you. Your liaison officer in New York came over all stuffed shirt several weeks ago when I enquired about you. I said that London must be crazy to let you go, and I don't think he welcomed my comment. But your story fits in and confirms all I have always suspected about Wetherby."

"My people don't take that view. That wouldn't matter so much if I could put my past behind me and concentrate on a new career. But how the hell can I when my life is under perpetual threat?"

"Tell you what I'll do, but it may take time. Under the Freedom of Information Act plus a bit of personal pull, I'll see what I can get on Wetherby out of the files, as there should be something on him. I'll also feed his name into my personal computer and see what turns up. I hope for some help this end because for a whole year now we have been worried about rumours of yet another mole highly placed in the British Establishment."

"So it looks as though it's back to the fifties again – the era of mistrust, Burgess, Maclean, Philby and Blunt, not to mention Blake, possibly the most professional of all."

"Not quite as bad as that. The English-speaking alliance will go on weathering the storms, but on security matters there is room for a hell of a lot of improvement. We've made our blunders, hell only knows. But we have a feeling that one reason your people held back so much from us so long on the defection of Vladimir Kuzichkin could have something to do with Wetherby. I hope not, but we still have to do some hard graft on both sides to find the perfect working arrangement. Anyhow, I'll be in touch again very soon – possibly later today."

It was during a glorious late summer heat-wave that Bram and I left the Tavern on the Green; and I just ambled around Central Park thoroughly enjoying the scene. There are those people, mainly ill-informed cosmopolitans, who will tell you that it isn't safe to go into Central Park today. This is rubbish; Central Park is still probably the finest and most attractive open space in the world today for a free and uninhibited people.

There were only twenty-five minutes in which I could prepare myself for my meeting with Zita. While it had been quite amusing to be introduced to her flatmates, their unexpectedly early arrival had prevented me from saying to Zita half the things which had been uppermost in my mind. This time I was quite determined that she should know exactly how I felt about her.

Yet was Central Park the best place for this? That, I knew, depended largely upon luck. On some days, chiefly at weekends, Central Park could seem as overcrowded as the waterfront of Hong Kong. Sometimes the area around Bethesda Fountain gave the impression of being simply a muggers' hunting ground, rife with petty crime of all kinds. But this was not a fair, or accurate picture. On other days (and this seemed to be one of them) it could present itself as a non-stop carnival, but with little oases of solitude under the trees where two people could curl up and nobody would notice them.

I paused for a few moments on The Terrace above the park, looking across to the hill paths and lawns known as the Ramble and the mock-medieval Belvedere Castle, and then turning my eyes down to the plaza below in the middle of which was Bethesda Fountain, crowned by the statue of the Angel of the Waters. It was hard to believe that this extremely pleasant lay-out was created out of an open sewer in the middle of the last century. There were youths and girls, arms on each other's shoulders, running round the ledge of the Fountain, making noises like an ancient steam train. A negro boy was playing the harmonica while his girl friend jigged around him wearing a T-shirt with the motto, "Safety in Speed." Occasionally there was a whiff of marijuana, then it became lost in some heavy and heady perfumes. Once I caught the chatter of drug pedlars, who seemed to be in their teens. A falsetto voice proclaimed, "I've gotta fix some scag for my pal."

This time Zita arrived on the stroke of 3.30. She was wearing a close-fitting cream-coloured outfit which set off her reddish hair and, as she came nearer, I saw that she had amethyst earrings.

"Well, I must say this is much easier to find than Lovers' Seat," were her first words. "And on a day like this it's lovely to meet out of doors. But what an extraordinary scene – these weirdos, I mean."

"Oh, we'll make tracks away from here now that we've met. But I thought you might like to see the Fountain."

"You're absolutely right. What a scene for a painter. Helen Bradley would have captured it superbly. At least, I think she would. My technique wouldn't measure up to it. But I should like to try to create a pictorial map of the park. Could we stop just a few minutes while I get out my sketch-book?"

"Of course. Probably the best vantage-point is up above on The Terrace, but you can get quite a lot of colour by sitting out at the Fountain Café. Let's go there now, sit down and have a Sangria. You can sketch while you drink."

We sat down, Zita took out her sketch-book and we both absorbed the scene around us. "If you see me make an odd note or two, it's to use for possible captions to put against certain landmarks of the park. Also I should like to record a few of the really groovy phrases we hear to pass on to Sandra and Julie next time I see them."

Two rather obvious drug pedlars among the teenagers passed by.

"It all seems so obvious. Don't they get arrested?"

"Oh, yes, they get copped sometimes. The police are fairly active, if inconspicuous. But of course there's safety in numbers and drug pedlars and addicts rely on that."

Zita sketched furiously. "I shouldn't dare sit here and sketch by myself. I'd be much too frightened."

"Talking of Sandra and Julie," I said, "they gave me quite an inquisition the other night. I almost felt they were prospective heroines themselves."

"Oh, Richard, I'm terribly sorry about that. Was it very embarrassing?"

"No, normally it would have been great fun. But I was wanting to talk to you. Also I didn't know how much they knew about the novel."

It was then that Zita told me all about the madcap quest for men which Sandra and Julie had propounded. "You would probably have done much better if you had engaged Sandra and Julie in your quest for a heroine. They are much more sophisticated than I am."

"I doubt if that's true."

"You just wait and see." I was puzzled at this enigmatic reply and it was not until much later that I discovered its meaning.

We left the plaza and turned into a path leading up to a mound on which was a group of trees. Here was gathered a party of Hari Krishna children who were handing around a shellacked conch shell and whispering. Out of the bushes suddenly appeared a man with a camera who asked the youngest girl (she couldn't have been more than fourteen) if he could snap the group. "You can snap me, OK," she replied. "But don't snap my soul."

"Have you jotted that down in your little book?" I asked.

"You bet I have."

We moved higher up and eventually came upon a slight hollow, surrounded by trees. Stopping, we were surprised at how quiet it was. "Like coming into a church from a busy street," said Zita. "Let's just sit down here and talk. I'll put my sketch-book away now. But, first of all, have you had any success in New York?"

"If you mean my problem, the answer is that I'm hopeful. But I fear it's going to take a long time to find out everything."

"Oh, dear, I was so hoping ... I mean I read in one of the papers here that the CIA were claiming to have discovered some botch-up in British Intelligence and I just wondered if that might help you."

"Adorable Zita, it's nice of you to think about these things, but they are problems I've got to tackle on my own."

"I wish I could share them with you. I know you can't tell me much, but I have thought a lot about what little I know. What's more, if there is anything I can do to help at any time, I promise you can count on me. I think I fobbed off Sandra and Julie with that story about the IRA, and I must say that really gave you a boost in their eyes."

"Thank you," I said. This was the cue I had been waiting for. Zita was lying down, stretched out, hands folded across her tummy. I bent down swiftly and kissed her on each eyelid and then a final, discreet and very light twiddle of the tongue across the lashes of one eye.

Curiously enough at this stage of a romantic fandango neither male nor female indulges in any memorable phrases. The great breakthrough is much more likely to be marked by the humdrum comment than the *bon mot*. Zita sighed "Oh, Richard", and, for once keeping a curb on my tendency to make outrageous comments, I just murmured, "A butterfly kiss for a flutterby girl."

And that was it. A silent, undeclared state of love without anyone making any move to make love. But there was this mutual discovery that we might be on the way to loving one another.

"Do you remember where we left off talking just as Sandra and Julie came in?"

"Oh, yes, we were talking about orgone therapy. I almost had a feeling we were going to see how it would work into a novel."

"That's right. What you just did reminded me of it. You see, part of orgone therapy is pleasure massage. I know that sounds pretty awful, but the aim is to create good bodily sensations. The strokes used are much the same as in energy-releasing massage, but much lighter and more subtle. This doesn't stir up emotions, but creates a sense of well-being."

"I think I see what you mean. There's a bit of a clue in that new in-phrase 'cuddles, not sex'."

"I don't suppose you've been to see Jack Klaff's show at the Battersea Arts Centre. He's tried to put that into words in a show called 'Cuddles'. In this play two lovers ask each other whether sex isn't overrated. I can't remember how the exact answer comes up in verse, but it goes something like this – 'if sex's meaning is completely ignored, cuddles with everyone must strike a chord'."

"I certainly think there's half a clue in what you say. 'Cuddles' is a lovely word, so much nicer sounding than sex. But I'm not sure that what you quoted isn't ambiguous."

We were playing some kind of charade with one another. At the same time I think we both sensed that behind this facade of abstract talk was an instinctive reaching out towards the other's heart.

"Cuddles," I said. "Cuddles," Zita smiled. Her red hair flaked across my face, she snuggled up against me. I probed with my tongue into her hair, darting this way and that among her tresses. "I love red hair," I muttered rather inconsequentially.

The next half hour was lit up by all the colours which make love seem real. Out under the shade of these trees all seemed radiant and beautiful. We suddenly became hooked up and unhookable on our own coloured glass minds, peaceful in each other's arms, unprogrammed and therefore able to tap out our private jargon, much of it monosyllabic. We would lie back and look up at the patterns of the trees and listen to the onomatopoeic rustling of the leaves, "rather like listening to the music of a thousand kisses," said Zita.

"You know," she added, "I've never been quite sure what colour your eyes are. This is one of the things about you which has had me guessing. I'm not sure whether they are grey, blue or green, or if they simply change colour from time to time, as I suspect they do."

"You, too, have a coloured glass effect about you. I don't quite know how to describe your eyes, but if I had to make a careful judgement, I should say they were like mixing green Chartreuse with a pale, mellow brandy."

I can't remember all we said. There were a few dreamy, mystical half-sentences with eyes tightly shut. I think the exceptional warmth of the late afternoon kept us in a state of fond inertia, not to mention the effect on me of three of Bram Stoppard's ultra-strong Daquiris, the recipe for which he actually dictated to the waiter. Twice some Central Park eccentrics wandered past very close to where we were lying. One was a barefooted girl wearing green lipstick and a coiffure dyed to look like a rainbow; she was holding hands with a male in a huge floppy hat and a scarf around the right leg of his trousers, his chest covered with exotic tattoos. Then a couple of young freaks sat down some short distance away to play Scrabble on the grass.

Somehow these interruptions didn't seem to matter. I think that was because not only were we just happy to feel in love, but we each wanted to fall in love slowly, much more slowly than I could ever recall having fallen (or thought I had fallen) in love previously. One could say that in the hollow under the trees it was sandwich love, with Zita's dress as bread, but with the sky dancing a waltz and the trees letting in little sparkles of light that matched the secret stars inside the sandwich. The secret stars were our respective fantasies which fanned our love, yet kept us from fulfilment. It was so many different things – it was laminated love, kaleidoscopic love, Venus on wheels skiing on sand, winging to the Moon, hopping from one cloud to another.

I must have said some pretty mad things as we lay clasped in each other's arms. For Zita suddenly aroused me with the comment, "I love it when you make up stories about you and me. It means you, too, must have fantasies like me."

"*You* have fantasies?"

"Why not?"

"What then?"

"Well, one of my fantasies is that I should really love to be a mermaid and to rise out of the water and tease a man by tickling him with the flip end of my tail."

"Go on."

"I should caress him with my tail, gently at first, then wrap it around him and dive into the water, come up and make faces at him. Oh, Richard, I wish I had a tail to wrap around you."

"I should like that very much. It ought to be a shimmering bluey-green tail, by the way. Better than any Reichian therapy."

We clung together as though we never wanted anyone to tear us apart. Yet all the time, as Zita confessed afterwards, we were each dreadfully afraid that someone would do just this. Perhaps it was as well we were in Central Park.

Zita's story about the play, "Cuddles", came back to me. To believe in cuddles was to believe in love. Without cuddles, what would love mean? We cuddled, relaxed, cuddled again.

When one is indulging in the preliminaries of love, all manner of visions flit across the mind, one takes in a thousand pictures in a matter of seconds. At one moment Zita reached up to kiss my nose and in a recollection of things long past it came back to me how the Touareg women of the Hoggar Mountains in the Sahara kissed the men's noses, but never their lips. Touareg women were the first liberated females in all Africa. I once watched an *ahal* night of Touareg men and women in the tents of the Sahara. I recalled the women singing in Arabic these words:

> "We shall love you eternally,
> We have the swiftness of the camel,
> We have the strength of the donkey,
> We are tireless in love,
> We shall lead you to paradise."

FIFTEEN

It was Zita who at last broke the spell. "I'm afraid I've got some more work to do before I go back to New Haven tomorrow. I really must be on my way."

"You will have dinner with me tonight."

"I fear that's just not possible, worse luck. I've got to call on an old lady who lives right the other side of Central Park. She is giving me a whole lot of data on the Walmsley family to take back to London and she's asked me to dinner and to stay the night."

"Can't you slip away for an hour or so? I have all manner of suggestions for eating out. We could go to Casey's in Greenwich Village where the *steak au poivre* is a speciality. Or even cut a real dash and go to Uncle Tai's Hunan Yuan on Third Avenue, a restaurant that looks like a garden."

"No, Richard, I'm sorry."

"What about meeting for half an hour at Rumpelmayer's in the St. Moritz Hotel where you could indulge your passion for the most delicious sweet concoctions and maybe some coffee."

But the answer was still no. Zita was a firm-minded girl where work was concerned. But, seeing my disappointment, she explained, "I should have made things clear when you telephoned me. I'm dreadfully, dreadfully sorry. More so because it's been a heavenly afternoon and I am looking forward to next time."

"But when will that be?"

Zita smiled in a somewhat mysterious way. I felt sure she was quietly planning something on her own account. Then she asked how long I would be staying in New York.

"I'd love to stay here as long as you are here, but that's

only part of the answer. My friend will get some action going for me, I hope, and that may take a few days or a few weeks. If it's stuff under the Freedom of Information Act it might take weeks or even months to get vital material declassified. I can't stay longer than a week, as there is too much to fix up back in England. I must push on with the novel and even write a few articles to justify my existence. There's also the sale of the flat and fixing up about the barge. Not to mention rescuing your flatmates from the chore of looking after Tortie."

"Don't worry about Tortie. I shall definitely be going back to London next Sunday. Meanwhile I've got an idea. Can you try to keep Friday and Saturday free?"

"Why yes, of course. What's your plan?"

"I'm still thinking it up. For a change will you let me do the planning of a rendezvous. It would be such fun. Tell you what, I'll drop a note in at your hotel tomorrow morning before I go back to New Haven. And now I must dash."

I escorted Zita out of the park and got her a taxi. Then I returned to the Barbizon Plaza Hotel to find a note from Bram Stoppard, asking me to ring him. I lost no time in dialling his number.

"Things are moving quicker than I imagined," he said. "Point Number One for you to bear in mind is that it seems that Wetherby has been responsible for a series of requests over the past few years for a stop to be put on the release of a whole number of documents concerning our mutual Services. Point Number Two is that Wetherby, according to my Latin-American expert, was partly responsible for playing down Six's intelligence reports of Argentinian invasion intentions *vis-à-vis* the Falklands.."

"Does this provide a link with C. A. Walters?"

"Say no more now. Meet me at Oscar's Salt of the Sea at 1155 Third Avenue at 20.00 hours. I can promise you some absolutely splendid stuffed lobsters."

Bram was a great trencher man who made a point of enjoying almost every type of food the world had to offer. He was a walking encyclopaedia on the best restaurants of the Middle East, the Balkans and Central Europe and he made dining out an absolute pleasure. "I have hit very little but dry holes to date as far as Wetherby goes. My impression is that he has left very little spoor. But the C. A. Walters angle is rewarding, for that name had had our people worried, too. No wonder that Wetherby was alarmed when he guessed you must have spotted his false signature in the hotel register. During the Falklands shenanigans two interesting facts emerged. First of all, having been told that C. A. Walters was conducting arms purchases for the Argies and especially that he operated in Paris, we made some enquiries. To begin with we came up against total silence. Then we made a check with our man in Buenos Aires. C. A. Walters was definitely an Anglo-Argentinian, speaking perfect English, having an English grandfather. But the big surprise is that eight years ago he went on a trip to Russia, spending several weeks in Moscow, Leningrad and elsewhere. He returned to B.A. and then almost immediately afterwards went to Paris and announced that he was going to live in South Africa."

"And where does that take us?"

"Since then nobody has seen him – at least nobody who could recognize him. There's a dead end to all inquiries, just as your SA security man seemed to experience when he made inquisitive noises. So our boys thought it worth while making an investigation. Walters had suddenly blossomed as an under-cover Argentinian agent for the first time just after he returned from Russia. The story was that he had brought back quite a lot of information from Moscow. That information was tainted. It smelt like a feed from the Soviets, even though some of it was useful and accurate. True, Walters had negotiated various highly favourable arms deals for the Argentine, but he conducts all his business without any of his former colleagues actually meeting him. What is more we have discovered that Walters secretly married a Soviet agent whom he met in Cuba only a few months before he went to Russia. It was almost certainly through her that he got his visa for the USSR. The Argies don't know about that secret marriage."

"In other words, Walters is now a Soviet agent who is so important that he needs to keep totally out of sight from those in the Argentine and in South Africa with whom he deals."

"That would be a fair deduction. I think he is probably aided in all this by Wetherby. We do know that in the weeks prior to the Argies' invasion of the Falklands that Walters was pumping through intelligence in Buenos Aires that you Brits would turn a blind eye to any landings. He was citing documentary evidence of this. Who else could that stuff have come from but Wetherby?"

"What makes you think that?"

"Our man managed to get hold of a lot of this stuff – unofficially, of course. It included copies of reports from the files of Six and the Foreign Office, names of personnel, what they were saying and doing. Some of the stuff was undoubtedly genuine, but a great deal was faked – enough to do damage, Maybe it was concocted by Wetherby."

Bram, one of the most forthright and high-powered of any of the agents serving the Western cause, was an old Harvard man who wore his learning lightly and modestly. Indeed, he seemed to go out of his way to play it down. But I knew by his assured manner and the way in which he kept plying me with splendid Californian wine that something important was coming.

He waited until the Bourbon and brandy stage before he made his revelation. "Richard," he said, raising his glass, "here's to your complete clearance of all the grossly unfair charges alleged against you. We are getting nearer to doing this because we have found out by a lucky chance that Wetherby and Walters were at Cambridge together – the same college. It was an elementary question to ask, yet why didn't your people ask it?"

"They may have done so by now."

"If so, it's time they produced some action. Mind you, we should never have linked Walters with Wetherby unless you had tipped us off. When you broke Wetherby's cover in Paris there must have been a lot of aggro all round. Not least for the Russians. Because make no mistake about it, they are after your guts. By the way, I've had you tailed ever since you left me in Central Park this afternoon and so far nobody has picked up even the smell of a spoor of any Russkie agent tagging on to you."

"You old bugger!"

"It was in your interests, brother. But be careful nevertheless. What precautions did you take when you left London?"

"Oh, the Special Branch engineered my departure rather

150

cleverly after I had changed cars twice en route to the airport."

Dear old Bram! He had done his stuff remarkably quickly. He was an astonishing man in that one minute he could be totally serious, but the next he could revert to his normal bantering and semi-humorous approach to life. I'm sure that more than one enemy agent has been lulled into complacency by thinking that Bram was crude and insular; in fact he was cosmopolitan and spoke three or four languages fluently. "I'm going to take you to a little night spot in the Village where there's a dame who plays the piano like she was in bed with you. But before pleasure, one final question, what baffles me still about this whole affair is how Wetherby arranges his alibi for being in England when your people checked back on him? Everything hinges on that, for it is the one factor which destroyed your case."

"It has baffled me just as much. So much so that at first I began to wonder if I was having hallucinations."

"Well, I guess there's an answer somewhere. Just as there must be an answer to the other thousand-dollar question of the moment. You know about this communications leakage at Cheltenham GCHQ which caught your people with their pants down. How the hell was it that Cheltenham of all places had town-twinning links with the Russian Black Sea resort of Sochi from the late 'fifties? How goddam chummier than that can you get?"

There's no doubt about it that Americans can very nearly kill you with kindness, and Bram was no exception. He took me along to the night club and we stayed there until about two in the morning. He listened patiently to my enthusiastic description of Zita and the work I was doing on the novel. Then he outlined his plan of action: he would see that the CIA head of station in London was fully briefed and, to ensure this, he proposed going down to Langley to see some of "the top boys in the Company", as he called the CIA. "It's as important for us as it is for you," he added. "I think you'll find it is in your interests to get back to London as soon as possible after the weekend. Have your fun now, while you can. By the time you get back we should have set things in motion."

I shouldn't think there was anybody in the world who could drink Bram under the table. What was more, as midnight passed by, his talk became even more erudite in an informal way, even upon the subject of love. "Did you know that the Company even gets psychiatric reports on some people as to the extent of their being love-prone? Awful phrase, isn't it? Michael Liebowitz, of the New York State Psychiatric Institute, set the trend when he asserted that there might be a specific chemical in the brain associated with being in love. The suggestion was that it could be phenylethylamine, a compound linked to the amphetamines. His theory was that love created a response similar to an amphetamine high. But what I always say is that you can't measure love like you can count orgasms. My own view, for what it's worth, is that people who live dangerously, or who live in fairly constant danger, are more prone to fall in love than all others."

"Maybe it works that way with me," I replied.

I woke next morning with a king of hangovers, the result of having consumed quantities of rye whisky, which is not one of my normal tipples. But when in New York one tends to embark on all kinds of activities which are out of the ordinary. Also, by the nature of my Intelligence work, I am conditioned to being a glutton for doing the other person's thing. It was nearly noon when I went down to reception where a note from Zita was awaiting me.

"Dear Richard," it began. "My mind simply hasn't been on my work since I left you. You really must be having a bad effect. I did try to cope, but I must have been a very boring dinner companion for Mrs. Walmsley. I really should have liked to stay with you the rest of yesterday and to have explored New York.

"Now it is my turn to make the rendezvous. It really has a most romantic ring about its name – Troubadour Island (I'm trying to find out how it got its name and wondering if the story is as romantic as that of Lovers' Seat). It's one of the Thimble Islands, of which there are about thirty, situated about half a mile off Stony Creek, a few miles east of New

Haven, Connecticut. New Haven is not much more than fifty miles from New York City, so it will not be a difficult journey for you, if you can spare the time to make it. Do please try to come, though I know you must have a lot to do. We could meet at Stony Creek, but phone me here in New York before midday as I shall be leaving for New Haven where the Junior branch of the Walmsleys lives shortly after one o'clock. If you miss me, here is the New Haven number.

"PS. Something odd happened when I got back to Mrs. Walmsley's last evening. Do you remember the girl with the green lipstick and the hair-do that looked like a rainbow in Central Park yesterday? Well, as I looked out of the window from behind the curtains I saw her with a man — not the boy in the floppy hat, but someone much older — on the pavement below and she was pointing out Mrs. Walmsley's residence. I suppose it's very silly of me even to mention it, but I just wondered if someone had been following you, me or both of us.

"Love from your very happy Mermaid,
Zita."

That postscript made me forget the rest of the letter and cured my hangover in an instant. Bram had been quite positive that there had been no indication of anyone tailing me in Central Park. I had not troubled to keep a look-out myself because I felt absolutely sure that I had got away from London without my movements being discovered by anyone other than MI6 and the Special Branch. I knew that Soviet Intelligence had a very long arm indeed, but it seemed improbable that even the KGB could have learnt so quickly that I was in New York. From what Hanson had said it also seemed that Wetherby was being kept in the dark concerning my movements, and, if so, no leakage could have come from him. Common sense suggested that the postscript should be ignored as recording a mere coincidence. But what alarmed me was the awful possibility that now Zita herself could be in some danger.

I looked at my watch. It was nearly one o'clock. Zita must have left that note for me at least two hours previously. I rang up old Mrs. Walmsley's residence and was told that Zita had left for New Haven only five minutes earlier.

Checking with reception, I found there was a train to New Haven leaving in about four minutes. There was no chance of reaching the station before Zita left.

A call to Bram's home informed me that he had already left for Washington en route to Langley, Virginia. My luck was out. I supposed it was the law of averages. Up to now I had been very lucky, well, lucky in love, if not in my career. Now the pendulum was beginning to swing against me. I must find Zita and convince her she might be in real danger.

I cursed myself for staying in bed so long and thus failing to telephone Zita in time. I also sadly missed the advice of Bram. With his local knowledge he could probably have assessed the chances as to whether or not Zita was being tailed. True, he had been convinced that there wasn't "any trace of a Russkie spoor", as he put it, but maybe the KGB were using new tactics in shadowing. Perhaps they were using flamboyant, punk-style teenagers in an attempt to cover for their professional tail-men. That could make sense and it might have been that Zita had seen one such teenager handing over her assignment to a professional. Another point to bear in mind was that anybody Bram had asked to keep an eye on me would not be following Zita as well, so he could quite easily miss any tail on her.

If Zita had been followed to the Barbizon Plaza Hotel when she delivered her note to me, then it would be reasonable to expect that my whereabouts would be known to the enemy. So I made a snap decision to leave the hotel speedily and go straight to New Haven, taking care to deceive any shadowers as to my intentions. I didn't want anything to interfere with the prospect of seeing Zita again, especially as the rendezvous on Troubadour Island seemed so attractive. But, above all I must do my utmost to protect her from any possible danger.

By this time I knew that I was fast falling in love with this green-eyed sprite of a girl. But how did she feel? She had said in her note that her mind hadn't been on her work and that I must be having a bad effect on her. Was that a good sign, or otherwise? Had she allowed herself to be carried away by the speed with which our relationship had suddenly blossomed? Librans, I knew from even a casual study of astrology, were supposed to be temperamentally responsive to romantic impulses. Or was I reading too much into what she had written? There were substantial reasons why she should reject me as a lover. I was twenty-three years older than her, my own professional career was in ruins and my future as an author a complete gamble, while all I had to offer as a home was a rented barge, masquerading as a houseboat. Zita, on the other hand, had a regular job which provided her with both variety and travel, a share in a flat which was at least on the fringes of Chelsea, and no particular reason why she should tie herself down to any kind of liaison, marriage or otherwise.

Then I argued with myself in more optimistic and typically Sagittarian mood. Luck was something one drew to oneself by one's attitude to life. That attitude was that the romantic, whether male or female, must be prepared to tilt at windmills, to overcome all odds, to indulge in the art of the impossible. For love itself is the achievement of the impossible in that it comes as a flash of lightning, suddenly, unexpectedly and seemingly by magic. And, after all, most Englishmen, except for those who are born middle-aged, do not really grow up until they reach the age of fifty. I did not feel any more mature than Zita, indeed possibly less so. I almost convinced myself that I should go to New Haven and tell Zita I would marry her, if she would have me. But I swiftly realised that this was neither the time, nor the place for making any such proposal.

I paid my bill, hastily packed and fixed a car to take me to Macy's store. There appeared to be nobody following the taxi, but I was taking no risks. I went swiftly through the store and out by another door, then catching another taxi to the station.

SIXTEEN

Zita takes up the story again.

It wasn't until I happened to look out of the window of my bedroom at old Mrs. Walmsley's that I realised at last that reading spy stories wasn't such a waste time. At least, not the modern type of realistic spy story; there's so much true life details in the narrative that one begins to think like a secret agent. And, of course, after learning that Richard was one of them – at least I think he's one of them – I began to see spies everywhere.

I was certain that there was an awful lot that Richard hadn't told me and that, if I knew the truth, I should probably be quite frightened. That was why I decided to put a postscript to my letter and warn him about the two people outside the Walmsley residence. There was no doubt about it, the girl was actually pointing up towards this apartment and I noticed that the moment she did so the man somewhat angrily slapped her wrist and appeared to remonstrate with her. Maybe, if he was a shadower, he was ticking her off for making such an obvious gesture. It was the fact that she was actually pointing out the apartment which made me suspicious.

Or was I being whipped up into some kind of spy-phobia of my own creation? I couldn't feel easy about the incident, whatever way I looked at it, and when I had finished taking notes from Mrs. Walmsley senior I dashed off my letter to Richard and took it round to his hotel. When he hadn't rung me by 12.30 I began to get worried. I rang up the hotel but they couldn't find him.

I couldn't wait any longer. I had to return to New Haven. But I really was worried – not about myself, as I couldn't imagine anyone wanting to shadow me, but for Richard's sake. He had been so vague about his enemies. Who were they? Not the IRA, he had said. He had come to the USA for help, so could it be the Russians? Or international terrorists like the Red Brigade? It must be rather a nasty business if the Special Branch were involved.

Then I looked out of my bedroom window while I was packing. On the pavement opposite I noticed the same man I had seen yesterday with the girl from Central Park. He was lolling against a wall, reading a newspaper. It was then I decided to put my knowledge of the world of spy fiction to good account. For a start, I must try to make sure I wasn't followed when I went to the station. If I ordered a taxi and left by the front door, my departure would be obvious and I knew from spy films that taxis can be very easily tailed by professional agents in New York. I spun a story to Mrs. Walmsley senior about having looked out of my window and seen a rather unpleasant man who had followed me around Central Park yesterday and tried to chat me up. Fortunately she accepted my story and showed considerable concern.

"My dear, you really should never have gone to such a dangerous place! Central Park is full of the most undesirable characters today. Probably some sex maniac prowling after you. But do not worry, I may be old, but I'm still resourceful. It would be risky for you to go out of the front door and take a taxi. He'd probably follow you by car. I know the type, they never give in. I've had a peek at him from my window and I see that there is a car parked quite near to him, with someone sitting in it. So you must go out the back way and I'll ring a friend of mine who'll pick you up outside and whisk you to the station."

Old Mrs. Walmsley really was a dear. Possibly she revelled in conspiracy, but, no matter, what British housewife would have been so co-operative? I began to wonder what else she might have thought up if I had told her the whole story, Richard included. Anyhow, it all went according to plan. I slipped out through the servants' quarters, down a covered-in passage way and was met by Mrs. Walmsley's friend. I caught my train to New Haven just in time.

In the train I had time to think. I was beginning to realise that I was becoming much more obsessed with thoughts of Richard than I had ever imagined to be credible. I had actually been thrilled to lie in his arms and talk nonsense the previous afternoon. Perhaps I had been too flippant, all those fantasies about pretending to be a mermaid. Was it all very silly and would he just laugh me off as rather a zany kid full of kinky dreams? I hoped not. I felt at the time that he enjoyed such fantasies as much as I did.

I was determined to ring up his hotel as soon as I got to New Haven. If we were going to make that Troubadour Island rendezvous, then precautions must be taken. If anyone stalked us over the island from Stony Creek, we should just be easy sitting targets and completely at the mercy of the stalker. For while I might have given my shadower the slip, someone else might still be stalking Richard unknown to him.

There was a great deal about him that I still didn't know. I mustn't get too carried away. I momentarily shuddered at the realisation that if anyone had told me a few weeks ago that I would be lying down in a hollow in New York's Central Park with a man I had only met a few days previously, I should have hooted with mirth. Yet that was what I had done and, though Richard was very, very nice, he could still turn out to be an easy-come, easy-go philanderer. After all, he hadn't telephoned me back.

With all this on my mind I took from my bag correspondence which Sandra and Julie, in bantering mood, had given me before I left London.

"Zita, my Poppet," read Sandra's letter. "There wasn't much time to talk last night as we had both got dates, and this morning you are out shopping so we shan't see you to have a natter before you leave for New York. So we've both decided to write you a letter instead.

"I am going away for the weekend and shan't be back until Monday. But Julie will set your mind at rest about looking after the cat. She is going over to her parents at Guildford for the night, but she'll be back tomorrow morning unfailingly. Personally, I think your man has a bit of a nerve to land you with the cat, or land us, I should say. After all it does involve some work. However, not to worry.

"Now about your man. I must say he wears well for forty-two even if he has some streaks of grey in his hair. He's tall and slim, but, oh, those eyes. They have a very wicked gleam indeed and you need to watch out for what they might imply.

Julie and I had arguments as to what colour his eyes are. She said blue and I say they are grey. What's your verdict?

"If you have fallen for him, do be careful. That story about the IRA being after him sounds rather tall to me. Do you think he's posing as a James Bond type? All those calls from the Special Branch were rather odd. I hope you won't think I was sending him up, but I thought a little gentle ribaldry was necessary to test him out. After all what was that chit-chat about orgone therapy, or whatever it is? It sounded downright kinky to me. He says he's open to ideas about actual love-scenes for his book. Why don't you test him out with a few really wild ones? That'll keep him guessing! I wonder if he really wants to learn, or if he's just playing along. Very deep, that man.

"Anyhow I will give him this. He played along with our teasing quite smoothly, which is more than some of my male friends would have done. I should think he could be quite amusing at a party, if he let himself go. But I had a hunch he was on his best behaviour with us. I wonder how he will go down in the States away from all the grunge of London.

"Julie and I have composed jointly memoranda (think that's what they call it) for you on the theme of the Romantic Novel: Vital Questions to be Considered. It was a bit of a giggle doing it. Most of the ideas are mine, but the cleverer and subtler ones are Julie's. Julie typed it. Hope you can take it in the spirit it's intended. By all means show it to your man, if you think it will help!!!

"Last night was fun – the wine and cheese party at Melanie's, I mean. We were tanked up on your Richard's wine to start with so Julie and I arrived in the right mood. I also scored a modest success by boasting that I has just had drinks with a man who was on the IRA hit list.

"Have a lovely time in New York. Hope it's not all work, your slightly scatty Sandra."

Julie wrote in slightly more sober mood, "Dear Zita, first and foremost, don't worry about Tortie. I promise faithfully to look after her and to make sure that Sandra behaves in a manner becoming one pussy-cat to another. She's rather sweet and no trouble. Missing her master, I feel. But that's a good sign. Never trust a man who doesn't like cats, I have always said. So the reverse must be true for one who does. But, to reassure you, I shall be back in the flat on Sunday morning before ten.

"It was fun meeting your Richard. I suppose we were rather outrageous in the questions we put to him, but I don't think he minded. And I hope you didn't.

"By the way, Sandra has shown me her letter to you and I should perhaps add that, though she adored bragging about having just had a drink with a man on the IRA hit list, she didn't mention any names. Thought I'd just mention this in case you were worried. I do hope Richard manages to solve his problems. He seems to take them pretty calmly. I only hope you don't get involved in anything too awful.

"Spies are somewhat in fashion just now with these two big cases coming up, and one at the Old Bailey. I wonder if they have anything to do with Richard? Not as an enemy agent, I don't mean, but somehow else. It's a jolly good job it's discreet little you and not Sandra who is hooked up with Richard, otherwise she might not be able to resist telling the world who he is. I'd give him two days at the most before his cover was blown, or whatever they call it.

"I must say Melanie's parties go with a zing. She served up some quite good snacks, so we didn't go hungry. And, God, did we need them as blotting paper after all that wine of Richard's which we drank first. Melanie is quite a changed personage since she married Hubert. She's all broody and cosy and Hubert flaps around like a butler on skates doing all the chores."

I paused while reading this. Looking around the carriage in which I was sitting, I noticed two men watching me closely. Oh, dear, was I being followed? It made concentration difficult, but I read on, "Sandra is very keen on this memoranda idea for you to submit to Richard. She thinks it will enable you to get him to talk on the nitty-gritty of the novel and, in doing so, see whether he's keen enough to put you first and the novel second. I should hate to see him say in the end, 'Well thanks for all the help with the novel, it's been nice knowing you' and then to disappear. Bye for now, Julie."

My flatmates had really gone to town with their memoranda. This consisted of a long list of questions, allegedly designed for helping Richard's book, but actually more of a tease for both of us. I couldn't at this stage make up my mind whether or not to show it to Richard. In a way it was intended to help him, though in a very skittish, spoofy manner.

Question Number One was, "How is he going to tackle the love-scenes when the hero and heroine get together? If Cartland is out, he hasn't got a great deal of choice. It's either (a) mildly erotic – i.e. the whole job minus the penetration part, or (b) soft porn or ultra-realism.

"Remind him that while female readers prefer romance to porn, they go abundance on things like foreplay and stylish preliminaries. They don't want what Wendy Perriam calls in her poem, *A Silent Movie*, 'How dare you make love to me like that, in that cold, silent, uncommitted way'."

Question Number Two asked did Richard know what turned girls on, or turned them off? "He ought to do, he's old enough. But he must be able to spell these things out. Lots of girls like getting bitten during love play (Sandra says 'only on the ear playfully and not on the thighs'; Julie says 'all biting is out'). He'll have to weigh things up."

I began to wonder if any of his other prospective heroines had written to him quite as outrageously as Sandra and Julie. Their next query was "Has he read the *Kama Sutra*? He ought to get genned up on all the various positions so that he can describe who gets which leg over what. This would seem to call for the most skilful writing as you would have to take the reader step by step into the delights of pre-copulation. These ancient Arabs had some marvellous names for the various positions, much, much nicer sounding and more exciting than any of our modern terms. Here are some of them: the Screw of Archimedes (the woman plays the male in this); frog fashion; the somersault (this is very complicated indeed); legs in the air; driving the peg home (sounds rather boring); fitting on the sock. And lots more. Perhaps Richard could invent a few himself – what about 'Spy's Delight' or 'MI69'?"

However, I must say that I did agree with the next point Sandra and Julie made. "What is really appalling about the awful, drab, drippy, unwashed and nasty scribblers of today is that they must call a spade a spade. So let Richard cut out all the nasty little, unimaginative single-syllable words which describe the various parts of the human anatomy. 'Prick' should be out. Who wants to be pricked? Both to male and female private parts he should give exotic names."

Frankly, until re-reading these letters and the memoranda which I had briefly skipped through on the plane coming out, I hadn't realised that either of my flatmates had so much to offer. I felt a tinge of jealousy because they made me feel that my offerings in letters to Richard must have been highly unsophisticated and not at all what was really wanted. "It might help a great deal if Richard tackled his book with the idea that it is much more fun to make love flippantly than in deadly earnestness."

There was one question which didn't touch on sex, "Where does his heroine get her clothes from? He must be able to describe her fashionwise. Maybe he won't bother. Men rarely do. But is she Gucci, Wendy Dagworth, Johnson in King's Road, Laura Ashley, Portobello Road, Sue Rider or Oxfam?"

I began to feel rather sorry for Julie who had obviously been asked to type out all this rigmarole. "What is the heroine's favourite tipple? You might say this is a useful thing to know in the light of a build-up for getting-it-together. Most girls like champagne, but some have the odd-way-out liking for drinks such as 'bloodies', a Pangalactic Gargleblaster or Manhattan Skydiver. Any of these could make his heroine sound real groovy.

"Beds. Very important, says Sandra. She thinks love on a water-bed might make for an amusing scene. Tell him love in a duvet is definitely *out*. Maybe one of those massive four-posters with gilded cherubs on them.

"Some really original love games might make for spicier reading. Straightforward love-making is rather boring when put bluntly in prose. The truth is we are both very much in the experimental and guessing stage, hoping, but not really believing that sex is all that's wonderful whichever way you tackle it. What about Tantric Sex? There's something full of Eastern Promise. We are a bit vague about it, but Paula has a friend who swears it keeps her marriage going. It's some kind of rhythm method (not to be confused with the RC Church's rhythm method, by the way) and you both go off into a delectable trance, while locked together. Or so she says. Some weeks ago Daphne Olroyd told us her husband had bought a vibrator. All very hush-hush and baited breath.

Good grief! She's only been married three months. For heaven's sake don't let Richard put any rubbish about sex-shop gadgets in his book. They are only for dreary, middle-aged housewives with inadequate husbands who give gin-and-tonic parties to their women friends in the mornings while some saleswoman tries to flog them these appalling toys. Hilarious for some, anathema for romance."

Maybe what they had to say was very amusing. Maybe Richard would have preferred their ideas to much of what I had told him in my letters. Normally, I should have giggled and laughed at almost all of it. Now it was a measure of the anxiety I felt for Richard and doubts about my own pent-up emotions that made me unable to concentrate on the thoughts of Sandra and Julie. Somehow their witticisms made me feel inadequate and that was something I deeply resented.

I lugged my suitcase off the train at New Haven and walked swiftly down the station platform. It now flashed across my mind that I had been incredibly stupid to have delivered that note to Richard by hand at the Barbizon Plaza Hotel. By this act of mine he could be in real danger, if I had been followed there. I was tense and near to tears when I reached the Walmsleys' New Haven residence.

SEVENTEEN

Richard resumes his story.

On the way to New Haven I kept a wary eye on my fellow passengers. I was fairly sure that I had given anyone who might be following me the slip, but clearly I couldn't leave anything to chance. The quest for Richard Deacon was hotting up. If that quest could be switched so speedily from one side of the Atlantic to the other, it was obvious that an attempt to silence me at all costs was being given top priority. But I was puzzled that Zita and not I had spotted a shadower and that it would seem that Bram had been deceived into thinking all was safe. These facts didn't quite add up.

I booked into a hotel at New Haven and rang up Bram's wife to give her my new address and telephone number. I asked her to get Bram to ring me urgently as soon as he could. I must keep him in the picture. Then I rang Zita.

"Richard," she cried in a voice which certainly sounded pleased to hear from me. "I have been worried stiff about you, as you didn't call back. Then I rang your hotel and they said you'd checked out for good. I began to wonder if you'd decided to fly back to the UK."

"I'm dreadfully sorry. I'm afraid I woke late and by the time I got your letter and rang you, you'd already left. Now, listen carefully. I'm very worried about your safety."

"I'm worried about yours. I'm pretty sure I gave whoever it is the slip in New York." She then told me her whole story.

"At first, when I read your letter, I thought you might be mistaken about anyone actually watching the Walmsley household. But now you've told me of the man still watching a day later, that's a different matter. It was very bright of you to plan a getaway from the back door. Assuming no car was round at the back as well, you should have given them the slip. Old Mrs. Walmsley sounds really alert. But I don't want to say too much on the phone. I'm only dreadfully sorry to have landed you in all this."

"Can we still meet?"

"Yes, if you care to risk it. But don't let's talk about where, only when. Hope you get my meaning."

"I think so."

"What time did you think of making it to your little bit of paradise?"

"Noon tomorrow. I shall have finished all my work by then."

"Keep your eyes skinned tomorrow morning and then make your own way to the rendezvous. Don't wait for me, but just go ahead to where you said. I'll get there in my own way. Don't worry."

"But how? You can only get there . . ."

I cut her short. "Say no more. I fully realise what you were going to say. I'll get there OK – the ultimate destination, not where we were to have met."

"I hope so." Zita sounded very doubtful.

"Cheer up. I won't let you down."

If Zita was puzzled as to how I proposed to get to Troubadour Island, so was I. It was mere bravado when I declared I would get there in my own way. Troubadour Island wasn't the sort of place one could go to without attracting somebody's attention. Half a mile was not a long way to swim, but I did not fancy attempting it. I should be a perfect target in the water if anyone had picked up my trail. I felt reasonably sure that Zita had thrown off her shadowers, but as we were both up against real professionals, obviously ordered to maintain a thorough surveillance, I couldn't be sure that by noon tomorrow they would not be hard on our tracks once again.

I did not want to leave the hotel in case I had a call from Bram, so I borrowed a map of the Connecticut coast showing the Thimble Islands, in which Troubadour was situated, and Stony Creek. This I studied carefully in my hotel room, making a swift pencil copy of the map. An hour later I got a call from Bram.

"I got your message. I guess you've got problems."

I gave him both mine and Zita's account of events.

"I'm at Fort Meade now. Things are moving fast.

Obviously our people boobed when they said nobody was stalking you. It's not altogether their fault because the enemy must be using new tactics in shadowing. But it's rare for them to use kids in Central Park. Anyhow, we've got to act fast; and first and foremost you must get back to London tomorrow. There's no time to be lost. I'm fixing a flight for you and you'd better be at Kennedy Airport by 23.00 hours tomorrow. I can't pull any strings to get you an earlier flight, or I would. Collect the ticket at the airport. I'm not going to give you any reasons for this panic, but I would have made this suggestion regardless of what you've told me. I've learnt a lot more down here and things are coming to a head. Meanwhile don't move from your hotel in New Haven. It's the safest place. I'm sending one of our E. and E. specialists along to see you. He'll be coming from New York, so he should be with you within the next three hours. But don't move from that goddam hotel and stick by your phone. The game is changing hour by hour. Our chap will make things easier for you."

I knew Bram wouldn't make suggestions such as these unless he had very sound reasons. He was not a man to panic. I was surprised to hear he had gone to Fort Meade, as this was the headquarters of the National Security Agency, which suggested that whatever developments there were came under the schedule of top priority in US security.

Bram's envoy to New Haven was one of those CIA men attached to a division known as Escape and Evasion. Their work ranged from sending a man to rescue a captured agent to preparing an escape route. "Call me Flickertail," he said, without a glimmer of a smile. "I come from North Dakota and it's as good a name as any." Flickertail is the nickname of North Dakotans.

He was ploddingly suspicious and cautious, going over my bedroom with the precision of an expert fumigator, as the CIA calls its de-bugging specialists. But he found nothing and seemed disappointed rather than pleased. All the time he chain-smoked cigarettes, occasionally asking me questions. "Bram says you want to meet some dame on one of the

Thimble Islands. Why the hell is that? It seems a dumb thing to wanna do when your life is at risk."

"It's a promise to a very special girl," I replied. "It's my last chance of seeing her before I leave New York tomorrow."

"I'd like to appeal to you to give up this plan."

"Sorry, but I can't agree to do that."

"Well, if that's your last word, you'd better know that I shall be chaperoning you all the way."

My face must have shown some misgivings because he was quick to say, "OK, don't fuss yourself. I'll just stick around. I won't get in your way. In fact, as long as I'm in earshot, I needn't even be seen."

"Thanks. If you think it's really necessary, then OK."

"It had better be OK. The girl's likely to be in danger, too."

Of course, he was right. In my longing to see Zita alone in what sounded like a superbly romantic setting, I had momentarily forgotten that if she and I were together, she was almost certainly in some, if not as much, danger as I was. Flickertail had a talent for minimizing conversation. I'll swear he could convey a wealth of instructions lucidly and precisely in a mere twenty words.

Tersely and unsmilingly, Flickertail revealed his plan to me. He would stay in the hotel that night and keep in touch with me if necessary, tapping a capacious inside pocket to indicate that he was armed. We would dine in his room, not in the restaurant. Before going to bed I was to ask the night porter to make sure I had a call at five o'clock in the morning as I wanted to go for an early swim, the beach being only a matter of fifty yards from the hotel. In the meantime I was to give my passport, money and any valuables to Flickertail to look after, while leaving clothes and other articles in my suitcase, which I should carefully lock. "And then," he said in a laconic voice, "you will go down to the beach, take off your shorts, T-shirt and sandals, leave 'em in a neat pile, put on your bathing attire and go for a swim. From then on, I'll take charge. You will simply stage your own drowning."

"Stage my own drowning? What do you mean? Does Bram know about all this?"

"He certainly does. It's not a certain method of keeping wraps around you, but for twenty-four hours it should work.

Before that time is up you will be aboard a plane for the UK anyhow."

"But how do I stage my own drowning? And what happens then? And why all this melodrama?"

"Last answer first. This is a darned sight less melodramatic than would be your murder by KGB agents on US soil. I have strict instructions that the last thing the State Department, the CIA or the NSA want is for an ex-British Secret Service agent to be bumped off on American soil. Answer to your first two questions I'll tell you how to fix your faked drowning and it mustn't look like suicide as that could get us too much publicity of an unwelcome kind, especially when you came to life again. And I'll tell you what to do after."

I suppose in a predicament such as I was in some tough, terse talking was called for. But it all sounded so melodramatic that I just couldn't believe it was happening to me. If I had been on my own, I think I should have kicked against such wiles and precautions. But as Zita was involved and we were both in another country, I felt it would be foolish to argue. In any case I trusted Bram totally.

At this juncture, having obtained my acquiescence to all this clandestine stuff, Flickertail briefly revealed a more human side of his E. and E.-conditioned personality, "Not to worry. Bram says he doesn't think anyone will have tracked you down here yet, and I'm inclined to agree. But we now feel sure that there is a full-scale hunt for you going on and that the KGB will have caught up with you by tomorrow morning some time."

I will omit the exact details of Flickertail's instructions. Suffice to say that I carried them out and set off for a swim at the uninspiring hour of five o'clock. He left nothing to chance and, presumably in case I proved to be a poor swimmer or developed cramp, gave me a lilo and a paddle "for double security". As I left the hotel the night porter mumbled something to himself about a "goddarn Limey nutter" and who could blame him. I left my clothes in a pile on the beach well above the high water mark and then pushed off into the water. The water rippled under the lilo as I swung round in a course parallel with the coastline some fifty yards out to sea. With paddle feathered I steadied the lilo and headed for two craft, anchored some thirty yards from the shore, taking care to keep the craft between myself and the shore so that briefly I was out of sight of anyone on land.

There was nobody aboard these craft, a fact which Flickertail had already ascertained. So I edged my lilo up against the hull of one of the boats and waited. It was quite chilly at this time of the morning. Within a couple of minutes I saw a speed-boat approaching. Suddenly shutting off its engines, Flickertail gently headed the boat in my direction. As soon as it was alongside I clambered aboard, leaving lilo and paddle to float away after we had got clear away from the anchored boats. Then, without a word, the boat headed off again at full speed towards the Thimble Islands.

Flickertail had retained my map of the islands and so knew exactly where Troubadour Island was. One has to hand it to these Escape and Evasion specialists. "I've never had an adventure, escapade, call it what you will, anything like this during the whole of my Service career," I said.

"You wouldn't have had it even now if you hadn't got yourself tangled up with a dame at the worst possible moment," was his rather sour comment. But I had to admit the Zita factor had made things immensely difficult for him. I had no doubt whatsoever that if I had been a CIA man in the same predicament, he would have ruled out the Troubadour Island meeting and ordered me to go with him straight-away to Kennedy Airport.

Troubadour was an attractive little island, only a few acres in size and one of the smallest of the Thimbles. It consisted mainly of low-lying cliffs and salt marshes, but was distinctly different from most of the other islands in that it had been planted with a few trees to protect its log cabin from the winds.

"You wouldn't have a key to that log-cabin, I suppose?" enquired my companion.

"No, I'm afraid we must wait for Zita. I hope she makes it without any trouble."

"She will, because I'm going to fetch her."

"You!"

"Yessir. It's all fixed. I spoke to her myself last night on the phone and then went over to present my credentials to her employers. I've told her she must be at Stony Creek at

11.45, or she'll be too late. And if there should be any nonsense, this little craft of mine is armed."

"You think of everything. How did you manage to fix up all this gear and the speedboat in so short a time."

"I'm paid to think of everything. But you've been lucky in one respect. I live at Bridgeport, just down the coast. So I know Long Island Sound and the Connecticut coast like the palm of my hand and this is my own little cutie of a speedboat. But for her, you would probably now be making tracks for New York. But don't think all this detailed planning is only for your benefit. It's in the interest of Uncle Sam himself that we're trying to keep you alive. What makes me so angry is that we have to take these kind of precautions against the KGB in our own country. If I were doing this job in, say, Poland, it would make sense. But over here it's farcical."

"How did Zita take the news about your coming to fetch her?"

"She just had to take it. I called on the Walmsleys, showed my credentials and explained that there was a security flap on – no more, no less. Your gal had no option but to agree either to come, or call it off."

I wondered whether the Walmsleys had tried to persuade her to call it off, but I said nothing.

Flickertail then gave me my suit, shoes, passport and money, insisting quite correctly that I gave him a receipt for their safe return. "Here's a holdall for you to replace that suitcase. I'm afraid it was essential to leave the suitcase and the other clothes behind at the hotel because your disappearance is bound to be reported fairly soon. I've got a pal who works on the *New Haven Register* and I am alerting him on my radio so that by this afternoon there will be a press report of your suspected drowning."

"I'm feeling famished right now," I said.

Flickertail scowled and produced a bottle of rye and two glasses. "You'd better have a swig of this after your spell in the water."

I gratefully accepted his offer. After that he opened a hamper and proffered some sandwiches and coffee. Gradually I began to warm to this very cold and dour man. Soon we were swapping stories.

"I like the very short stories best," he said.

"Such as?"

"That about the man who had women on the brain so much, he bled from the nose once a month."

Flickertail set off in his boat shortly after 11.30 and it was not long before I saw him returning with Zita standing up in the bows, a slim silhouette in jeans. She jumped ashore and ran straight to me, shaking her head almost in mockery.

"What kind of a spy story are you letting me in for now?"

"How much do you know?"

"A little more than I did. It would seem that you're almost as important in the United States as in your own country."

"Probably far more so as of today."

"I gather you've got to return to the UK tonight, so we shan't have long together. Have I got to keep on pretending you might have drowned? I'm not a terribly good actress."

Flickertail cut in, "You've got to remember that, officially, you haven't seen your boy friend, and that he's missing. That goes for up to midnight. After that it doesn't matter."

"Well, I can't pretend to understand a quarter of what is going on and I suppose I mustn't ask questions. So we had just better try and enjoy the few hours left to us."

At that moment Flickertail announced that he was going to have a siesta under the tree. Zita led me towards the log cabin. "I've been lent the key, so we can go inside and talk. But what do you think of the island?"

"It would be absolutely marvellous if we hadn't got this awful problem hanging over our heads. I hope this hasn't upset things for you with the Walmsleys."

"Oh, no. I think they probably understand better than I do. Your minder, or whatever you call him, seemed to satisfy Mr. Walmsley. In any case my assignment over here is at an end."

"I shall feel happier when I know you've got back."

"Not to worry. Apparently I'm to be looked after, too. By the way, Mrs. Walmsley junior is quite an authority on the Thimble Islands."

"They own this island?"

"Yes, they sometimes spend weekends out here. Apparently, centuries ago the Walmsleys were a group of Puritan emigrants from Massachusetts and they purchased the island from the Indians."

"Have you found out the story behind the island's name?"

"No, but Mrs. Walmsley thinks the birds had suggested the name, as the Walmsleys themselves call them the troubadours. The island attracts quite a variety of birds. Apart from seabirds and ospreys there are even a few bobwhites and redwinged blackbirds."

Zita showed me around the log cabin which consisted of two bedrooms and a sitting-room. It was sparsely furnished, but immaculately clean and lit by kerosene lamps and supplied with bottled gas for cooking and refrigeration."

"This," I said, "is Lovers' Seat, the barge and Central Park all wrapped up into one. It really is a paradise."

"I felt very much like that when the Walmsleys brought me out here a few days ago. I just had to ask them if I could bring you along to see it."

"I'm glad you did."

"Tortie would love prowling around the island. She would be absolutely safe here, no traps and no predators."

"Yes, she would have completed the picture."

I then told Zita the story of how Tortie saved my life that night when an intruder crawled through the window, intending to kill me. There was no longer any point in witholding these facts from her. She was quite horrified.

"I knew you must have been in some kind of danger, but never dreamed it was as bad as that. Do you really mean to tell me that the very day after that happened all you could think of was to make a date with me at Lovers' Seat?"

"Well, not the only thing, but it was certainly uppermost in my mind. I suppose the whole seering experience had made me a little light-headed. I was determined not to allow that episode to stop me from seeing you."

"And even today you are behaving just the same. You shouldn't have come here, should you?"

"Well, I'm sure old Sourface down among the trees isn't too pleased about it."

"I ought not to be pleased either, but I'm glad you made the effort. And now that you've told me that story about Tortie, I shall adore her more than ever. The poor little mite must have been terrified."

"Talking of Tortie, dare I ask you to keep her a little longer when you get back after the weekend. It looks as though I might have quite a lot to do for a few days. I promise to pick her up by, say, the middle of next week."

"Not to worry. Of course, I'll look after her. You will have so much to do – having your furniture moved down to the barge, negotiating it's purchase and selling your flat. Not to mention sorting out all your other problems, and the horror of being permanently under threats to your life. But how much longer is this going on? When will it all end? It seems so damnable that you can't be safe on either side of the Atlantic."

"You mustn't trouble your pretty little head about it. I promise it will all work out fairly soon and then we can see one another normally."

I began to think there was never going to be a right moment for me to tell Zita how I felt about her. Certainly this was not a propitious moment for romantic proposals of any kind, especially with Flickertail hovering in the background, though I must say he maintained a low profile. Once or twice he got up and went to his boat and I imagined he was operating his radio rig. If ever a man seemed totally dedicated to the most irritating assignments in a deadpan sober manner, Flickertail was he. I made a mental note to tell Hanson that what MI6 really needed was more Flickertails. Zita went into the miniature kitchen and prepared lunch – a delightful Spanish omelette of her own concoction with hot bread rolls, salad and nectarines. She mixed me a Rum Sangaree.

"You've obviously been picking up some tips about drink-mixing while you've been in the States," I said.

"You approve? I hope it's all right, but I did notice how Mr. Walmsley made Sangarees the other night."

"I approve very much. And if you'll give me another Sangaree, I'll try to explain to you the whole complicated situation in which we find ourselves."

I discovered that in telling Zita what was happening, she had been given some fairly positive facts by Flickertail – "a nudge and a wink was how he did it", she said. But this time I had no inhibitions about telling her that I had good reason to believe there was a mole in the SIS in London and that it was because I took this view that someone, presumably in the KGB, had ordered my killing. If I hadn't told her, she wouldn't have known what to think. The whole situation was as bizarre as it could be, and I could only hope she would accept my word. Fortunately, in this respect, Flickertail had been a useful ally. She didn't say very much afterwards, but looked thoughtful and anxious. Then, a quiet smile appearing on her lips, she commented, "We have swopped information on our western signs of the zodiac, but did you know that in the oriental art of astrology we both come under the sign of the Cat?"

"Meaning?"

"I have worked it out that by Chinese astrological processes we were both born in one of the Years of the Cat, which come at twelve-yearly intervals. One can actually combine the two forms of astrology and apply our respective birth dates to the Cat Years. I should add that a Libran Cat is a mighty cautious and elusive person, but she's not aggressive or interfering."

"And what about me?"

"Ah, that's what I was leading up to. According to Suzanne White, who has done an extraordinary amount of work on the subject, including her *Book of Chinese Chance*, you, the Sagittarian male Cat, are the 'pick of the litter'. Just read what it says."

She handed me the book and I read, "Ordinarily it is difficult for Cats to bear the consequences of disaster, but here his spirit is infused with courage . . . Sagittarians endure adversity."

"I think that's very apt as of this moment," said Zita. "It would be interesting to know what sign Tortie was born under and if she could also belong to the Cat Years. Nice to think we made a Cat Trio."

"We'll make her an honorary Cat."

There was a pause in our conversation. I think the tension surrounding what might be happening on the beach had made each of us unable to focus our feelings about one another. I could not help wondering whether the police and coastguards might be searching for my body. And how did Flickertail propose to smuggle us back to the mainland? Zita cleared away the lunch utensils and I went outside to scan the coastline. A few minutes later she joined me and we went for a stroll around the island.

"If only we could spend the whole weekend on Troubadour Island entirely on our own," I said. "We could have such fun and you could do some painting. You see, Zita, I think I ought to make it abundantly clear that while all this started as a result of my writing a novel and looking for a heroine, now I've actually found her, it's no longer a game. I'm not putting this exactly brilliantly because this isn't the best of moments for being serious. But let me put it this way – being with you is more important than writing the novel. I'd just like this afternoon to last a whole week."

"I'd love that, too. The swimming is heavenly in these waters – at least at this time of the year it is. There are even low cliffs for diving off. The Walmsleys spend quite a lot of time fishing here and then end up with a glorious clam-bake."

"A perfect setting for a mermaid."

She took my hand, looked up at me and tried to smile, but her lips just quivered. "Oh, Richard, this isn't at all how I had planned things. I was so looking forward to this trip to Troubadour Island. Somehow the magic seems to have gone."

"No, it hasn't. Things have not gone as we expected, but the magic is still there. And for me the real magic is how you have taken all this, the way you've accepted my appalling problems."

"Perhaps. But it's so maddening that we can't be just as carefree as we were in Central Park."

"Not carefree, possibly, but what happened in Central Park is still very real. It means we still have something to look forward to."

We sat down in a little crevice below cliff level, but well above the seashore beneath. I put my arm round Zita and she put her hand on my shoulder. "To make love to you is rather like drinking a very special liqueur," I said. "One needs to sip slowly."

Zita's eyes seemed to glisten and I was aware she was very near to tears. We hugged one another and I suppose that like Raymond Peynet's two lovers we each retreated into a wondering childhood as though we were each about to discover the facts of existence. I had made love often enough before and sometimes in unusual surroundings. But this was fumbling one's way towards love-making on the accompaniment of a slow tango, slower in fact. For me it was rather like being on a time-scale escalator. I was going forward and upwards, eager for the future, worried about the present and with some instinct telling me, "Try walking backwards, beat the escalator and return to the zaniness of youth."

Zita jumped up, saying, "Let's go back to the cabin. There's something I want you to hear." I was rather perplexed by this sudden change of mood, but back in the cabin she switched on the music-centre and I at once recognized the Iberia Suite. "You once told me that my voice was like the tinkle of an *étude* by Albéniz. I never knew anything about Albéniz before that and then, the other day in New York, I found this cassette in a shop and bought it. It would be marvellous just to lie in each other's arms listening to it."

"So you like it. I'm glad because I've always felt that Albéniz composed such happy music."

We lay for a long time, absorbing that superb Iberia Suite with its twelve movements all distilling the atmosphere of different parts of Spain. Yet all the time each of us was conscious of the external threat to our happiness, though we both pretended to ignore it. A small bird somehow strayed through the window and perched at our feet.

"You remind me of a wild goose," said Zita, without explanation, and I was too lazy to ask for one. If she saw me as a wild goose, there were moments when I saw her as a rather gorgeous ginger pussy cat with large green eyes. Like such a cat, she was someone to be held close, but not too tightly, to be caressed with hands which skimmed the surface of the body, the face, the head, the breasts, the thighs, carefully cossetting her through emotional storms. Deep down in our hearts we each knew that this was not the moment for the great get-together, but we were as certain that it would come in time just as we were that the sun would duly set, so delaying it did not seem to matter.

Zita kicked off her beach shoes and we cuddled and snuggled together on the huge couch in the log-cabin's sitting-room. We greedily kissed each other from face to toes. For what was a mere few minutes we relaxed sufficiently to be able to make a few amatory jokes. "I think you should concentrate on my toes for the time being," laughed Zita. Momentarily, she had cast off her worries by trying hard to be flippant. So for the rest of the time in the log-cabin lovemaking became a five-toe exercise. This may have been ersatz love (I think we both realised this), but it was fun. I recalled those lines of Sir John Suckling, written in the seventeenth century:

> "Her feet beneath her petticoat,
> Like little mice, stole in and out,
> As if they fear'd the light."

How absolutely delectable a foot, or a glimpse of one, must then have been. But Zita's neat, trim, tiny little toes even in this latter part of the twentieth century aroused similar sentiments in myself. For what other reason should I suddenly break into French and give each of her toes both a kiss and a French name – Françoise, Frisette, Marie, Solange and Yvette.

But suddenly there was a knock on the cabin door and Flickertail announced that it was time to go.

EIGHTEEN

I always thought that the business of staging a faked drowning of myself was overdone and not really necessary. It had inevitably cast a cloud over our trip to Troubadour Island and caused unnecessary anxiety for Zita. When we left the island she was very close to tears and made me promise to telephone her as soon as I got back to London.

"You must take great care for my sake," she said tensely, "for we are both in this now."

"You must take care, too. I wonder after all you've been subjected to that you can stand seeing me around."

Flickertail took us by speed-boat to a remote point of the beach on the Bridgeport side of New Haven. Two cars awaited us, one to take Zita safely back to the Walmsleys, the other to deliver me, in the company of Flickertail, to Kennedy Airport. I still had no idea why keeping me alive was so vitally important to the American Establishment, especially as I was no longer in the Service. I couldn't believe that even Bram with all his influence could have fixed up all this so speedily. Somebody much higher up must have given permission for this type of operation. Maybe it was all for the best in the long run. At least Zita was being given the same kind of protection. That, in the normal way, would have been more than I dared hope for.

On the flight back to London I tried to puzzle out what was really going on. I hated being a pawn juggled and fought over by three secret services. It all seemed too ridiculous. At the back of my mind I felt there was one factor in the events of the past few months which I had overlooked and that, if I could recognize it, I might solve the whole problem. I was certain that it had something to do with the unsolved query as to how Wetherby had fixed his alibi with MI6.

When I arrived at Heathrow I was beckoned to one side at customs and taken straight to an office. There I was met by my old friend, the Special Branch inspector, and an American who knew Bram. Undoubtedly telephone wires between Washington, or Langley or Fort Meade and London had been carrying quite a lot of traffic on my behalf. I was told that a car was waiting to take me down to Cucking Manor. The chauffeur was none other than dear old lugubrious Vaughan. "It's nice to see you again, sir," he said in his graveyard voice. But I felt he meant it.

Hugo Hanson was at Cucking Manor to greet me. He looked as though he hadn't had much sleep for some days, but he slapped me on the back, saying, "You certainly have a penchant for putting the cat among the pigeons. But it would seem your pal, Bram Stoppard, has worked wonders. Tell me all about it."

I explained the whole situation in great detail, but said that I was completely in the dark about the latest developments. "What really is happening? And why have I been brought to Cucking Manor?"

"First of all, it's a matter of security – not yours so much as ours and the Americans. Secondly, there is to be a certain amount of unofficial interrogation, nothing like last time, of course. Finally, your furniture and belongings were not moved out of your London flat and into storage until yesterday and it will not be until Monday morning that they will be taken down to Rye Harbour. So stay happily here until Monday morning and then Vaughan can drive you down to the barge. After all, Cucking Manor is more than half-way towards Rye."

I felt that Hanson knew a lot more than he was telling. I tried to probe him, but he was evasive. "There's been quite a battle inside Six. 'Uncle Bob' and the Wets have declined to believe half the intelligence they have been getting from Washington in recent months. They say it's clever disinformation, disseminated among the CIA by Soviet sleepers."

"What else have you found out?"

"We now know that your assailant was a KGB man working under diplomatic cover in London. Seamus

O'Donovan, by the way, was not watching you. He may have been watching someone else, but there was no link between him and either you or the Russians. As we haven't finally closed your case satisfactorily, it was decided to ask the Soviets to withdraw their man quietly without publicity, rather than have an official expulsion. I think Uncle Bob made a mistake there."

"So my would-be killer is back in Russia?"

"We sincerely hope so. At any rate he's left the country. So I think we can say there will be no more attempts on your life."

Hanson was present at my interrogation which concentrated wholly on questioning me in detail as to what had happened in the USA and which CIA officers were involved and how much had other American departments come into all this. On the latter queries I couldn't enlighten them, but only make intelligent guesses. As soon as the interrogation was over Hanson and I had a meal together and then he left Cucking Manor. Meanwhile I had telephoned Zita to say I was back in Britain and safe. Time dragged on wearily over that weekend. I had become so used to non-stop action of one kind or another that I was greatly irked by staying put. I wanted to get back to a normal life again, to put the barge shipshape and restore a happy, stress-free relationship with Zita.

I telephoned her again the following night after she had returned from London. I couldn't say very much, knowing that any calls out of Cucking Manor would be carefully monitored as standard practice. Zita was tired, having only just got back, but she said she had no new assignment as yet, only the continuation of the old one and that was a relatively leisurely job calling around at Somerset House and St. Catherine's House looking up wills, and birth and death certificates. So, she said, she could bring Tortie down to Rye on the Tuesday, if I would meet her at the station. This I agreed to do. It was after this telephone call that I vowed I would never again let myself be divorced from my rig. From now on Zita and I would keep in constant communication this way, whatever happened, and, as far as possible whenever we were separated.

I had been lucky. For once in my life there had been people

who believed in me and were prepared to see things through however difficult they were – Zita, Bram and perhaps I ought to include Hugh Hanson. It was then I wondered whether romance without difficulties and dangers was remotely possible. I am not sure that even now I know the answer to that, but I am sure that turmoil can be an aid to romance whereas a boring, plodding routine can kill it. Of one thing I was absolutely sure. Without the excuse of researching a heroine for a novel, I doubted very much whether, in so short a time, Zita and I would have learnt enough about each other to be able to effectively confront the hazards besetting our love affair. I knew I should finish the novel, though now it would be somewhat delayed. But out of our love affair I had come to realise that the trivialities and fantasies of love were sometimes of more importance than love itself. I recalled Somerset Maugham's advice that "a novelist must preserve a child-like belief in the importance of things which common sense considers of no great consequence. He must never entirely grow up." This advice seemed to apply equally to the lover as well as the novelist.

On the Monday I went down to Rye Harbour and saw my furniture and belongings safely aboard the barge. Gradually this ramshackle old craft began to take on some semblance of a real home. Only now did it dawn on me what kind of a shack I had induced Zita to visit that day we first met. Yet, provided I could clinch the deal to purchase the barge and then have it painted inboard and outboard, there was the prospect of tolerably comfortable living accommodation. In fact the barge accommodation was larger than that of the flat, so I really needed to buy some more furniture.

I went into Rye to arrange for my bank account to be switched from London and to purchase stores. These I took back to the barge by taxi, making a mental note to enquire the price of a second-hand MGB roadster I had seen in Rye, but wanted to inspect next day. I was still busily putting things straight up to 9.30 that night. Then, having set up my rig, I decided to try to call up Zita. There was no response. I tried again at quarter-hour intervals because I had mentioned the previous night I should call her up as soon as my rig was set up. Still there was no call-back. I began to get worried and set off for the nearest telephone-box. I dialled the number of the Ifield Road flat and Sandra answered.

"Hello," I said. "Terribly sorry to trouble you at this time of night, but is Zita there by any chance? I've tried to reach her by radio, and had no luck. She was coming down to Rye tomorrow and relieving you of the chore of looking after Tortie. I really am most grateful to you both for coping with the cat."

"That's all right, Richard, but I'm glad you've rung up because Julie and I are rather worried. Zita had a telephone call early this evening from one of your colleagues, I believe, and afterwards she seemed very agitated and acutely worried. She couldn't say what it was about, but she went out for about ten minutes and, when she got back to the flat, started to pack a suitcase. She said she was going away for a night or two. We asked if she was going to see you at Rye, but she shook her head and said 'No, don't mention Rye to anyone. I'm not going to Rye.' She added that if anyone rang up, other than you, of course, we were to say nothing. 'Be as dumb as you like' were her words."

"What happened then?"

"She rang for a taxi and took Tortie with her. That's what puzzled us. If she wasn't going to meet you, why should she take Tortie?"

"It's certainly very odd. It looks as though she intended to come down here, yet you say she said she wasn't going to Rye."

"That's right."

"Do you know the name of the colleague of mine who rang her up?"

"I'm fairly certain it was one who has rung up before. Let me see, I think the name was Aston, or something like that. Yes, I remember now – it was Hanson."

"Well, thank you for telling me all this. It is rather worrying as Zita hasn't come down here. Is there anything else you can remember that might help to clear up the mystery?"

"Not really. But Zita was desperately worried, almost in tears in fact. I can't think what she did when she went out for ten minutes, as she seemed far more agitated then than when she had the phone call."

I thanked Sandra, explaining that I wasn't on the telephone, but would call up in the morning to see if there was any news. I felt sure that something really important must have happened to cause Zita to go away like that. I was myself seriously worried about her, more especially because she had been so secretive to her flatmates about what she was doing. The reason for that secrecy, I assumed, was something to do with me.

Why had Hanson telephoned her? That was the biggest puzzle of all. Why, if she wasn't going to meet me, had she taken Tortie with her? Returning to the barge, I felt in no mood for sleep. By now it was nearly 11.30. I just paced the deck and pondered on what could have happened. Then I went back to my cabin, poured myself a large whisky and tried to go back over all the facts and search for a clue. What for instance had Zita done in those ten minutes she was away from the flat? Why was she more agitated when she came back? Could she have been lured away from the flat on the pretence that someone was going to take her to see me? Nothing quite added up to making any sense, yet all the time I had the feeling that the answers to these riddles were tucked away in the recesses of my mind.

I tried to reconstruct what conflicting facts I had. Those ten minutes Zita was out of the flat – she wouldn't be shopping early in the evening, so what was she doing? A phone call from a telephone box? Highly unlikely as there was a phone in the flat. But, wait a moment, if she wanted to preserve secrecy it was reasonable to assume that she might make a call outside so that the girls wouldn't hear. But who would she be likely to call?

The mechanism of the mind is a peculiar thing. It doesn't have the advantages of a master-computer in that one can dial up the answers to one's queries. But it has one great advantage over computers in that it can supply an imaginative interpretation which bridges the gap between the facts in one's mind and the unknown facts in the outside world. Thus it was that suddenly an almost inaudible mental alarm bell began to ring steadily in my brain, forcing me to try to bridge that gap. What it told me was that the clue to what had happened to Zita lay in obtaining the answer as to how Wetherby fixed his alibi that night in Paris.

So what was that clue? What was the common factor?

Another thought came to me – why had I had no call from any member of the Special Branch since I had been back aboard the barge? True, Hanson had told me that my assailant had left the country. But if the KGB had thought it worthwhile to pursue me in the USA, I could be in just as much danger over here on an isolated barge with no telephone. I tried to console myself with the thought that the report of my suspected drowning might have filtered through to the KGB. But, knowing how suspicious was the Russian mind, I felt certain that by now they had found out that I was alive, and back in London. They had their own methods of getting lists of travellers on planes and watching departures at airports all over the world.

It was then that the clue to all these mysteries revealed itself in one of those imaginative flashes by which a brain can beat a computer – Hugo Hanson.

In most senses it was impossible to accept that his name provided the clue. He was my friend and I liked him immensely. He had stuck up for me all along, or so it seemed. He had concurred with my going to New York and seeing Bram. He was the most reliable of all the MI6 hierarchy with an impeccable background. I went over every possible reason why Hanson could not provide the clue. But then I examined the case against him. In retrospect it was formidable. It was Hanson who first heard through me about Wetherby being in Paris. If Hanson had been in league with Wetherby, he could have covered for him and given him an alibi until he got back to London. It would be Hanson who would have laid the facts before "C". Then again it was Hanson who had constantly kept in friendly touch with me after I left the Service. Hanson knew the lay-out of my flat in De Beauvoir Town. I had often wondered why the attempt on my life was so skilfully planned from the rear of the block of flats.

Hanson again knew that I was going to New York. It puzzled me that he should have been so enthusiastic that I should go to see Bram Stoppard, but it could have been that he felt the KGB could wipe me out more easily over there than in London after the failure to kill me in my flat. If Hanson knew where I was, then he alone could so speedily have informed the Russians of my movements and the hotel where I was staying. Knowing that I should be seeing Bram

Stoppard, he had warned the KGB of this and they decided to keep tabs on me by tailing Zita rather than risking having their shadows spotted by any CIA men that Bram would have brought into action. That interrogation at Cucking Manor, when I got back – again, it was Hanson who was controlling events and asking me what had happened in the USA. And he knew I was back on the barge. I remembered that he had been particularly ingratiating when he spoke on the telephone to Zita on a previous occasion.

Why had he telephoned her now? There was no reason for him to do this and certainly no reason for him to alarm her. So was he setting me up now? Had he not informed the Special Branch where I was? Had he conned me into thinking all was relatively safe because a certain Soviet diplomat had been asked to leave Britain?

All this mental probing made me feel somewhat sick. I liked Hugo Hanson. I found him a splendid companion with very much my own sense of humour and underneath it all a mocking view of the Establishment. It didn't make sense. I had even thought that, if Zita and I married (I had already considered this possibility), Hanson might make an admirable best man. But then I remembered other people one had liked. Kim Philby had always been somewhat of a charmer and so, according to all accounts, had been Guy Burgess, though I never knew him. Anthony Blunt had sidled through the corridors of Buckingham Palace with the air of being "one of us". The mind boggled, but my writer's instincts told me that however pally we had been, Hanson must be the villain of the piece. I should have been on my guard long before. But how or why could he act in this way? I thought I had some inkling of human nature. I instinctively mistrusted Wetherby, but with Hanson it would seem I had been totally deceived. I could have sworn he was the best and most reliable of friends. Was my hunch right or wrong?

But it was Zita who mattered and I came to my senses asking myself just what I could do about her. Then, just before midnight, I heard footsteps approaching the barge. I went up on deck and was confronted by a police officer in uniform. "Excuse me, sir," he explained. "I just wanted to be sure you were all right. I think somebody will be visiting you shortly to explain things."

"That's all right, officer. Glad to see you around."

What he said could only mean one thing – that the Special Branch had been alerted. Once again I was given protection. Somebody obviously considered this still necessary even if Hanson didn't. But why hadn't I suspected Hanson earlier? Many other little suspicious details came back to me now. For example, on one visit to my flat in De Beauvoir Town, Hanson had asked if he could take a look at my internal alarm system and had not only examined it very thoroughly, but had asked questions, too. I also realised that, while I had made a number of character delineations on the strength of studying people's handwriting, to the best of my knowledge I had never seen any of Hanson's writing, not even a signature.

Then just before midnight I heard footsteps approaching the barge. I rushed ashore and made my way in their direction. It was a dark and misty night and not easy to see. Then, out of the gloom, carrying a cat-basket and holdall was Zita herself. I whooped for joy and ran to take her in my arms.

"Thank God, you're safe," I cried.

"Thank God I've found you, too. Oh, Richard, I've been so dreadfully, dreadfully worried I hardly knew what to do."

I took the cat-basket and led Zita up the gang-way on to the barge, taking her into what I had now somewhat ambitiously named the saloon.

"What a change!" cried a delighted Zita. "You've got all your furniture in at last."

"Today. It's fitted in quite well, really."

"First of all, we must let a very plaintive cat out of her basket. She's been quite good travelling, but has been mewing a lot this last hour. I managed to give her some milk when we got to Rye and I was waiting for a taxi."

"The cabin doors are locked, so she can happily wander around now. I'll get you a drink and fix Tortie with a saucer of milk and some food. What will you have?"

"Anything you've got. I'm feeling rather weak."

"So am I in one sense. I've been going through a thousand hells in this past hour or so."

"I'm so sorry. I suppose you phoned the flat."

"Yes, I tried to get you on my rig first of all, but no luck, of course. Then I rang up and spoke to Sandra. Whatever happened?"

While Zita told me her story I opened a bottle of Liebfraumilch and poured out two glasses. Tortie was meanwhile sniffing around the furniture to try to re-establish her bearings.

"During the evening the telephone rang. Sandra took the call and said your friend, Hugo Hanson, wanted me. He asked if I was Zita Stanway, muttered something about our having spoken to one another before, and then said, 'Have you spoken to Richard tonight? I wondered what news you had of him.' Well, I thought that was extremely odd because, though you hadn't said anything, I felt certain he must know where you were and what your movements were. So I said that I hadn't spoken to you since yesterday, but that I gathered you were returning to the barge today. Then he started to ask me questions about what had happened in America and if I had been interrogated by anyone over there. Finally, Hanson said that if I was thinking of going down to the barge to see you, it would be best if I postponed any such trip for a few days as it could be dangerous for me.

"That really had me worried. I replied that surely the British were going to give you as good protection as the Americans and hadn't that already been done? If so, I didn't see it would be any more dangerous for me than for you, and I had promised to go anyhow. Then he went on to say that things moved more slowly over here and that it wouldn't be possible to arrange full protection for you for at least another twenty-four hours, so he really must appeal to me to keep out of the way.

"So my mind was in a whirl. I felt Hanson was agitated, too. Before he had been very charming and cool on the phone. But not last night. I felt something was wrong, but I didn't know what. Then I remembered that I had made a note of the telephone number and extension of that Special Branch inspector friend of yours. He had asked Sandra, Julie and me to try to find you, so why shouldn't I ring him up and ask why you weren't having proper protection?"

"Zita," I said, laughingly recollecting my ultra-serious friend of the Special Branch. "You really took a chance there. What happened?"

"I didn't want Sandra and Julie to know what was going on, as they were all agog. So I went outside and phoned from a call-box. Luckily, I got hold of the inspector and, to my astonishment, he didn't know you were down at the barge."

"If nobody had told him, he would think I was nice and safe at Cucking Manor."

"Where's that?"

"Never mind. It's a secret hide-out for people like me and others. So what did the inspector say?"

"He was terribly nice, said I had done the right thing by ringing him up and that there must have been some blunder by somebody that he hadn't been told before. He said he would see that some action to protect you was taken at once. Then I asked if it would be all right if I went down to see you, and I told him what Hanson had said. When he heard what Hanson had said he hum-hummed down the phone, but said 'as we shall be alerting someone to be on the spot right away, it would be absolutely safe by the time you get down there by train.' So I went back to the flat, packed and then ordered a taxi for Charing Cross and came down to Rye. I missed the first train at Charing Cross by a whisker – that's why I'm so late. Also I had a long wait for a taxi in Rye. By the way there's a uniformed police officer nearby and he wanted to know my name and also asked to examine my handbag. So I suppose the inspector has done his stuff. I didn't tell the girls where I was going because I was afraid Hanson or someone else, even someone sinister, might ring up and ask questions. So I lied to Sandra about not going to Rye."

I took Zita in my arms again. "So you thought you'd come and warn me tonight rather than wait until tomorrow?"

"Yes. I couldn't be sure that the inspector would fix protection so quickly and I really began to fear you were in dire danger again. I was more or less ready to come anyhow. I had spent the day doing a stint at Somerset House researching a will of an eighteenth-century Walmsley who lived in Dorset. But I would have come anyhow. Anything is preferable to sitting alone in the flat and not knowing what's going on."

"We must ensure our rigs are permanently in working order in future. I didn't get mine fixed up until quite late. By then you had gone."

"This barge really is rather snug now. So much so that I

could contemplate coming here in winter and still enjoying it."

"You must be starved. Let me get you something to eat."

"Tell you what, I'd love to have a go in the barge's galley. Have you any eggs?"

"A dozen in the fridge which is now installed."

"Then I'm going to make us scrambled eggs on toast."

"Go right ahead," I just said "that's wonderful." And wonderful it was. Totally bemused by all that had happened in the past hour or so, I was finding it hard to know what to talk about first. Scrambled eggs on toast aboard a clapped-out barge was hardly the most romantic moment to make a proposal of marriage. But after what had happened I was determined to pop the question before dawn.

NINETEEN

A few minutes later there was a knock at the cabin door and a voice called out, "Inspector Sulgrave here." It was the Special Branch officer who had been handling my case all the time. After asking him in and exchanging greetings, Sulgrave commented, 'You owe a very great deal to your bright lady friend. She has not only been most helpful, but she may even have saved your life."

"I'm sure you're absolutely right," I said.

"We had no information about your coming back to Rye Harbour. As far as we were concerned you were supposed to be staying at Cucking Manor indefinitely. So you can imagine my astonishment when Miss Stanway rang up. I couldn't get hold of Hanson, but one of his colleagues confirmed what she had told me and seemed very surprised we didn't know."

"It seems to me that we are all going to find many more surprises before long," I said grimly. "And they won't be pleasant ones."

"No," said Sulgrave, stroking his chin thoughtfully. "It comes as a shock to find one has been working with wrong 'uns. But there's one good bit of news."

"What's that?"

"The threat to your life is to all intents and purposes finally removed. I haven't got full details myself, but I think you can probably fill in the gaps for yourself when I tell you that the chief villain has at last been unmasked. That means the Russians no longer have any need, or indeed interest, in trying to wipe you out. I'm not going to waste your time with a lot of talk now, as there's considerable work to be done. We shall keep the guard up all night, just to be on the safe side. There's always a chance that someone on the other side hasn't yet had the 'call off' message. I shall be staying in the neighbourhood and will see you in the morning with rather more news, I hope."

"What about Hanson?"

"Ah," said Sulgrave enigmatically. "Now there is a question we can't answer just yet. And I hope, Miss Stanway, you will be very discreet about anything you may hear."

"Of course."

"I assure you, inspector, she is the soul of discretion. Not even her flatmates know she has come down here, or what exactly is happening."

So Sulgrave departed and Zita resumed cracking eggs in the galley. "Has there been an awful muddle in communications between your people and the Special Branch?"

"I'm afraid it's rather more serious than that. But don't let's talk about all that right now. I seem to be on the verge of freedom once more and that's what matters."

"Yes, I agree. It's just wonderful to feel that this awful ordeal is almost over."

"It means we can really be our light-hearted selves again and as zany as we wish."

We sat down to scrambled eggs and coffee. "I have been in two minds as to whether to keep something very quiet and just between Sandra, Julie and myself, or whether to consult you on it," said Zita.

"Which means you've made up your mind to consult me."

"Yes. First of all, let me make it quite clear that this is supposed to be entirely to do with your novel. That's what started Sandra and Julie off. You saw for yourself how they questioned you."

"I did indeed."

"It would be grossly unfair of me if I hid anything from you which might concern your novel, however outrageous or ridiculous it was. So I think you'd better read what Sandra and Julie have concocted. This will be a two-way test for you – both on the novel and real life. Either you will be shocked into believing that we are a dreadful trio, or you'll be able to laugh it off. Or even adapt some of it. Read these while I clear away, and yes, I'd like another glass of that wine."

I read the letters and memoranda. "They are quite right," I replied. "Absolutely right. One builds up a picture of hero and heroine, what they are like, what they do, their likes and dislikes, recreations etc., but the vital part of the book is, without doubt, the secret of their respective chemistries – the love-making and how they do it. Now, if I had started off asking questions on this theme – at least in the early stages – I should either have been discarded at once by you and other prospective heroines, or regarded as some kind of voyeur or kink. Nobody would believe I wanted this for a novel."

"So?"

"Where I have a problem, especially with the novel, is that since I grew up there has been a sexual revolution. I think a romantic novelist's task was easier in the past in that there was still supposed to be an awful lot about love and sex which young girls knew nothing about. Sandra and Julie have now demonstrated just how far a new generation has been educated in such matters. So, yes, it is helpful to hear what they have to say. It just shows how much, er . . ."

"Scope?"

"Yes, scope, I suppose. How much more freely one can write and how many more things are to be taken into consideration. I can see that Sandra and Julie have both written with tongues in check, out as much to tease you as me. But it is very helpful. And what's your reaction?"

"At first I thought they were both teasing me unmercifully. We are all three of us pretty knowledgeable about things considered taboo twenty years ago, but I think Sandra and Julie believe that the sexual revolution has somehow washed itself each side of me and not right over me, if you know what I mean. Between ourselves we sometimes have quite outrageous talks, but I wouldn't say I was as sophisticated as either Sandra or Julie. I became angry when first reading their letters because I thought they were trying to send you up. Thank God you are not pompous, as, if you were, this could have caught you out."

"Tell your flatmates I'm deeply impressed. They have given me some of the answers I wouldn't until now have dared ask you for. Tell them I've read the *Kama Sutra* and *The Perfumed Garden*. I know nothing about middle-aged housewives' mid-morning sex-aid parties with or without gin-and-tonic. Nor have I come across a Pangalactic Gargleblaster."

"Let's forget the novel for a while. What about the other women in your life? There must have been others besides your wife."

"I suppose so. But they now seem to have faded into insignificance."

"Oh, come now, Richard, that's really avoiding the question."

"I'm not really one to dwell on the past. My wife was a brunette, a year younger than myself, tall and slim. She was very much a party type. That's what brought us together."

"And the others?"

"Nothing much in recent times. One American girl who was great fun, but not the marrying type. Oh yes, and a rather beautiful Hungarian defector who in many ways was more English than the English. But there were problems there."

"Problems?"

"Yes, there was a real problem concerning my job. It could have been awkward all round."

"You mean duty came first?"

"Something like that."

"You still sound very reticent."

"I'm reticent because I have not been involved with any woman for a quite a long time and I just want to forget the past. During the past few months, for example, the only females I have known have been you, the other prospective heroines, only one of whom I actually met once, and a teenager named Lucie."

"A teenager?"

"Yes, she helped me with my chores." As that explanation sounded inadequate, I told her the whole story of Lucie even down to the detail of how she wanted her toes tickled while drinking rum and coke.

"I had noticed you were an expert toe handler."

"I didn't touch Lucie's toes. I think you would like Lucie. She was devoted to Tortie and for that reason I think she should be asked down here sometime."

I suppose this was a bloody-fool, thoughtless kind of thing to say, but fortunately Zita just said, "I'd like to see her."

"Then you will. The tragedy of the Lucies of this world, the children of broken marriages and homes, is that they suddenly become adults while still children, and so they miss out on a real childhood. While other kids are still playing with their dolls, they are actually cooking meals."

"Richard, you seem to be quite perceptive about women, though hesitant to speak about them."

"That's because I'm apt to say outrageous things and give a false impression."

"Such as?"

"Well, one woman I remember more than any other was a Chinese girl I only knew for one night. We stayed awake until dawn solely because between each bout of love-making she insisted on making tea."

"I can only think of an awful pun – that's not quite my cup of tea."

"Nor mine. Love-making and sleep represent my programme. And I mean sleep for both."

Here we were again, indulging in verbal fencing. Zita asked if we could go up on deck. "Why not?" I replied, "It's probably less misty now. We can take up the rest of the bottle of wine and drink it on the bridge."

We clambered up the steps and walked towards the bow of the barge. A few stars peeped out at us from a break in the clouds. Otherwise there was nothing but a dark curtain of scud and mist. Holding hands, we looked out towards Camber Sands.

"I wonder if you understand that there are other young girls like myself who think and talk a lot about sex from time to time, but quite honestly tend to want to postpone the Big Thing? We love cuddles and we love to be loved. It is being loved that turns one on – not the act, but the feeling, even when the person is far off, that *he* loves one."

"I can understand it because I think it was how I felt when we were together in Central Park. I've felt much the same ever since."

"I see love as a kind of partnership, but with each person requiring his or her own space."

"Me, too."

"But at the same time I'm very frightened – frightened things won't last."

"You mean the magic might go."

"Something like that. Do you realise we haven't quarrelled yet?"

"We don't have to."

"No, but it will probably happen some time."

"We've had quite a lot to test us."

"I think this gloomy night is making us gloomy. Let's go below."

We went down the companion ladder to the main deck and then into the saloon. "I suppose we should turn in," I said rather lamely. "You had better have my bed, as I'm sure you're all in."

"Do you really feel like resting?" Zita seemed to have recovered her spirits and was looking at me with rather a challenging smile.

"Not really."

"Nor do I."

"They say that when Sagittarian Man meets Libran Girl the air seems full of static electricity. Then everything takes off with the speed of lightning."

"I rather feel that now. Look, Richard, I'd be much happier if we shared your bed and snuggled up together until dawn."

"You mean that? Well, the bed's made up. Would you like to go ahead on your own? I'll make sure that Tortie's got something to eat and drink during the night. Is there anything you want?"

"Promise me two things," said Zita, heading for the cabin in which I had installed my bed.

"Name them."

"First of all, I shall put the light out when I get into bed. When you come in, please don't switch it on. I have a thing that darkness is made for love-making."

"And the other thing I have to promise?"

"Do you snore?"

"I don't think so. Well, not unless I've been drinking."

"Then when you come to bed you must repeat three times before you go to sleep, 'I must not snore and keep my Zita awake'."

"I'll promise. But does it work?"

"It should work. Sheer will-power plus the fact that it's the last thing you think of before going to sleep."

I felt a trembling sensation in the legs and a distinct speeding up of the tempo of my heart as I busied myself below deck preparing food and drink for the cat. "Wish me luck, Tortie," I whispered to the cat. "I shall certainly need it because I'm almost as unsure of myself as a schoolboy having his first affair." Then I made sure that all the scuttles on the ports were properly secured and all doors locked, deciding to get undressed in the saloon rather than strip off in the darkness of my cabin. While the art of undressing is something which women have perfected and turned into an artistic skill, it is a mere routine to men which they perform in a singularly ungainly fashion. Many a first night of love has been at least partially marred by male clumsiness in discarding garments, hopping around on one leg getting out of trousers, or inelegantly kicking shoes into a far corner with unmusical thuds. The truth of the matter was that I had been taken completely off my guard by Zita's sudden appearance that night. Had I had any inkling that we were about to go to bed at last, I should at least have put a bowl of red roses in the bedroom cabin and tidied up.

I poured myself a neat Armagnac and drank it swiftly before tapping on the cabin door. A soft, but clear little voice said "Come in". I opened the door, went up to the bed, knelt on one knee beside her. Zita put her arms around me as I bent over to kiss first her lips, and then her breasts. We were in total darkness, as she had wished, so that we could make love in the jungle of the night, feeling and hearing, but not seeing. "Darkness makes it so much nicer," whispered Zita.

This was not how I had intended things to happen. All this time I had been wanting to ask Zita if she would marry me and for all else to follow according to her answer. Now we were in bed before I could put the question. In a curious way that I had never encountered, this gave me inhibitions. "Do you realise that what we are doing is rather like bundling in the last century?" I asked, trying to break my inhibitions by getting a laugh.

"That's what Victorian parents sometimes allowed their daughters to do with an approved fiancé, isn't it? But what exactly happened?"

"They were allowed to get into bed together but not take off their undergarments. If they seemed to like being together by the morning, they were told to get married quickly. If it didn't work out, then they never saw each other again."

"I'm sure they had more protection than we have."

Ours was a passacaglian getting together, like that slow Spanish dance from which the adjective takes its name. As each of us tentatively explored one another's bodies with wandering hands and lips, so the fact that we could not see each other gave us a desire to talk in madly erotic improvisations of words. We began to invent a language of love of our own, the more delightful because no one else would understand it. Sometimes Zita, sometimes I, made up the words. "You must write them all down tomorrow," she murmured, "and make sure we don't forget them."

"Not to tell Sandra and Julie, I hope."

Zita playfully slapped me. "For us alone."

The momentary joke gave way to oblivion. It was this fairy-tale quality about Zita which I found most endearing. For all I know her bedroom chatter with its elfin sense of mischief might irritate some men. To me it lifted the whole game of love on to a much more decorative plane.

There was one unexpected interruption, at first alarming and then wildly hilarious. I had left the cabin door open and we heard a noise, as though something had been knocked over in the saloon. Then a soft little body glided swiftly over us, perching first on me, then on Zita. Tortie had decided to leave her cushioned sleeping box and invade our privacy. I should have anticipated this as the cat had been in the habit of sleeping at the foot of my bed in De Beauvoir Town. She mewed and miaoued and then started to purr. Yet it didn't seem to matter and Zita insisted that Tortie should share the bed with us for the rest of the night. The cat was, however, in no mood to settle down, but prowled around the bed in somewhat of an erotic state herself and seemingly anxious to join in our fun and games. Eventually Tortie curled up quietly on my tummy. "Just leave her as she is," giggled Zita. "I think I shall try to get some sleep. Don't forget your promise not to snore."

Zita was soon fast asleep and as dawn came I was able to gaze on that tranquil face, enhanced by those long eye lashes. I might have been on the verge of sleep myself once or twice, but I kept on thinking about Hanson and wondering whether my diagnosis could be right. But what had been his purpose in telephoning Zita? Did he think I might have left the barge and wanted to know where I was? Or could it be that, though committed to conniving at another assassination attempt on myself, he was trying to save Zita from becoming involved in it? Even traitors can have quirkish qualms of conscience which result in chivalrous gestures.

I didn't go to sleep. By the time dawn arrived I wasn't even tired. So I stole out of bed without waking Zita, gave the cat some food, washed and shaved and then went up on deck. I had a hunch that when Inspector Sulgrave said he hoped to have more news for me in the morning that it would be early news rather than late. It wasn't just Zita's intervention that had brought him down to Rye Harbour. True, she had sparked off a new situation, but I imagined that by now what was going on in Washington, Forte Meade, the hierarchy of MI6 and the Special Branch respectively, not to mention MI5, had combined to produce a highly explosive situation.

My hunch proved correct. As I leaned over the barge's side I saw Sulgrave striding briskly towards me. He gave a curt wave and walked up the gangway. If this dedicated Special Branch officer was dour and not altogether possessed of a great sense of humour, these were hidden strengths rather than weaknesses. There was no slap on the back, hail-fellow-well-met tactics about Sulgrave. But he was incorruptible and, though a plodder, he could see for himself the frustrations and obstacles with which our Intelligence and Security Services hampered him. So his first words were sober and to the point.

"I hardly expected to see you up and about, but I thought you ought to be informed as soon as possible that all danger for you and the girl is now past. Everything, well, nearly everything, is cleared up."

"And they've left it to you to give me the news?"

He shrugged his shoulders. "I'm afraid so. It's the old, old story, nobody wants to admit to blunders – least of all to you, the chief victim of such blunders. I am told that somebody from your own department will be contacting you later today.

No doubt there will be apologies and, I trust, some compensation.."

"To hell with that. It can wait. But has Wetherby been nailed? What has happened to Hanson?"

This was the first time I had mentioned the name of Wetherby to the Special Branch man.

"Wetherby has been arrested. MI5 tipped us off and we pulled him in late last night. He is now being interrogated and charges will be brought. Hanson, on the other hand, has slipped the net. I should never have thought he was a guilty one. And a pal of yours, too. Yet he was the cleverest of the lot. It was because Hanson had told the Special Branch that you would be staying at Cucking Manor indefinitely that we didn't take any steps to protect you down at Rye Harbour, because by that time the Americans had put us wise as to the dangers you faced. Hanson obviously never thought that your lady friend would act in the way she did."

"You say he has slipped the net. What happened?"

"Once Wetherby was caught, Hanson had to go. He must have known that Wetherby would shop him when interrogated just as Wetherby knew that the Russians would be quite prepared to let him be arrested as long as they could be sure Hanson stayed on as a prime informer. And that is where the Russians would seem to have miscalculated. For Hanson has vanished."

"Any idea where?"

"So far none. He flew to Paris last night after he spoke to Miss Stanway. Interpol believes he crossed into Switzerland and is probably now inside East Germany. But one can't be sure."

"What about that report of mine that Wetherby was in Paris when I was there?"

"Oh, that is now accepted. It seems that Hanson was the man who provided Wetherby with an alibi. It was Hanson who told 'C' that Wetherby was in this country all the time he was supposed to be in Paris."

"What I don't understand is why Wetherby made no attempt to disguise himself on those secret missions abroad."

"Good question. But there weren't many such trips – only that one in Paris. Apparently the Russians insisted that Wetherby must deliver the documents personally to a character known as C. A. Walters in Paris, and that Walters would be accompanied by a KGB man who would personally identify Wetherby. For that reason they insisted that Wetherby should not attempt any disguise. They wanted to be absolutely sure that nobody was substituted for him. This was in the middle of the Falklands affair, so it was urgent. They fixed the meeting for the Île St-Louis as being suitably off the beaten track."

I offered Sulgrave a drink in the saloon, but he said not only was it too early for him, but that he was far too tired to absorb any alcohol. "These last twenty-four hours I feel I've done a whole month's work. But let's meet next week and celebrate properly."

When Inspector Sulgrave left I went back to the cabin and saw that Zita was fully awake. "I heard voices," she said. "So I thought I'd better get dressed."

Briefly I told her what had happened. She was very shocked at the news that Hanson was a traitor. "It seems unbelievable. And he was one of your best friends."

"Yes," I replied, "I've not quite come to terms with the facts myself as yet. But now I can put to you the very question which all last night I longed to ask, but never got around to. There is no romantic moonlight now, only the harsh light of day, so I won't waste time with verbal preamble. Zita, will you marry me?"

She was silent for a moment and then said very quietly, "I hoped you would ask that."

"Does that mean yes?"

"I think so. After all we have been through these past few days and weeks I don't think I could say anything other than yes or no. I couldn't say 'perhaps', so it must be yes."

I kissed her very gently on each eye in turn. "I suppose it is quite mad to make a proposal of this kind before breakfast. But I just want to shout to the whole world 'I want to marry Zita Stanway'. That's how it is, that's how it feels. I've nothing to offer you but my body, my barge and the proceeds of my novel."

Zita grinned, "That's rather a nice way of putting it."

"Where would you like to be married?"

Zita, in the middle of wiping her eyes where one or two tear drops had gathered, thought a moment and said, "If it's possible, I think I should like to be married out at sea, away from everything and with just the music of the seagulls."

"That's fine by me. Yes, it is possible, though I think we have to get a notary or commissioner of oaths to conduct the ceremony."

"I don't want to leave you one little bit, but I must go back to London this morning. I need to finish off this research on the Walmsley family. But I'll come back to you on Friday night, if not before. What's more I'll buzz you on the rig each night at nine o'clock and keep on buzzing till I get you. So don't hide out in the William the Conqueror pub about that time."

"I promise. It was an ecstatic night, wasn't it?"

She kissed me again. "But for Tortie it might have been more ecstatic. Though even that was fun. Anyhow we can look forward to a thousand and one ecstatic nights now, can't we?"

"And afternoons as well sometimes."